Death in Hellfire

Death in Hellfire

DERYN LAKE

ISIS
LARGE PRINT
Oxford

First published in Great Britain 2007
by
Allison & Busby Limited

Published in Large Print 2008 by ISIS Publishing Ltd.,
7 Centremead, Osney Mead, Oxford OX2 0ES
by arrangement with
Allison & Busby Limited

British Library Cataloguing in Publication Data
Lake, Deryn
    Death in hellfire. – Large print ed.
    1. Rawlings, John (Fictitious character) – Fiction
    2. Pharmacists – England – Fiction
    3. Great Britain – History – 18th century – Fiction
    4. Detective and mystery stories
    5. Large type books
    I. Title
    823.9'14 [F]

ISBN 978–0–7531–8054–9 (hb)
ISBN 978–0–7531–8055–6 (pb)

Printed and bound in Great Britain by
T. J. International Ltd., Padstow, Cornwall

For Jane Ray,
my friend and co-researcher.

Acknowledgements

I owe this book entirely to two doctors: Dr Ann Ferguson and Dr Peter Heaney, both of whom were speakers at the Crime Writers' Association Conference in 2006. Dr Ferguson is an expert on curare and was able to tell me all about its introduction into this country and the symptoms it would produce. She did all this while suffering from a detached retina herself so I owe her a special debt of gratitude. Dr Heaney told me all about the Great Pox or syphilis and was generally a great help when I telephoned him and asked him medical questions. Thank you to both of them.

I also owe a debt of gratitude to Beryl Cross, a descendant of Pierre Langlois, who was able to tell me all about her ancestor and his son-in-law, Dominique Jean, including details of the sums of money owing to them.

Thanks are also due to Keith Gotch for his assistance with the state of the bodies, to Nick and Jane Ray for their kind hospitality, and to Teressa Tedman, manager of the gift shop at the Hellfire Caves at West Wycombe. She was very considerate and courteous and made me feel most welcome.

Thank you all.

CHAPTER ONE

The sound reverberated round the room, filling each corner and growing in intensity as it did so. It was an infectious noise, the sort that one wanted to join in with. So much so that John Rawlings put back his head and laughed, loud and clear, delighted to blend his humour with that of the Blind Beak himself, Sir John Fielding.

The two men were sitting in Sir John's upstairs salon, the shutters back and the noises and stinks of the street rising undaunted into the room above, yet unable to dispel the atmosphere of bonhomie which seemed to pervade the entire building.

Eventually, Sir John raised his black bandage and wiped his sightless eyes with a large handkerchief, saying, "Damme, Mr Rawlings, I haven't had such a chuckle in an age. 'Tis a fine thing that you have returned to London. Indeed it is."

"I was away too long, sir. Far too long."

"But now you have returned to us. And most welcome you are. Tell me, how is Rose?"

"I sent her to Kensington for a fortnight but she is back with me at the moment and blooming like her namesake."

1

"I presume she was with Sir Gabriel?"

"Indeed she was."

Sir Gabriel Kent, John's adopted father had become an almost legendary figure, partly because of his habit of dressing in stunning ensembles of black and white — black and silver for high days and festivities — and partly because of his great age. The man whom John regarded more highly than any other person alive was now in his eighty-third year and as lively and spry as ever, his great delight being when his five-year-old granddaughter came to stay with him. Picturing them together in Sir Gabriel's garden in Kensington as they examined a flower, Rose's red head leaning close to that of her grandfather, who insisted on wearing an extremely old-fashioned three-storey wig, made John smile. Fortunately the Blind Beak could not see him and busied himself with pouring out two glasses of summer punch. He handed one to John as deftly as if he were sighted.

"Here, my friend, drink deep. I've a favour to ask of you."

"Oh?"

"A favour that might appeal to you."

John smiled to himself. He was back in London and the month was July, the year 1767, and despite the fact that he was now parted from Elizabeth di Lorenzi — perhaps permanently — he felt happily resigned to his fate. It was good to have returned to his old way of life.

The Blind Beak rumbled another laugh. "I hear from your silence that you are not enthusiastic."

"I'd hardly say that, Sir John. I was waiting to hear what the favour was."

There was a pause while John Fielding drank a goodly draught. Then he said, "You know that last year a new Postmaster General was appointed?"

"Sir Francis Dashwood? A friend of Wilkes's I believe."

"Indeed he is. And that is one of the reasons why I want you to investigate him."

"Investigate, eh? Is it your opinion that he is up to no good, sir?"

Sir John paused. "That I don't know. But certain rumours have reached my ears."

"Of what kind?"

"Of a most profligate nature. Apparently Sir Francis runs some kind of club close to his home at West Wycombe."

"Is that harmful?"

"That is what I have to find out. But I believe it to be a place of orgy and sexual excess. And, worse, Wilkes was a member until, for some reason or another, he was expelled."

John sat silently, thinking. John Wilkes had been a thorn in the side of the established order since he had first appeared on the political scene several years previously. Born in 1727, the man had been elected a member of parliament for Aylesbury at the age of thirty, having previously served as High Sheriff of the county of Buckinghamshire. Violently opposed to the monarch-ridden government, he produced a paper called the *North Briton* in which he flayed them with scurrilous attacks. In issue Number 17, published on 25th September 1762, Wilkes launched a broadside at the painter William Hogarth, who had been appointed sergeant-painter to George III, using the words, "I think that this term means what is vulgarly called housepainter". Hogarth, by way of revenge, produced a cartoon of Wilkes with his wig shaped like the Devil's horns and a saturnine expression on his face. On seeing the cartoon, George III exclaimed, "That devil Wilkes," a description which had been made of the man ever since.

Eventually, nothing daunted, in 1763 Wilkes produced a blasphemous and pornographic publication entitled *Essay on Woman* which Lord Sandwich, himself a rake of notoriety, insisted on reading aloud to the House of Lords in a tone of pious horror. After each stanza he paused dramatically and apologised to their lordships for scandalising their sensibilities. To which the assembled peers cried out, "Go on! Go on!" The upshot was that at Christmas of that same year Wilkes travelled to France — some said to see his daughter, others that he had gone to recover from a duelling wound, perhaps a combination of both — and had stayed there ever since. The thorn had been removed though nobody knew for how long. Now, though, it seemed that his former friend, Sir Francis Dashwood, was giving cause for concern.

John looked at the Blind Beak, who had relapsed into one of his customary silences.

"You were saying, sir?" he prompted politely.

"Yes, indeed. I was wondering exactly what goes on in this club in West Wycombe. Whether sedition is preached. Or whether, as seems more likely, it is merely a place for sexual pastimes. But take a look at this, if you would. It is a previous list of members which has come into my keeping."

John glanced at the piece of paper which had been handed to him.

"Sir Francis Dashwood, Lord le Despencer," he read. "The Earl of Sandwich, First Lord of the Admiralty; Thomas Potter, son of the Archbishop of Canterbury." His eye flicked to the bottom of the list and saw, "John Wilkes, MP; William Hogarth, Painter".

One of the Apothecary's eloquent eyebrows rose. "A motley crew indeed."

John Fielding raised an expressive shoulder. "But also the cream of society, wouldn't you agree?"

"Indeed I would. But the list must be fairly old. Hogarth is dead and Wilkes is in exile."

"Certainly. But nevertheless it shows the calibre of the people who joined the wretched organisation."

John looked thoughtful. "And you want me to find out all I can about it."

"I do. If that is agreeable to you, of course."

The Apothecary appeared momentarily weary. "I was just about to release Nicholas Dawkins from the shop and send him to Kensington."

The Blind Beak looked magnanimous. "Dear Nick. That was a good day when I asked you to take him as an apprentice."

John Rawlings smiled, remembering. The Muscovite — as Nicholas was known because of his exotic Russian ancestry — had been a thin, pale youth when the Magistrate had suggested that John might like him as an apprentice. Somewhat reluctantly, the Apothecary had agreed. But his doubts had been totally allayed. Nicholas, now no longer under indentures but a qualified apothecary in his own right, had proved himself both a worthy pupil and also a staunch and loyal friend.

Sir John spoke again. "I hear the doubt in your voice, Mr Rawlings. Would you rather that I ask someone else?"

John hesitated, part of him longing for time at home with his daughter, the other more than aware of the adventure that such an enterprise could involve. After a few moments of silence, he said, "No, sir, I would like to discover more about the Hellfire Club on a personal level. You have intrigued me with what you have to say about it. I shall go."

"Then it's settled?"

"It is."

"Obliged to you, my friend. I shall inform Jago of your decision."

"And give him my kindest regards when you do so."

"That I most certainly will do."

Walking home through the crowded and noisome streets, John Rawlings wondered whether he had done the right thing. Much as the thought of attempting to infiltrate the circle of Sir Francis Dashwood — a politician who had long intrigued him — appealed to the Apothecary, the idea of leaving Rose at so interesting a time of her life, frankly did not. Even as he approached his house in Nassau Street he felt his heart lift and running up the steps to the front door, he hastened inside. Rose was nowhere to be seen and John turned to one of the footmen who came hurrying up.

"Where is Miss Rose, Frederick?"

"She's gone out to Leicester Fields with her grandfather, sir. They are taking the air."

"Then I'll go and find them."

And as quickly as he had come in, John turned and made his way back down Gerrard Street, into Princes Street, left into Lisle Street, sharp right into Leicester Street, then into the Fields themselves.

Behind him lay Leicester House, formerly the residence of Frederick, Prince of Wales, father of the present King, George III. To John's left was the former home of William Hogarth, who had died three years previously. The sign of The Golden Head, which had hung outside for so many years, had been taken down and the place had a somewhat desolate air. John stared with interest, wondering exactly what had been the painter's connection with Sir Francis Dashwood. But his thoughts were distracted by his glimpse of a tall figure leaning heavily on its great stick, but for all that walking well and still upright, holding the hand of a little redhead.

"Father," he shouted, "Rose. I'm here."

The child heard him, for truth to tell Sir Gabriel had grown somewhat deaf with the passing years, and turned in John's direction, waving her free hand enthusiastically.

"Hello, Papa. Come and join us."

John ran forward, suddenly immensely happy, feeling that life was good, given point and meaning by the advent of Rose. Coming up to the pair, he bowed swiftly to Sir Gabriel then scooped his daughter up, lifting her high to his shoulder.

She squealed joyfully, full of the sunshine that only a five-year-old can know. "You are so funny, Pa." Then she removed John's hat and placed it on her own head, concealing almost all of her face in the so doing.

The Apothecary tickled his daughter under the chin, the only part of her features visible. "You think so, eh?"

"Yes, I do." She raised the hat which fell to the ground. "Oh sorry, Papa. I'll pick it up." She wriggled downwards and rushed to retrieve the headgear while John and Sir Gabriel looked at one another and laughed.

"A most engaging child," said the older man. "It is always a pleasure when she comes to stay."

John cleared his throat. "Talking of that, I'm afraid I have to ask you a favour, sir."

"Oh?"

"You know that I went to see Sir John today?"

Sir Gabriel's golden eyes lit with inner amusement. "He presumably wants you to work on some affair of his? And you would like me to take Rose to Kensington while you do so? Am I right?"

"As usual, perfectly." John sighed. "How have you mastered the art of knowing exactly what I am about to say?"

8

Sir Gabriel smiled and said, "I have known you since you were a small boy, remember. I would be a poor creature indeed if I was not aware by now of how your mind works."

The Apothecary gave his adopted father a swift kiss on the cheek. "What an amazing being you are."

The older man responded with a deprecatory wave of his hand. "Think nothing of it, my child. But tell me, are you going out of London? Is that why you want me to care for Rose?"

"Yes, indeed I am, sir. I am off to West Wycombe; the reason why, I feel I should keep confidential."

Sir Gabriel bent to take Rose's hand once more. "Investigating the wicked Sir Francis, no doubt?"

"Perhaps."

"I see you will not be drawn and for that Sir John Fielding should be proud of you. Of course I will care for my granddaughter. It will give me infinite pleasure to do so. But may I ask you a favour in return?"

"Name it, sir."

"I would prefer to spend a month in town, staying in my old house in Nassau Street. Indeed that is the reason why I brought Rose back personally from Kensington. Occasionally I get an urge to see London once more. And this is one of those times."

John put his hat — offered to him by an anxious Rose — back on his head. "But, Father, that would be an ideal solution. I can't think of anything better than you keeping an eye on the place in my absence."

"And what about your shop?" asked Sir Gabriel with a touch of acerbity.

His son pulled a face. "Alas, I have to leave it in the hands of Nicholas Dawkins — again."

The older man sighed. "Poor young man. One of these days you will have to release him."

"But Father, he doesn't want to go. He swears he is greatly attached to me — and to Shug Lane."

"Nevertheless he is of an age now when he should have his own premises."

"I know," said John, looking miserable.

"I rather imagine him in Kensington."

"So do I," the Apothecary answered heavily, and thought of the apothecary's shop that he and Sir Gabriel had bought between them which had mostly been managed ever since by apothecaries seeking experience before they went on to premises of their own.

Rose interrupted. "Papa, can I climb a tree?"

"No, sweetheart, only boys do that."

"How unfair. Why can't girls?"

"Because of their attire," Sir Gabriel answered succinctly.

"I could wear trousers," Rose protested.

"Like Lady Elizabeth," said John, and instantly had a vision of the woman he had fallen in love with, her supple body encased in men's clothes, her dark hair pulled back and hidden beneath a concealing hat, her beautiful face intent on the task she had set herself.

He must have made a small involuntary movement because Sir Gabriel said, "How I would love to meet that lady. You speak of her with much fondness, my son."

"Perhaps one day you will, sir. As for the second part of your sentence, let us say I have developed a certain *tendresse*."

"And held it for quite some while, I believe."

John merely smiled ruefully, aware that his father could read him like a book. He changed the subject. "How do you think I should present myself at West Wycombe?"

"As a dissolute young rogue I would imagine."

"Doing what precisely?"

Sir Gabriel paused. "That I'm not certain about. Allow me to give it some thought."

Rose interrupted. "Pa, please can I climb a tree? I promise to dress like Mrs Elizabeth if I do."

"We'll have to see about that," answered John, and thought he sounded exactly like Emilia used to before her terrible and tragic end.

CHAPTER
TWO

That evening they had supper with Serafina and Louis de Vignolles, their two greatest friends in London. There were also two surprise guests whom John had often thought about but had by way of accident rather than design, missed seeing for some considerable time. Samuel and Jocasta Swann, parents of one child and with another on the way, came to the dining table rather late and somewhat self-importantly, or so John thought.

He had known Samuel since he had been a small child and loved him like a brother; in fact in all of his life he could think of every important event and associate Samuel with it. But Samuel had married an heiress and gone to live in Curzon Street, while his goldsmith's business had gone from strength to strength, and consequently he had put on weight both physically and in character. John, embracing his friend warmly, felt Samuel draw away and could have wept.

"My very dear friend," he said, pretending not to notice, "you look so well. And Jocasta, motherhood becomes you."

"Thank you, John," she replied stiffly, and the Apothecary thought that they had both changed and not for the better.

Sir Gabriel, sensing John's discomfiture, came in, saying urbanely, "How delighted I am to see you two young men reunited. It has been unfortunate that John has been away so much recently but now that he has retaken his position in town I feel certain that we shall be seeing more of you."

"Let it be hoped so," Samuel replied without enthusiasm.

Serafina came in. "I called at your shop in Shug Lane t'other day, my dear. I was quite taken aback by the charm of Nicholas. What a truly delightful young man he has grown into. Why, I nearly included him amongst the guests for this evening and would have done so were it not for the fact of embarrassing you."

"Oh, you should have asked him," answered John, "I wouldn't have minded in the least."

Samuel said rather pointedly, "I most certainly wouldn't expect my apprentice to be asked to supper when I was present."

"Nicholas is now a qualified apothecary, Samuel. Did I not tell you?"

"No, I don't recall you doing so. But remember, John, I have only seen you twice since my wedding."

So that was it. Samuel had taken offence, egged on no doubt by Jocasta who would have considered it rude and unmannerly of the Apothecary not to be a regular visitor at their grand home in Curzon Street. But this sort of thing needed threshing out privately. John composed himself as best he could and merely gave his old friend a seraphic smile.

The supper as usual was superb, Comte Louis proving an excellent host with both the quantity and quality of his wines. All having imbibed well, the conversation came round to the subject of children.

"My dears, I am feeling positively elderly," said Serafina. "My daughter is ten years old and her brother two years younger."

"You have had no more?" asked Jocasta, clearly interested.

"No. Louis and I decided that two were enough."

And Serafina smiled at her husband who gave her a very knowing wink.

"And you, John," Serafina continued, turning towards the Apothecary, "you have the delightful Rose."

"Whom I haven't seen for a year," said Samuel pointedly.

"I shall bring her to you tomorrow if that would be agreeable," John countered, still smiling broadly.

Samuel looked towards Jocasta. "Would that suit you, my dear?"

Yet again she replied without enthusiasm. "Yes, I think so."

John caught Sir Gabriel's eye and felt rather than saw his raised eyebrows. "I shall arrive at eleven o'clock if that would be in order," he said.

"I shall be at my shop at that time," Samuel answered airily. "Perhaps you could make it nearer the dining hour."

The Apothecary felt the first pangs of irritation. He had known Samuel for as long as he could remember and though admittedly there had recently been years when they had not met — particularly the times when he had been on the run, accused of the murder of his own wife, and otherwise engaged in the West Country — there was no need to treat him like a mere acquaintance.

"I'll come at whatever time you like," he replied, an edge in his voice.

Jocasta gave a polite cough. "Perhaps you would bring Rose to dine with us, John."

Controlling himself, John said, "How kind of you to invite us. At what time do you have your dinner?"

"Rather late, I'm afraid. At six o'clock. It's because Samuel is so busy at work."

"That will be convenient, thank you," the Apothecary answered, thinking that he would have to have the child put to bed in the afternoon in order to ensure that she didn't fall asleep at the table.

Serafina, sensitive to the undercurrent, suggested a hand of whist at this juncture and made up an unusual game with all six of her guests included. John found himself partnering Samuel, while Louis gallantly bowed to Jocasta. The only two good players in the room, Sir Gabriel and Serafina, were forming an unbeatable team against which the others had no chance.

Samuel, however, had either improved his game or was having a run of early luck for he won the first hand and appeared somewhat smug about it.

"Well done, Sam," John exclaimed, to be rewarded with a strange look which he could not interpret.

John played half-heartedly. He had never been fond of cards, unlike Sir Gabriel, and his attention soon started to wander. He had been thinking more and more of late that he must employ a full-time companion for Rose. She was five years old and divided her time between London and Kensington, being transported between the two by Irish Tom, as reliable a guardian as one could wish to find. And though she had a nursery maid she lacked a mother figure, someone to whom she could chat and talk as one female to another. He decided that he must place an advertisement in *The Public Advertiser* immediately and see what this brought forth.

His mind wandered on to Elizabeth, as it frequently did. He presumed because of his recent treatment at her hands that their relationship must henceforward be one of friendship and friendship alone. And bitter though it was to accept this, he knew that he must, for the sake not only of his daughter but also his sanity. Elizabeth had more power to disturb him than any woman he had ever met — including both his beloved Emilia and the glorious Coralie Clive — and the only way forward that he could see was to make a great effort to put her to the back of his mind, almost impossible though this was going to be.

Samuel said something and John jerked back to attention. "I'm sorry, Samuel. What did you say?"

"I said that I am pleased you are coming to dine tomorrow."

John looked him straight in the eye. "I'm glad you mentioned that because I wasn't sure that you were."

Samuel dropped his gaze, saying quietly, "Shall we speak outside? Privately."

"Yes. I am bored with cards. Probably because I've never been any good at 'em."

Something like Sam's old familiar grin spread over his features. "I confess my liking of them has increased since my marriage but I am certainly quite happy to throw in my hand."

John stood up. "Comtesse, will you forgive Samuel and me if we take a stroll round your beautiful garden? We haven't seen one another in an age and have a great deal to catch up on."

Jocasta looked up with a bright stare but Sir Gabriel gave a nod of approval. "About time you two lads had a conversation *à deux*. At one time people used to think they were brothers, you know."

He looked round him benignly and the Apothecary thought that he was being terribly cosy, suspiciously so. He gave his father a swift grin and left the room.

Descending the delicately curving staircase side-by-side with Samuel, he made his way out through the large French doors that led on to the terrace. The scent of the summer garden hung heavy in the air and the sun was descending behind the house. It was high season, the weather was hot and all should have been at peace. Yet despite this, John knew perfectly well that the criminal classes were hard at work, stealing, whoring and murdering. At that moment he was sorry that he had to argue with Samuel, but the air had to be cleared for once and for all. Making his way to a shady seat, he sat down and motioned for his friend to do likewise.

"Now, Sam, tell me why you are angry with me."

Samuel adopted his pompous face, a look that John was not used to seeing. "I don't know what you mean," he said.

"You know perfectly well. Why have you and Jocasta turned against me?" Samuel started to explode and expostulate but the Apothecary cut across him. "Don't try to deny it. You have given me black looks ever since I arrived here."

Samuel stood up and walked a few steps, then he said over his shoulder, "I was more hurt than annoyed, John. Why did you stay away so long?"

"Godammit, man. I know that I have seen little of you over the last few years but if you will recall I was accused of my wife's murder and had to go into hiding. And that meant not seeing anyone, not even my father. But I did come and visit you as soon as I could and admired your son and tickled him. And after that I went to the West Country a couple of times. But now I am back and it ill becomes you to be so petulant with me. I beg you, Sam, if I have given cause for offence please forgive me. If I have caused you pain let me assure you that it was completely unintentional."

Samuel's back was a masterpiece of various emotions. Rigid at first, it slowly began to relax, then to quiver very slightly. John realised to his horror that Samuel was silently weeping. He got up and put his arm round the other man's shoulders.

"Sam, please don't. I truly am sorry if I've hurt your feelings."

The Apothecary realised, even as he said the words, that he was now apologising profusely, had, indeed, taken on the role of the bad boy, but frankly he didn't care. It was not worth upsetting Samuel just to prove a point.

The big man turned, all the pomposity gone from his face, which shone large and round in the last rays of the sun. He gazed at John earnestly.

"What was it about the West Country that so appealed to you, my friend? Was there some woman there that you wanted to see?"

Lying in his teeth, John answered, "No. I just like the place, that is all."

Much as he had once loved Samuel, he knew that to mention Elizabeth's name would be fatal. Sam would tell Jocasta, who no doubt would pass such a juicy bit of gossip on to her circle of women friends, and soon half of London would know how besotted the Apothecary had been and conjecture as to what would happen next. Which, John knew in his heart of hearts, would be precisely nothing.

But now he held Samuel close to him. "My dear friend, please can't we get back to the relationship we once had? I treasured it deeply, you know."

"It can never be quite the same," Sam answered honestly. "Because now I have Jocasta and Tobias and another child on the way. But as to my friends, I confess that none has ever come as close to me as you once did."

"Then can we agree to start again?"

"Gladly," said Samuel, producing a large and sensible handkerchief with which he dabbed his eyes.

"Then you still wish me to dine with you tomorrow?"

"Of course I do. It will be a great opportunity for us to reminisce."

"Indeed it will. Now, let us rejoin the party."

"And get slightly drunk."

"Why not," said John, and clapped his friend on the shoulder.

What had begun as a disaster ended as a most cordial evening. With the tensions between John and Samuel clearly resolved, the rest of the company — even Louis de Vignolles who had been blissfully unaware of anything — relaxed and engaged in frivolous conversation, abandoning their game of cards, somewhat to the annoyance of Sir Gabriel. Jocasta too, who had obviously turned against the Apothecary for reasons best known to herself, was clearly not sure where she stood and remained huffily silent until carriages were called for. Then she turned a frozen cheek toward him and murmured, "I shall see you at six o'clock tomorrow."

"I'll be delighted," he beamed back, disconcerting the poor woman completely.

Afterwards, as he and Sir Gabriel were driven home by Irish Tom, John said, "Sam has changed, of course. But I think he and I can get our friendship back on an even keel."

His father considered the remark in silence, then said, "That woman — his wife — was she ever in love with you? A long time ago, during the Aidan Fenchurch affair I mean."

John thought about it. "Possibly. I've never really considered it."

"Well, think about it. I believe therein your answer might lie."

"What do you mean?"

"What I say, my boy. It is very easy for a love once held to turn to hatred you know."

"You might be right at that."

Sir Gabriel turned on him a piercing glance. "What do you mean, might? I am always right in matters concerning the heart." And with that he pulled his hat forward and appeared to go to sleep.

CHAPTER
THREE

"Really?" said Samuel, his eyes widening in his round face. "Good gracious! I do envy you, John. I truly do."

The Apothecary, flattered despite himself, looked down modestly. "Oh come now, Samuel, you have a highly successful business, in fact you are spoken of as one of the principal goldsmiths of London. How could you leave such an enterprise?"

His friend surprised him by answering, "Very easily. Nowadays I have two assistants and several apprentices. I could hand the business over to one of them and get away for a few days."

John sat silently, thinking of the times when Samuel had been given tasks to do by the Blind Beak, tasks that even a child of five could have carried out. He remembered his friend's over-exuberant manner with witnesses, frightening the life out of them. He also recalled with fondness Samuel's great enjoyment, his relish in working on an investigation. And now he felt certain that by admitting he was about to undertake an enquiry on behalf of the Magistrate, Samuel had once again got the bit between his teeth. He looked at the Goldsmith and smiled, rather feebly.

"So your quarry is a prominent member of parliament, eh?" Samuel asked excitedly.

John sighed inwardly. The dinner had been excellent — clearly a peace offering — and Jocasta, though frosty, had warmed up a little during the course of the meal. Rose had behaved impeccably, sitting silently and straight, but had jumped up as soon as dinner was done and had gone with Jocasta to the nursery to play with three-year-old Tobias. Left alone, the two men had imbibed rather a lot of port with the result that John had said too much about his latest quest. Though not mentioning Sir Francis Dashwood by name, he had told an avid Samuel as much as he dared about the new commission given to him by John Fielding. And now Sam's face was taking on a conspiratorial expression as he narrowed his eyes.

"D'ye know, John, I've a mind to accompany you wherever it is that you are going. I could adopt a disguise if you like."

The Apothecary allowed a fleeting smile to cross his features before he answered, "I don't know about that, my friend. I would have to admit to the Blind Beak that I had told you something of what lies ahead."

"I don't see why," Samuel protested. "Supposing I just went independently and stayed at a nearby inn. I mean to say, I am free to travel where I please without Sir John's say-so."

There was no arguing with this logic but nonetheless John answered, "But you don't know where I *am* going, do you?"

Samuel gave him a pathetic glance. "You surely couldn't withhold that information from me, John. After all, all I want to do is help you."

The Apothecary drained his glass, then held it out for a refill. "If you must know I am going to West Wycombe in Buckinghamshire."

Samuel goggled. "But that is the home of Sir Francis Dashwood, is it not? Good God, my friend, is he the subject of your next investigation?"

John grinned ruefully. "The trouble with you, Samuel, is that you're too clever by half. You worm out even my deepest secrets. But swear to me that you will tell no one else of this. I promise you that Sir John would have my head if he thought I had confided in anyone."

The first part had been said in jest, of course, but Sam turned on him a look so earnest, so overjoyed at his own supposed cleverness, that it moved the Apothecary almost to tears, and he felt ashamed and cheapened that he should have made fun of his old friend in such a way. Humbly, he put out his hand.

"Listen, my dear, if you should want to visit West Wycombe at the same time as myself then of course I cannot stop you. But be warned I might disappear for several days. That is if I am lucky enough to get an invitation to visit the house."

The Goldsmith looked mysterious, an expression which was so at odds with his happy moonface that John fought to control threatened tears.

"You're planning something," he said.

"I was actually thinking how good it would be to accompany you once more on an investigation," Samuel answered reflectively.

"It will be helpful to have you," John answered, and prayed that he would be forgiven for such a downright lie.

Later that evening, sitting in the quiet of his house, with Rose gone to bed and Sir Gabriel out calling on friends, John penned an advertisement for *The Public Advertiser*. It read as follows:

A Gentleman of London seeks a clean, honest, educated Lady to act as Companion to his motherless Daughter.
Must be proficient in Speech and Sewing, Music and Dancing and not be above the Age of Thirty-Five. Applications should be made to J. Rawlings, Esquire at 2, Nassau Street, Soho.

This done he sealed it and sent it round with a footman, together with a shilling to pay for the insertion, to the Editor, Henry Sampson Woodfall, at his office nearby.

Then he sat down in the library and took a book from the shelves. But he could not concentrate, his mind wandering over the fact that he was going to be forced to conduct this investigation with Samuel, hearty and keen, panting by his side. Yet, when all was said and done, did the years of friendship, the hours of devotion and somewhat poor advice given, count for nothing? How could he in all fairness turn aside so loving a comrade? Angry with himself, John Rawlings tried desperately to concentrate on the printed words but found himself unable to do so.

A picture of Elizabeth came into his mind and he saw her beautiful face with its ugly scar as clearly as if she were in the room. Memories of their first meeting, of how he had kissed her and known even then that she was dangerous for him, came back to taunt him with their bitter-sweet recollections.

He sighed and stretched in his chair and then he heard Sir Gabriel come in.

"Father," he called, "I'm in the library. Come and join me."

There were the sounds of the older man removing his cloak and then progressing towards the room. John opened the door and peered into the hall, seeing Sir Gabriel advancing, leaning on his stick, the only outward sign of his father's great age.

"My boy, I thought you might have retired. How was the dinner?"

"It was very good. And your granddaughter behaved impeccably. I believe she has thoroughly endeared herself — to Samuel at least."

"Madam Jocasta still unfriendly?"

"She's warming up."

Sir Gabriel sipped his brandy and looked at his son over the rim of the glass. "Mark my words, my dear, she must once have had a passion for you. And now she is angry that you have come back to annoy her. But she will slowly see reason."

John poured himself a glass and said, "I'm not so sure of that. Samuel has discovered that I am off on behalf of Sir John and wants to come with me to help."

"Will that be allowed?"

"There is nothing I can do to stop him. He says he will stay in an hostelry close by and watch points, as it were. Besides, Papa, I don't wish to upset him. Our friendship is just starting to restore itself. It would be a tragedy to undo all that."

"It would indeed. He is too valuable a companion to risk a further breach. I think, my son, that you will have to consider this as a case of when the maggot bites."

"I agree. But I shall reveal nothing to Sir John. If he gets to hear of it I shall say it was pure coincidence that Samuel was staying in the same place."

"And do you think he will believe you?"

"It is all the same to me whether he does or does not," John answered with far more assurance than he actually felt.

The Apothecary set off for work early the next day and reached the shop while Gideon Purle — now well established as an apothecary's apprentice — was still sweeping out.

"Good morning, Gideon," he called cheerfully.

"Good morning, sir. Master Dawkins will be along soon."

"Before he comes I would like to have a word with you."

"Yes, sir?" said Gideon, and put down his broom.

John went through to the compounding room and striking a tinder managed to light the little brazier upon which stood a well-used kettle. He looked up as his apprentice came into the room.

"Tell me, Gideon, is Master Nicholas contented working in Shug Lane? Or would he rather have his own establishment?"

Gideon looked cautious. "I don't care to gossip about him, sir, but he seems happy enough to me."

"Good, I'm pleased to hear it."

"And he's moved his lodgings of late to Bow Street, where he is a great deal more settled."

"I see." John sipped his tea reflectively. "And lady friends? Does he have any of those?"

Young Purle, who was now nineteen and had shot up to an enormous height, looked down at his master.

"I think not, sir. But you had better ask him directly."

So the apprentice was not willing to chat about the man whom he considered his master even though his indentures had been signed with John. The Apothecary gave a crooked grin.

"Well said, my friend. I consider myself reprimanded."

Gideon blushed a deep rose red. "I'm sorry, sir . . . I didn't mean —"

"Don't worry," John interrupted, and laughed. "I was being inquisitive — a naughty little habit of mine. You were quite right to stop me in full spate."

At that moment the subject of their conversation walked into the shop and John rose to greet him.

28

"Nicholas, my dear chap. I hear you've moved to Bow Street. Tell me all about it."

"Well, sir, I saw an advertisement for some rooms in *The Public Advertiser* and I went round immediately and got them. And very pleasant they are too. On the fourth floor and not at all stuffy."

"Are you anywhere near Sir John Fielding?"

The Muscovite gave an attractive smile and answered, "Two doors down, sir."

He was now in his late twenties and had a special place in John's affections. He had been suggested to the Apothecary by the Blind Beak himself; a pale, starving, thieving boy from the poorest of backgrounds. But he had turned out to be a wonderful apprentice and John gave sincere thanks that he had, albeit somewhat unwillingly, taken the youth on. Walking with a slight limp — a fact which the ladies seemed to find attractive — he was tall, dark and pale, another feature which they seemed to think appealing. Yet, despite his obvious charms, Nick had never got himself a wife, having a penchant for picking women who were either impossible to capture or who loved someone else. John was beginning to worry about him. Now, though, he gave Nicholas a broad smile.

"Familiar territory for you, eh?"

"Yes, indeed. I was working for Sir John when you first took me on, sir."

"And Mary Ann? Have you seen anything of her?"

"I have seen her from my window and must say that she has become a very highty-tighty wench — if you'll forgive the phrase, sir."

John, remembering the incident when Mary Ann had been kidnapped and Nick had been dying for love of her, merely smiled.

"Enough about that young lady. I'm afraid I have to ask you another favour."

"And what might that be, sir?" asked Nick, removing his caped coat and putting on his long apron.

"I want you to stand in for me yet again, I'm afraid."

Nick pulled a quizzical face. "I have been here so long now I feel as if I practically own the shop." Then seeing the expression on John's face, added hastily, "But I love the place, sir. I truly do. It is no hardship to me to act as your deputy."

John sat down and poured out two cups of tea, motioning Nick to a chair.

"I promise you, my friend, that one day you will be rewarded for this. And I am not speaking lightly. One day this shop will be yours."

"But supposing you should have a son, sir."

John grinned. "No chance of that, I fear."

Nick looked at him over the edge of the tea cup. "Why not? You might well remarry and have another family."

"I have no plans to do so. Absolutely none."

Dawkins gave a disconcerting wink. "You never know what is round the corner," he said.

For some reason this remark made John pause and think about his life. Perhaps he should marry again and put his great passion for Elizabeth behind him. Perhaps he should marry for the company, for the contented routine that living with somebody brought in its train.

Perhaps, indeed, he should try and have another child to give Rose some company.

"No," he answered Nicholas slowly, "you don't know, do you." And he slowly sipped his tea.

Some hours later he returned home to sense a change in the atmosphere. Even as he put his key in the lock and opened the door he could tell that something in the place had changed. There was a faint perfume in the air, a smell of summer and roses and sweetness of the fields.

"Grey," he said to the footman who came hurrying to take his coat. "Has somebody called?"

"Not only called, sir, but is waiting for you in the parlour."

"And who might that be?"

"A young lady, sir. She's come about the advertisement you placed in the newspaper yesterday. I thought it best that she should wait, sir. I hope you don't mind."

"No, of course not. I'll just go and wash quickly and then I'll present myself."

"Very good, sir."

Hurrying up the stairs to his bedroom, John doused his hands and face in cold water, brushed at his clothes then, on a whim, changed his cravat, his other looking somewhat soiled. Then he sauntered downstairs and into the parlour.

The girl was standing looking out of the window as he came in but turned immediately and dropped a curtsey. John bowed slightly, then straightened up to look at her.

It was a neat little parcel of humanity that he was staring at, everything perfectly proportioned and concise. But it was the girl's face that held his attention, huge dark blackberry eyes and a large smiling mouth, smiling so broadly in fact that John had no option but to grin back. Hair, black as midnight, showed itself beneath her lilac hat, which matched her open robe beneath, her general smallness belied by the girl's hands which were long and fine.

"Madam," said John, and bowed once more, this time a little more deeply.

"I am Octavia da Costa," she answered, and the Apothecary knew at once that she was not a native of these shores, not just from her name but also from her very careful use of the English tongue.

He should have been totally in control of the situation, calmly speaking about the advertisement and her qualifications in answering it, but there was something infectious about her good humour, about her precise use of his mother tongue, that just made him want to laugh. Instead he smiled.

"Miss da Costa, I am John Rawlings. Do sit down. Would you care for some wine?"

"Oh yes, I would like that very much," she answered, removing her gloves and revealing her hands which were truly distinctive as he had guessed.

John rang a bell, then said, "Tell me, Miss da Costa, where do you come from and what is your history?"

The blackberry eyes beneath their thin dark brows flashed him a slightly apprehensive glance. "I was born in Portugal, Mr Rawlings, of a Portuguese father and

32

an English mother. Unfortunately my father, though a good husband and parent in every other way, was addicted to gambling; in particular he liked to back horses. It was my mother who taught me English, by the way."

"And very well too," John answered, finding her accent charming.

"Anyway, Papa died leaving a string of debts and I'm afraid my mother and I were forced by dead of night to take the packet from Lisbon and escape to this country." She looked at him to see if he was shocked but gathered from his relaxed expression that he was not.

"It was very honest of you to tell me that," he answered as a footman came in carrying a tray.

"I know, but I thought it best. I think any relationship should start off with the truth. The lies can come later."

John laughed aloud, at the same time pouring her a glass of rhenish. "Here, Miss da Costa, try this."

"Thank you, Mr Rawlings. I will."

She drank deeply and John noticed the way she supped, so that her generous mouth was bedewed with tiny droplets of wine. He knew then that providing she did not reveal anything terrible about her past, he would employ her. Trusting both his gut and his instinct, he found her refreshing and pleasant and felt already that she would be a good influence on Rose.

"So what happened next?" he asked.

"My mother and I got lodgings in London, in Clare Street behind the Strand to be exact. She worked in a dressmaker's and I took employment with a milliner. But then she got ill and I left my work to look after her. But, alas, she died last month and I knew that I must find some other occupation — preferably one which demanded I lived in — to make ends meet. So here I am, Mr Rawlings. I can provide references from Madam Violet, the milliner, and also from my mother's physician if they would suit."

"Yes," said the Apothecary, attempting to act like an adult, "I should very much like to see them."

Miss da Costa produced two documents from her reticule and finished her wine while John perused them. He could see out of the corner of his eye that she was regarding him while he did so. He looked up.

"Yes, they seem satisfactory. Tell me, madam, what you will teach my daughter?"

"How to be a good woman," she answered.

John stared at her, quite dumbstruck, never having heard anything like it in his life. "And what of the more conventional things?" he heard himself ask.

Octavia laughed. "I shall teach everything of everyday life as well, until she is old enough to go to school. You do intend to send her to school, I take it?"

"Yes, I certainly do."

"Well then, sir, I shall leave you to think things over. Perhaps you would be good enough to send round to my lodgings with your reply, that is when you have interviewed the other candidates."

"There are no other candidates at the moment," John answered.

"I see," said Octavia, and pulled a grave face.

34

"But I am sure that there will be."

"Indeed yes."

"So in the meantime would you like another glass of wine?"

"Yes, I would relish one," the girl answered, and smiled her warm-mouthed smile.

CHAPTER
FOUR

At breakfast the following morning, John told both Rose and Sir Gabriel about the lively Miss da Costa and how suitable he thought she would be.

"But why do I need a governess, Papa?" asked his daughter. "I am perfectly happy with you and Grandfather."

"Yes, but we cannot always be here to take care of you, sweetheart. Besides, you lack feminine company. It is time you had a woman friend."

"But supposing I don't like her."

Sir Gabriel interrupted. "I would suggest, my dears, that Rose be the person to make the decision. Why not call Miss da Costa to join us this afternoon and see how she gets on. Surely that would be the sensible way out."

"You're right as usual, Papa," said John. "Though convention decrees that the decision is mine, I will let Rose make the choice."

"Thank you, Father," she said, and rising from her place at the table planted a moist kiss on his cheek.

Breakfast done, John made his way to his shop but not before he had looked through his correspondence which the postboy brought early to Nassau Street.

There were several replies to his advertisement which the Apothecary put on one side against the fact that Rose might take a dislike to Miss da Costa. Not that he could imagine such a thing. Wondering what his daughter would make of the situation, he entered his premises in Shug Lane.

"Good day, Mr Rawlings," said Nicholas, who this morning was looking decidedly in need of mothering in his dark clothes and impeccable white cravat, which only served to enhance his pale complexion and slim body.

John turned to look at him. "Nick, don't you think it is time that you addressed me as John?"

His former apprentice looked quite shocked. "Oh no, sir. It would be difficult for me to do that. You were my master for many years and that is something that cannot be forgotten."

"No indeed. But nonetheless I would like it if we ceased to be so formal."

"I will try to accede to your wishes, sir."

John gave a quizzical smile. "I'm glad to hear it." He looked round. "Where is Gideon?"

"I have sent him out to administer a clyster of Good Henry."

"Really? Is he ready for that?"

"More than ready, sir. As you know I have a dislike of giving clysters — always have had, I fear — so I made sure that Gideon was fully trained in that discipline. He does most of the bowel work nowadays."

"Don't tell me he enjoys it."

"He seems to have a rough and ready approach which most of the patients find commendable. All except the young females which I do myself."

"I'm sure that makes it as pleasant as possible for them," said John drily.

"I like to think so, sir," answered Nick seriously. He changed the subject. "When will you be off in pursuit of your quarry?"

"In a day or two. I am going to see Sir John tomorrow evening and will get my final orders from him."

"Very good."

The Apothecary suddenly felt a wave of compassion. "Look, Nick, why don't you come round and dine this evening. As I am going away I would relish the chance to talk to you. And you look as if you could do with a good meal."

His former apprentice grinned, transforming his features into those of a most becoming young man. "Oh, I eat well enough, sir. It's just that I was born to be thin. But I would very much like to accept your invitation. At what time shall I call?"

"I'm afraid we dine late because of the shop. Shall we say six o'clock?"

"That will give me time to race home and change."

"Indeed it will," John answered.

Before he left the house he had scribbled a quick note to Miss da Costa asking her if she could call on him that afternoon. And while he was away at his shop a reply had arrived at Nassau Street saying that she would attend at four o'clock and apologising for the lateness of her arrival. John guessed at once that she had applied for another post and was being interviewed. Remembering the freshness of her and the general jollity of her manner he prayed that Rose would choose as he had.

He returned home at three and called his daughter in from the garden where she had been playing with Sir Gabriel. Sending her upstairs for the nursery maid to clean her up, his father too retired to the upper regions.

"I just thought I would sit in on the interview and see the young woman for myself," he had remarked casually, his lower foot on the bottom stair.

"I will value your opinion greatly, sir," answered John, well aware that his adopted father was bursting with curiosity.

"Then I will go and prepare myself," Sir Gabriel had answered, pulling his old-fashioned three-storey wig firmly down upon his head.

Punctually at four o'clock the bell rang and Miss da Costa, today wearing a sky blue hat with matching open robe and cream petticoat, was ushered into the library to be greeted by three pairs of eyes, all regarding her with different expressions. The old man, dressed to the hilt in black and white, was eyeing her as if he could see into her soul, which he probably could, she thought. Mr Rawlings, on the other hand, was smiling at her. But it was to the child, whose dark blue eyes seemed as large as an opened flower, that she was drawn. Miss da Costa saw ancient mystery in those eyes, knew at once that the child was gifted, to the point where she exclaimed, "Oh, you little beauty, we shall have such chats, you and I."

Rose got up and came towards her, putting up her arms and drawing Octavia's face down to be level with hers. Then she kissed her on the cheek and turning to her father said, "If I have to have a governess, then I want this one please."

The two grown men laughed, both having got to their feet when Miss da Costa entered the room, and now John bowed to her.

"Well, Miss da Costa, that would appear to be that. I promised my daughter that she should choose and it would appear that she has done so."

She made a deep curtsey. "I think I will be very happy here, sir."

Rose, who had not let go of her hand, said, "May I show her the garden please?"

"Perhaps Miss da Costa would rather rest."

"No, sir, if it is all the same to you I would like to see the garden very much."

"Then inspect it you shall," answered John, and bowed once more as the two females passed him on their way out. He turned to his father. "Well?"

"Well indeed. A very comely young woman if I may say so."

John smiled. "I am dining with Sir John tomorrow evening."

"Excellent. Then you will be leaving us shortly I take it."

"Yes. I shall be off very soon afterwards."

"Tell me, will you have to impersonate another character? Adopt a guise of some kind?"

"I think," John answered carefully, "that I will have to pose as a member of the minor nobility."

"To gain entry to wherever it is you want to go?"

"Precisely."

Sir Gabriel rested his chin on a long, thin, elegant hand. "Perhaps try the Irish aristocracy. They are so much more difficult to check."

"You have a very valuable point. But wouldn't that mean I'd have to adopt a phoney Irish accent? I don't think I could keep that up."

"Nonsense. A great many of them send their sons to England for their education. You could just say the odd word here and there with a strange intonation."

John burst out laughing. "Father, you truly are an inspiration — and a master of all that is ridiculous. However, I do take your suggestion seriously."

Sir Gabriel rose and helped himself to a small sherry. "Now, let me think. Who could you be? Perhaps some relation of the Earl of Cavan — one of the smaller counties, don't you know."

"No, I don't, to be perfectly honest. Is there such a man as the Earl?"

Sir Gabriel sipped his sherry thoughtfully. "I have no idea, my son. That is why I suggested that particular place."

"I see." John looked pensive. "I could pretend to be one of his sons perhaps."

"Why not? I doubt that your quarry, however well informed, would be able to check that fact."

"Father, you're right. I'll put it to Sir John tomorrow night."

Sir Gabriel finished his glass. "And will you be mentioning Samuel, my son?"

"No, I think not, don't you?"

But the answer never came for at that moment they were rejoined by Rose and Octavia da Costa both looking pink as the roses they had just been sniffing.

"Would you like a sherry, Miss da Costa?" the Apothecary asked.

"No, thank you. I must return to my lodgings and pack up my belongings. Would you mind showing me my room before I go?"

"Of course, how remiss of me not to do so before. Come this way?"

He led her upstairs to the first landing and opened the door of the best guest room, feeling that to put her upstairs with the servants would be to pay her insufficient respect. She went into it, clearly delighted.

"Why, it's most pleasant, sir. I hadn't expected anything like this."

John laughed, glad that she was happy, and at that moment the front doorbell rang. Looking down the stairs into the hall below, the Apothecary observed the footman go to answer the summons and Nicholas Dawkins arrive, pale and intriguing as ever. Unaware that he was being observed, his former apprentice removed his caped coat and was ushered in the direction of the library.

"Who was that?" asked Octavia, then blushed a little at her forward manner. John, however, ignored it.

42

"My ex-apprentice. Name of Nicholas Dawkins."

"Oh, I see. Well, I think the room is delightful. When would you like me to start?"

"In two days' time if that would be convenient. I have to go away and I will leave Sir Gabriel Kent, my father, in charge of the household. I'm not quite sure at this stage how long I will be."

Miss da Costa nodded. "Oh, I see. Well, we must do our best without you." She started to make her way downstairs, John close behind her, but four steps from the bottom she turned and placed her gloved hand in his.

"Do call me Octavia, sir. Miss da Costa is such a mouthful and I would far prefer to be addressed by my Christian name."

"Very well, then, I will. But by that token I suppose you should call me John."

But for the second time that day he met with difficulty. "Oh no, sir, that would never do. You will always be Mr Rawlings to me."

Sir John Fielding was not in the best of spirits. Joe Jago, who came to the bottom of the stairs leading off by the Public Office, winked and said, "Be careful of the Governor, Mr Rawlings. He's in high stirrup, I warn you."

"Why?" John whispered back as they climbed.

"Had a lot of rum cases today, sir. Including a woman accused of murdering her children. It's affected him badly."

"I shall try to be pleasant," the Apothecary answered, with a sinking feeling in the pit of his guts.

The Blind Beak was sitting in the little room he used as an office, irritably calling out, "Jago. Jago. Where the devil are you, man?"

"Here, sir," his clerk called back, "and I've got Mr Rawlings with me."

"Have you now. Good, good."

John as always made an elaborate bow, regardless of the fact that the Blind Beak could not see him. "Good evening, sir," he said, then added, "I hope I find you in good spirits."

"No you don't," Sir John retorted sharply. "I have had a terrible day in court. The standard of morals in this country has plunged to a new low, I tell you."

"I'm sorry to hear it," John answered, knowing that he was learning nothing new.

"Whores, thieves and beggars, the lot of them. As for Francis Dashwood and his bunch of cronies — members of parliament, peers of the realm and God knows what else — they are setting no standards for the rest of the population. The sooner a halt is put to their activities the better it will be for mankind. Those who look to them for an example will have a sorry time of it."

The Apothecary regarded the Magistrate carefully and thought that the signs of strain were distinctly visible. His face, usually so full and florid, was looking decidedly pinched and had a strange whiteness about it, while his nostrils and lips were both constricted.

"You don't look well, sir," he said tentatively.

Sir John made an impatient gesture. "There's nothing that a few weeks in Kensington wouldn't put right. It's just that today filled me to the brim with despair."

And the Blind Beak suddenly plunged his face into his hands, looking lost and bereft.

Joe Jago rose silently to his feet and poured out a large measure of gin which he guided into the Magistrate's hand.

"Here, sir, drink this. It will make you feel better I promise you."

"I have no wish to drown my sorrows," Sir John said tersely.

"May I have one, please?" John asked, not only because he needed a drink but in the hope that it might encourage the Blind Beak.

Sir John straightened up again. "I am forgetting my manners, Mr Rawlings. For a moment I thought you were a member of the family, which is a great compliment to you, sir. But you are a guest and should be treated as such. Certainly you can have a drink."

Joe Jago winked and nodded at John, then poured the Apothecary a measure before helping himself to a glass. "Good health, sir. Same to you, Mr Rawlings."

The Blind Beak drank his glass down then held it out for a refill. "I would like to propose a toast."

"And what might that be, Sir John?" asked John politely.

"That the scum of the earth might all be brought to book."

The Apothecary sighed. "I don't think that will happen in my or any other lifetime, sir."

The Magistrate echoed his sigh. "I believe you are right, Mr Rawlings. Alas I do."

Joe pulled his nose. "Perhaps some of them might make good if given a chance, sir."

"Precisely. That is why I started my Seminary for Sailors and my Plan for Preserving Deserted Girls. To keep young thieves and villains and child prostitutes off the streets of London."

"And very well they have worked too, sir," put in John, somewhat over-heartily.

The Blind Beak brightened. "Is that the general consensus?"

"I should think it is!" the Apothecary replied with gusto. "Why it is the talk of the town."

He caught Jago's eye over the Magistrate's head and watched as the Clerk gave a slow, blue wink.

"Well, well," said Sir John. "Who would have thought it." He slapped his thigh and it was the Apothecary's turn to wink. The Magistrate's mood was restored and they could now get on with enjoying the evening.

It was after an excellent dinner and two bottles of wine that Sir John addressed himself to the real reason why John had come.

"I've been hearing more about this infernal club. Seems there could be some form of Satanic worship going on."

John shivered. "Really? Have you any proof?"

"No, just hearsay. But I want you to get down there as soon as possible."

"My father suggests that I pose as the son of an Irish peer. Says they are more difficult to trace."

"A good idea. Who have you decided to be?"

"I thought of the Honourable Fintan O'Hare, a son of the Earl of Cavan."

"Splendid. Will you speak with an Irish accent?"

"Glory be to God, no I won't," answered John in a stage Irish voice. "I'll just have a slight drawl."

"Very wise," replied Sir John dryly.

"And what is your plan?" asked Joe.

"To book in at an hostelry in the nearby village, then perhaps call at the big house on some pretext or other."

"Um." The Magistrate cogitated. "Well, be careful. I believe Sir Francis to be a wily old bird. But then I need hardly warn you of that."

"I promise, sir, that I will be very careful indeed," John answered thoughtfully.

CHAPTER
FIVE

The village of West Wycombe stood bathed in summer sunshine, its ancient cottages closely packed on either side of the High Street giving a friendly yet guarded look, as if the place would stand firm against any intruder whose aspect it did not care for. Behind the cottages rose a hill, its velvet green sward dotted with trees and at this time of year, early in the month of July in the year 1767, alive with meadow flowers. But it was not to this great medley of colour that the eye was drawn but to the buildings on the summit. For there, dominating the surrounding landscape, was a church with a huge golden ball set upon its tower. While almost immediately in front of it stood a somewhat nightmarish building, quite new judging by the excellent state of the brickwork, hexagonal in shape and faced with flint. It was a strange construction that made John think of a Scottish sepulchral enclosure and something about it made him grow quiet at the very sight.

He had left London the day before, driven by Irish Tom, his coach-driver, taken as far as Maidenhead where they had spent the night at The Bear. The next morning, Tom had returned to Nassau Street to attend to Sir Gabriel's wishes, while John had gone to the livery stables and there he had hired a chestnut stallion with a friendly eye. These days he found this very important in view of his ill luck with hired beasts which constantly threw him, or refused to move, or misbehaved in some way or another which left him — a rather unconfident rider — looking a total idiot. However, judging this horse to be as good as it was possible to get in such an out-of-the-way place, he paid his money and took to the saddle.

The horse, called Rufus because of its red hair presumably, behaved well other than for one fault. It slowed right down whenever they passed an inn. John assumed from this behaviour that it had a regular rider who frequented such places and eventually gave in and dismounted outside The King's Head situated in a small village. Ordering a pint of ale for himself, he sat quietly in a corner and tried to formulate a plan. First of all, he thought, he would somehow have to engineer a meeting with Sir Francis Dashwood. Secondly, he would have to think up a good story to cover the fact that one of the sons of the Earl of Cavan was out wandering the countryside in lonely Buckinghamshire. Then it occurred to him that perhaps he could combine the two; that the Honourable Fintan had come in search of the Postmaster General. But why?

Like a flash of lightning he knew the answer. They were considering introducing the penny post in Dublin. What better excuse than to question Sir Francis about it and say that as an impoverished younger son he was trying his hand at writing and would like the baronet's views on the postal system in general. Suddenly cheerful, John ordered another pint and took some water in a bucket out for the horse.

An hour later he had entered the village of West Wycombe and as he proceeded up the High Street felt his eyes drawn to those two incredible landmarks on the skyline. If these represented Sir Francis's power locally John would have to play his part incredibly well. For reassurance he patted the pocket in his riding coat inside which were some freshly printed cards bearing the inscription "The Honourable Fintan O'Hare, Ballyconnell Castle, Co. Cavan". He just hoped that the baronet had no connections in that particular part of the world.

The one and only coaching inn caught his eye and he headed for it purposefully, handing Rufus to an hostler then making his way within. It was cool and shady inside and he was greeted by a rather charming maidservant who told him that the landlord was at market. Booking himself a room for several nights, John made his way into the taproom. Settling down in a dark recess, complete with a jug of ale, the Apothecary concentrated on listening to the local gossip.

His heart sank as he heard a loud voice say, "Sure, I'm waiting for my master to arrive," in an accent that was unmistakably Irish. He strained his ears.

"Oh, that's what you're about, is it? We did wonder," came the reply.

"He'll be here soon enough," the first voice said. "He's a bit of a lad, you know and might have got distracted on his journey."

There was a rumble of half-hearted laughter and the Apothecary surmised that the Irishman had been boring them half to death ever since his arrival. But his presence in the inn, together with that of his awaited master, could prove disturbing. With their knowledge of Ireland his stratagem could be unmasked almost before he had begun it. He listened on.

"Well now, lads, let me be buying you all a drink," said the Irishman.

This time there was a note of enthusiasm in the reply and John guessed that the fellow had an audience of three or four. There were various cries of, "I'll have an ale, Governor," and then silence while all quaffed. The Apothecary felt that he could not bear the suspense any longer and strolled round the corner to have a look at them.

The Irishman, who had his back turned, was a big fellow with a strange-looking brown wig on his head. He wore breeches tied round the ankles and a pair of working boots, while on his top half he boasted a sensible coat of fustian. His hat was low brimmed and wide and not like any style John had ever seen before. He stood silently while one of the yokels spoke.

"Whereabouts do you come from, sir?"

"Why, 'tis only a small county. Name of Cavan. Have you heard of it?"

The Apothecary virtually reeled back. What evil coincidence could possibly be at work to produce an Irishman from exactly the same place that he was purporting to come from? He stood hesitating, literally rocking from one foot to the other, trying to make up his mind whether to bluff it out or flee — and then the Irishman turned round. John found himself gazing straight into the face of Samuel Swann. There was one awful second while they stared at one another before they both burst out laughing.

"Sam, you old devil," said John, with just the hint of an Irish burr, "you got here before me."

"Glory be to God, sir, so I did," Samuel replied, and winked at him with a little blue eye.

"Well, now, would you like to go to my room and unpack my clothes for me?"

"Sure and I will. Have I time to finish my pint, sir?"

"You most certainly have," said John with an air of sudden generosity. "In fact I think I'll buy you a jug of ale and have one myself."

He settled comfortably in a high-backed chair and put his boots on the table in what he hoped was a typically younger-son-Irish way. Samuel, meanwhile, after seeking permission to sit with his master, waved to the yokel who was acting as potboy to get them their order. John leant forward and lowered his voice to a murmur.

"How the devil did you find me?"

Samuel gave a grin that oozed self-satisfaction. "Easy, old boy. I called round to your house yesterday morning to discover that you had already gone. I presume that you were going to write to me?"

"Yes of course," said John hastily. "But how did you find out about the Irish younger son?"

"Easier still. You left some newly printed cards in the library. I picked one up as soon as I arrived." Samuel looked decidedly smug. "You'll have to be more careful, John. Someone important could find out what you are up to."

John bit back his rude reply. His relationship with Samuel had only just healed and this was not the moment for a witty answer. Instead he said, "Point taken," and laughed.

Sam beamed. "I thought it was rather clever of me. I wormed out of Sir Gabriel the fact that you were posing as a son of the Earl of Cavan . . ."

John found it hard to imagine anyone worming anything out of Sir Gabriel but made no riposte.

". . . and then I wended my way to West Wycombe, to find but one coaching inn." He spread his hands. "The rest you know."

The Apothecary looked him up and down. "And you are meant to be my manservant, I take it?"

"Irish version, old chap. Wouldn't be as formal as an Englishman."

Mentally John shook his head, finding it hard to imagine anyone as terrible as Samuel looked in his homespun garb being anything but a labourer. The potboy approached.

"Oh, Samuel," the Apothecary said loudly. "How kind of you to help out when poor old Flaherty fell flaherty."

Samuel stared blankly.

"Oh, he was a wonderful servant, so he was," John continued. "Why, would you believe, that I looked on him as a father. And now there he is with two broken legs and an arm in jeopardy. But, praise be to the Holy

Virgin, you volunteered to accompany me to England, rough old fellow that you are, to make sure that I wouldn't have to look after meself. You've earned the drink I'm getting for you, so you have, you son of the soil, you."

Samuel looked dumbstruck and said "Eh?" and the potboy appeared thoroughly alarmed.

"Well now, laddie," John went on, getting into full spate, "would you be after having a pint of ale yourself?"

"Oh, no thank you, sir. Not when I'm on duty, like."

"Very creditable in a young fellow. Tell me, my boy, do you know Sir Francis Dashwood?"

"Of course, sir. He owns the village. Everyone recognises him."

"Does he come in here?"

"From time to time he does."

John lowered his voice. "He's not here now, is he?"

"No, sir. As a matter of fact I don't think he's in residence at the moment. I believe he's down in London."

Both John and Samuel made a simultaneous sound of disappointment.

"Oh, glory be, and there was me hoping to call on him. You see I'm very interested in the postal system in Dublin."

This was obviously beyond the potboy who just gaped at him, open-mouthed.

"Yes," said the Apothecary, expanding. "I had hoped to interview him on the subject. Him being Postmaster General and all."

"I don't know much about that, sir. I suggest you call at the big house."

"A splendid plan, thank you, I will." John raised his glass. "And now a toast. To Samuel O'Swann. The most cunning manservant in all Christendom."

Samuel, reviving, said, "Thank you, sir. I'll drink to that," and they clinked glasses.

John had been given a large and interesting room. Straddling the archway which led into the inn's courtyard, it had a window on one side, which looked down into the yard towards the stabling block and the greenery beyond, while the other side had two windows overlooking the street. The inn sign swung rather noisily and in something of a sinister manner beside one of them. Samuel, walking in, whistled beneath his breath.

"I say, this is a bit of all right. I've been relegated to the upstairs part."

"That's because you're a servant." John sat down on the bed. "Sam, are you sure you want to continue with this?"

"I should absolutely think so!" Sam answered with enthusiasm. "I went to quite a bit of trouble to track you down. I'm not going to miss out on the fun now."

"But it could be a bit awkward, particularly if Sir Francis discovers we're acting for Sir John."

"That all adds to the excitement." And Samuel beamed at the Apothecary in such a disarming manner that John decided he must say no more and for the sake of a long and steadfast friendship must endure Sam's occasional blunders. He stood up.

"I must unpack my trunk. It was sent here by cart, by the way."

"Where from?"

"Maidenhead. I parted company with Irish Tom there and hired a horse."

"Why did you do that?"

"To enhance the role I'm playing. I had a feeling that an umpteenth son of Lord Cavan might not be able to afford such a luxury as a coach."

Samuel looked guilty. "I must confess I took a flying coach from London to Maidenhead where I donned a disguise . . ."

John hid a smile.

". . . then I made my way here by farmer's cart. You know, John, it was quite extraordinary, but along the route I'd swear that we passed a coach in which sat Coralie Clive."

"Really?"

"Yes. She was accompanied by a dissolute young man — that would be the heir to the Duke of Sussex who, as you know, she married. They also had a child with them; a girl."

John sighed. "Yes, I knew she'd married some years ago. I'd forgotten about the child. It must have been born when I was occupied elsewhere."

"It would be about ten or so. I'm sure it was Coralie. So much so that I ducked behind a large lady next to whom I was sitting."

"You were travelling on the roof, I take it?"

"You are correct." And Samuel gingerly put a hand to his buttocks.

56

"I wonder where she was going?" said John thoughtfully.

"That," answered Samuel, "we shall probably never know."

He dined alone that evening, Samuel having been dismissed to another parlour in which the servants' food was served. His thoughts roamed wildly as he ate. First he wondered how Octavia was getting on with Rose. Then he thought of Coralie Clive and he pondered again the fact that she had been travelling on the same road as Sam and her possible destination. He remembered how much in love with her he had been all those years ago when he was just a young man and she even younger, determined to make a success of her acting career. Then he thought about her husband, the heir to a dukedom, and a cynical smile crossed his features. She had aimed high and she had achieved her objective. A mere apothecary would not have been sufficient to support the lifestyle she wished to enjoy. John's mind turned to what might have been and he felt himself growing depressed. He deliberately determined to walk as soon as dinner was over to try and shake off such disheartening ideas.

Slipping out of the George and Dragon, John made his way down the street, away from the great house, walking in the direction of High Wycombe. And then he heard the sound of wheels and drew back to let the coach pass. It was a great beast of a thing, painted black and as large and fearsome as anything he had ever seen. There was a crest on the door but one which the Apothecary did not recognise. Standing by the cottage he shrank back as it passed and was rewarded by a brief glimpse of a white face staring out of the window before the blinds were pulled abruptly down. It was the face of a child, a thin, sad face that seemed to quiver as he watched it pass. Then the coach was gone, thundering off in the direction of West Wycombe Park, leaving John standing alone, full of strange conjecture, as it disappeared from view.

CHAPTER
SIX

It was an uneasy night. John slept fitfully, waking several times and turning over again and again when he did manage to drop off. He dreamt that the little girl he had seen in the coach was standing in his room, gazing at him with sorrowful eyes and never saying a word. Indeed on one occasion he could have sworn he actually saw her as he awoke, only for her to fade from view as he returned to full consciousness. John was relieved when it was morning and he was able to rise and eat a hearty breakfast to restore himself.

Samuel, who was buzzing around but not actually doing much work, joined him as he left the guests' dining parlour.

"Well, sir," he said cheerily, "and what are your plans for today?"

"Where have you been, Samuel?" John asked in a slightly irritable voice. "I had to dress myself this morning and not a sign of you anywhere."

Samuel looked contrite; an expression that John always found immensely touching.

"Oh, sir, forgive me please. I must have overslept."

"I see. Well, don't let it happen again. Now let us go to my chamber. I intend to call at West Wycombe today and I must attire myself suitably."

Once inside Sam said, "Oh, John, I'll swear this wretched place is haunted. I hardly got a wink all night."

"I agree. I had a terrible time as well. I dreamt of a child I saw last evening in a coach. She looked so sickly and she was going in the direction of the Dashwood house. I wonder who she could have been."

But Sam was too full of his own stories to pay much attention. "Honest to God, John, I heard nothing but banging and rattling all night long. It was the most frightening experience of my life."

"Did you see anything?"

"No, not exactly." Samuel admitted this with a certain reluctance.

"Well, it was very windy. Probably all you heard was the building shaking. Old places do that you know."

"This inn isn't *that* old."

"But it is possibly built on the site of something much older." John warmed to his theme, watching Sam's face. "Perhaps a monastery. The ghost is probably a phantom monk with a cowl and no face."

"Thank you for that. I shall stay awake and watch for him."

"That I find somewhat hard to imagine. Anyway, I'm going to call on the Dashwoods this morning. What shall I wear?"

They decided on a suit of dark green with a velvet coat, doeskin breeches and an extremely elaborate cravat. John also wore a rather uninhibited ring which he had bought in the market in Cheapside and which his father would have declared as being not fit for a gentleman. However, it had certain merits as far as the Apothecary was concerned and he put it on with great élan and much shooting of his cuffs.

Samuel surveyed the ring with a professional eye. "A nice piece of workmanship that."

"My father hates it but I think it rather charming."

It was a design of a mermaid coiled round an aquamarine into which she appeared to be gazing as if the stone were a mirror.

"Perhaps more suitable for a lady."

"Nonsense, it is far too big. You are not going to put me off it, Samuel. Anyway, it is just the sort of thing that a roguish younger son would wear. Now, which hat?"

They chose a French cocked style, slightly out of fashion, which, they decided, would again point to someone who shopped in Dublin as opposed to London. Then, satisfied that he looked the part, John set out on horseback leaving a somewhat reluctant Samuel behind.

He had his cover story ready, indeed was rehearsing it under his breath as he went along. But thoughts of it were driven from his mind as he entered the parkland by the eastern drive, passing between two lodges as he did so. At the inhabited lodge — the other being got up as some kind of temple — he dismounted and spoke directly to the keeper, asking him if Sir Francis Dashwood were at home. The man confirmed that Sir Francis was in London but that Lady Dashwood was in residence.

"Would it be possible to see her?" John asked, an Irish burr in his voice. "I am the Honourable Fintan O'Hare, fourth son of the Earl of Cavan. I do not have an appointment, however."

"By all means go up to the house, sir. The servants there will be able to tell you more."

The gates were opened and John and his horse went within.

He found himself in an impressive avenue approaching the mansion from the east, the roadway lined with tall and majestic trees. The Apothecary, staring round him, felt a sense of awe as the trees stopped and he found himself skirting a large and magnificent lake on which was moored a frigate. Narrowing his eyes, he observed a figure sitting on the deck taking its ease in the sunshine. Shaking his head at the sheer impudence of having a manned ship moored on one's own private waterway, John guided his horse on.

To the side of the lake was a delightful grotto or cascade. It was built in the form of a huge jagged arch of colossal stones which enshrined a statue of a river god, lying on his back but propped up by one arm. Water trickled round him and on either side of this statue were two little waterfalls formed by the centre of two smaller arches. All these drained into a lower lake which, John observed, had been created by damming the River Wye. Beyond this impressive tract of water a large Broad Walk, very green and attractive looking, could be seen. John reined in his horse to gaze down into the waters.

The colours were brilliant, each droplet reflecting the sunshine of that summer day, and raising his head the Apothecary saw that the lake almost looked real, rather than man-made. It had a wooded island in the middle, within which some building work had been started and John, observing it closely, thought he saw a figure moving about inside.

He moved his horse onward and suddenly the house came into view, standing proudly on an incline. Once again John reined Rufus in to get a better look at the home of Sir Francis Dashwood.

West Wycombe was built in the style of Palladio and was in truth not enormously big. Indeed it was a villa, decorated with porticoes and colonnades, that would not have looked out of place in Italy. Facing John was an entrance with four Doric columns giving the overall impression of a temple. It had a rise of several wide steps leading up to it and a centrally placed door between two large windows. Above the church-like top stood three ornate stone ornaments.

John hesitated, wondering whether to dismount and knock at the door. Yet something told him that this was not the entrance generally used. Instead he walked Rufus round to the south side of the house and there slid down to the ground. Manners dictated that he should take the horse to the stables before he called but a very real fear of being shown away made him hang on to the reins.

"Can I help you?" demanded a woman's voice behind him.

The Apothecary spun round and found himself confronting a vision in grey. For not only was she dressed in that most boring of colours but had eyes, skin and hair to match.

He gave a deep bow. "Madam, I do apologise for appearing like this. I was hoping to see Sir Francis Dashwood and discuss the possible introduction of the Penny Post in Dublin with him. But, alas, I was informed at the lodgehouse that he is in London. Therefore it was my intention to see his wife and ask her if I might have the honour of being granted an appointment with the Postmaster General at some time in the future."

The ugly face stared back at him, not moving a muscle by way of changing its expression. Eventually it opened its mouth. "Who did you say you were?"

John gave an even deeper bow. "I didn't, ma'am. Allow me to present you with my card."

He produced one from an inner pocket and handed it to her with a flourish.

She became slightly human. "I cannot read it without my spectacles. Be kind enough to do so out loud."

The Apothecary cleared his throat. "The Honourable Fintan O'Hare, Ballyconnell Castle, Cavan, Eire. And may I ask, madam, to whom I have the honour of speaking?"

"I am Lady Dashwood," she said coldly.

John gave the deepest bow of all. "Madam, I am overwhelmed. Truly."

He said this last with a definite Irish accent and looked up with a twinkle in his eye. The lady did not respond but continued to regard him with a grim visage.

"Why do you wish to discuss the Penny Post with Sir Francis?" she asked.

"Well, madam, as the fourth son of the Earl of Cavan it has befallen on me to make a living for myself and I am trying my hand at writing a little in Dublin newspapers and journals. I thought that an interview with the Postmaster General would be a grand thing, so it would."

He was trying the Irish charm to the best of his ability with a stunning lack of success.

Lady Dashwood gave him an icy stare. "I cannot speak for my husband. You'd best come back when he is in residence."

"Of course I will. Thank you so much. When are you expecting him?"

She hesitated, wondering whether to answer him, then reluctantly said, "He is returning from town tonight."

"Then I shall call tomorrow if I may."

"As you wish. I cannot guarantee that he will see you, mark you."

"No, naturally not. I shall just have to rely on fate."

All the time he was talking John's eyes were taking in the beauty of the landscape and of the delightful villa, wishing that she would take pity on him and invite him inside. And then as luck would have it the central door in the colonnaded entrance facing him opened. A very sickly looking man of about thirty-five appeared in the doorway, shielding his gaze against the high sun, then strolled out onto the terrace, sinking down into a chair.

"Sarah," he called in a feeble voice, "Sarah."

"I must go to my cousin," Lady Dashwood said abruptly. "He is rather poorly. I bid you good day, sir."

"Can I help at all?" John asked, momentarily forgetting his pose.

She shot him a poisonous look. "Most certainly not . . ."

But at that moment the man on the terrace let out a terrible scream, tore at his cravat and fell with a loud thump onto the stone floor. John did not hesitate but ran forward, followed by Lady Dashwood, panting a little as she ran. Reaching the invalid first, the Apothecary picked him up and was rewarded by the creature being violently sick all over him.

"God's wounds," said John, side-stepping as the man retched profoundly once more.

Fortunately this avalanche missed him and hit the floor of the terrace, spattering as it landed. The Apothecary spared a thought for the wretched servant who was going to have to clean it up.

Lady Dashwood came puffing up. "My dear Charles, what ails you? Is it the heat? You'd best go back indoors."

For answer Charles heaved for a third time, all over himself and the base of the chair. John deduced that the entire thing had been brought on by the fellow having imbibed too well the night before.

"He's in a terrible state," he announced to Lady Dashwood, who had stepped back adroitly and thus missed being hit. "Can you call a servant and I'll help him indoors."

"There's no need," she answered stiffly.

"I think, madam, that there is. The Earl of Cavan insisted that all his sons be trained in the art of caring for the sick. We all had to study for one year."

She was shaken out of her usual forbidding manner. "Really? How unusual."

"The Earl of Cavan is a very unusual man," John replied solemnly. He hoisted Charles up by one arm which the Apothecary placed round his shoulders. Then he started half dragging the man towards the house. Sarah Dashwood in the meantime had frantically started ringing a hand bell which was placed on one of the many tables scattered about. A footman appeared.

"Help Mr . . . ?"

"O'Hare."

"O'Hare . . . to assist Lord Arundel to his room if you please. And send someone to clear up the vomit."

"If I might beg a change of clothes, madam," said John as he pulled the stumbling figure within. "Anything will do."

For the second time since they had met Lady Dashwood appeared almost human.

"Of course. Gollins will see to it."

"Then I'll just put the patient to bed. I cannot forgo my early training. Father would be very angry if I did."

"There's really no need."

"There's every need," John replied firmly, and took the lolling figure indoors.

He found himself in a beautiful entrance hall which, for all its charms, seemed somewhat in need of decoration. But John's eye was drawn to the magnificent staircase which rose up to his left. Made of mahogany, it had balusters of walnut and treads inlaid with marquetry in satinwood and ebony. Yet it was to the frescoes decorating it that the Apothecary found himself attracted. Depicting biblical and mythological scenes, they were vibrant and alive, arresting full attention. But as he lugged the unconscious figure of Lord Arundel upward, the footman straining on the other side, John saw that as one ascended to bedroom level the paintings became more and more erotic, while on the half-landing a portrait of Angerona, the goddess of silence, raised her finger to her lips enjoining discretion. It became perfectly obvious at that moment that Sir Francis Dashwood was certainly very interested in matters pertaining to the boudoir.

"Second bedroom on the left, sir," the footman grunted.

"Very good. Let's get him down and best leave a bucket beside him, that is if he's got the wit to use it."

"Yes, sir."

They reached the bedroom and laid the figure on the bed, John removing Lord Arundel's stained and unpleasant clothes. For good measure he took off his own coat and shirt and threw them on top of his lordship's. The footman scooped them up and holding them at arm's length disappeared from the room.

The Apothecary turned to the window which overlooked the lake. It was rarely that he had seen a more beautiful vista. The waterway, the sun gleaming upon it, stood calm and motionless in the summer day, its three little islands adding an air of mystery to the landscape. In the distance he could see the cascade, pouring water into the lower lake, while the frigate which he had passed earlier bobbed happily on its surface. In the distance John could spy the church with its great golden orb atop its spire and the grim mausoleum, the substance of nightmares, standing nearby. But this one blot on the landscape was totally obliterated by the rest of the warm and happy vista stretching before him. With a contented sigh, the Apothecary rested his hands on the window sill and gazed out.

At that moment the door opened behind him and John turned to see who had entered the room. Suddenly aware that he was stripped to the waist, he saw that it was a woman. His eyes, dazzled by the sunshine outside, believed that she was surrounded by an aureole of gold, that she was a creature of legend, and then the optical illusion wore away. His heart leapt, then plummeted to his stomach. He was, after all that had passed between them, looking once more on the face of Coralie Clive.

CHAPTER
SEVEN

They stood gazing at one another, she peering somewhat short-sightedly John thought. Eventually she spoke.

"John? Is it you?" she asked huskily.

"Yes," he answered, suddenly finding that that was the only word he could manage to utter.

"But what are you doing here?"

"Coralie, I can't tell you that. Not now at any rate. Just believe that it is for a good purpose."

At this point the creature on the bed moaned loudly and Coralie slowly made her way towards him. Sitting down, she looked at him, shaking her head.

"Oh, Charles, Charles. What in God's name has happened to you?"

Suddenly everything became crystal-clear to the Apothecary, who felt a consequent pang of unreasonable pain.

"I take it that he is your husband?"

"Yes."

"How long have you been married?"

"Twelve years. I have a daughter of ten."

"I see."

But see was one thing he didn't do. The close relationship between him and the actress had ended because she refused to marry him, choosing instead to follow her career upon the stage. So he had wedded Emilia, a kind and good girl whom he had adored, only to have her snatched from him by a cold-hearted murderer. But it was to Coralie that he had given his youthful heart. She had known his hopes and fears, his dreams, his obsessions. He had loved her long and well only to have that love thrown back in his face.

The actress looked up at him. "Do you?"

"What?"

"See. I'd wager a guinea that you are very far from that emotion, John."

"Coralie," he said, with a definite edge in his voice, "I would like to discuss this with you but this is neither the time nor the place. So we must save that conversation for the future. I have a far more pressing favour that I have to ask you."

She turned her head in his direction. "Which is?"

"I am here under false pretences. I'll tell you briefly that I am acting on behalf of Sir John Fielding . . ."

"What a surprise!" she said sarcastically.

". . . and I am posing as the Honourable Fintan O'Hare, a son of the Earl of Cavan. I beg you not to give me away. A great deal depends on my masquerade."

Coralie got up and came towards him. "And does the Honourable Fintan make a habit of receiving lady visitors stripped to the waist?"

"Always," he replied, and just for a second saw a glint of her old humour.

There was a knock on the door and John hastily stepped away. "Come in," Coralie called.

It was Gollins the footman bearing some clean clothes for John. He looked quite shocked at seeing him in a state of disarray in front of a woman.

"Oh, beg pardon, my Lady. I didn't know you were in here."

She turned on him the serene gaze that only a consummate actress could have achieved.

"That's perfectly all right, Gollins. The Honourable Fintan and I are old friends. Now, I see you have brought him some fresh apparel so if you would be kind enough to show him the dressing room he can complete his toilette."

"Thank you, my Lady," said John, and made a deep bow, half naked as he was.

He followed the servant along the corridor and was shown into a room in which was placed the very latest in toilet tables, namely a wash-stand in a corner, the top a quadrant with an upstand to take a large basin. Someone had also thoughtfully brought a jug of hot water. John explored the room and found a water closet set in a niche, the door so close to the seat as to hide it only when not in use. Despite this disadvantage he made full use of it, then washed himself thoroughly, sponging his doeskin breeches where blobs of vomit had adhered. He then put on the shirt and jacket — both thoroughly unfashionable — and made his way downstairs.

Coralie had gone down before him and he could hear her voice as he descended the staircase.

"My dear Lady Dashwood, I have known the Earl of Cavan for some time. I met him when I acted in Dublin. He is a grand old gentleman and I believe it is a stroke of fortune that one of his sons should have presented himself here and given aid to poor Charles."

"Oh," answered the other in her usual flat monotone, "I am glad you are able to vouch for him. Do you think I should invite the young man to dine?"

"Most certainly, yes. It would be a pity . . ."

Coralie's voice broke off as she saw John approaching.

"My dear Lady Dashwood," he said, making a deep bow to the senior woman. "It is time I took my leave of you. Thank you for your hospitality."

She gave a little snort. "It has hardly been that. I am grateful to you for caring for my cousin. Lady Arundel has just been telling me how she met your father in Dublin, by the way."

"I thank Lady Arundel for her kind words," said John, regarding Coralie with the merest hint of a twinkle in his eye.

"Perhaps you would care to come and dine tomorrow night. Then you may quiz Sir Francis about the Penny Post."

"I should be delighted to do so, ma'am. At what time do you sit down?"

"At four o'clock. We are in the country here."

"I shall be here at ten to, if that would be convenient."

"It will suit well enough. Good day to you."

"Good day, madam. Good day, Lady Arundel. I hope your husband soon recovers."

"Thank you. Farewell Mr O'Hare."

He left through the main front door and went round to the stables in search of his horse, his mind in turmoil. To see the woman who had once been the love of his life so unexpectedly was bad enough. But to find her married to a drunken roué, a feckless wastrel of a husband who could not hold his liquor, was beyond the pale. And then John was forced to the conclusion that the fact that Charles Arundel was heir to the Duke of Sussex had been the factor that had decided Coralie into making such an alliance. Feeling thoroughly depressed, he entered the stable yard.

A child on a white pony was there before him. A pale, wan girl who was lifted from the saddle and placed on the ground by the groom who had ridden with her. She turned on hearing John's footsteps and he looked into the face of Coralie Clive as she must have been years ago. The only difference was that this particular girl had pale blonde hair and blue eyes. Other than for that the likeness was stunning.

John made a bow. "How do you do, miss? A beautiful day, is it not?"

"It is, sir," she replied listlessly.

"And do I have the honour of addressing the daughter of Lord and Lady Arundel?"

"You do."

The groom had moved closer in a protective manner, eyeing John somewhat suspiciously.

"Allow me to present myself," the Apothecary said, more for the servant's benefit than the girl's. "I am the Honourable Fintan O'Hare and I have just been calling on Lady Dashwood."

The child made no response but the groom immediately saluted. "You've come for your horse, sir?"

"Yes. It is a chestnut stallion. I take it it is here?"

"I'll go and find it, sir, and bring it round."

He disappeared leaving John alone with Coralie's daughter. He gazed at her, fascinated by her likeness to her mother. Yet, for all their physical resemblance, the girl was but a poor shadow in contrast to the actress, for she had inherited much of her father's pallor and general lassitude.

"Tell me, young lady, what is your name?"

"Georgiana Arundel."

"I have a daughter," said John unguardedly, then realised that he had spoken out of turn.

"Oh," answered Georgiana, disinterested. She gave a little cough.

"Have you suffered from that for long?" the Apothecary asked.

"Yes, for some time now."

"I must try and find a cure for it."

"Do you know about things like that?"

"I have a certain knowledge."

"Oh," the child answered once more, in that same disinterested tone.

At that moment a nursemaid bustled from the direction of the house and swooped down on Georgiana.

"Oh, there you are, miss. I've been worried about you. Come on in and have a cold drink. Did you enjoy your ride?"

"Yes, fairly," the little girl answered and would have left without saying farewell to John had he not made her a sweeping bow and said, "Goodbye, Miss Arundel. No doubt we shall meet again."

She dropped him a very small curtsey. "Goodbye, Mr O'Hare. I hope we do."

John stared after her and was still doing so when the groom brought Rufus round, saddled up and ready to ride. The Apothecary slipped him a coin and set off down the east drive. At the lake, however, he had to draw into the side to make way for a rather vivid man also riding a horse and talking to himself.

"*Merde*," the fellow was muttering under his breath. "*Merde, merde.* How could they be so damnable careless? That is what I want to know."

He had a pronounced French accent and was riding quite recklessly so that he did not see John until the last minute.

"Watch out!" John called.

The Frenchman pulled his horse to the side with a sudden jolt. "A thousand pardons, *monsieur*. The truth is I did not see you. You are not 'urt, I trust?"

"Too busy chattering away to yourself," John answered without malice.

The Frenchman grinned. "It is a 'abit I have. I tell my wife it is because I am such a good conversationalist. Forgive me."

76

"Think nothing of it," the Apothecary answered, and regarded him.

He was a cheery-looking little man, with dark hair and bright eyes very reminiscent of a cock robin. He wore a hat which was slightly too small for him which he had crammed down over a wig that had seen better days. His suit, too, was workaday and in a sensible shade of brown. But the hands which held the reins belied his somewhat pedestrian appearance. For they were the hands of an artist, of someone immensely creative. Short and square they might be but the fingers were sensitive, beautiful almost. John was fascinated.

"You're going to see the Dashwoods?" he asked, stating the obvious.

A cloud crossed the Frenchman's face. "Careless lot," he muttered. He raised his voice and said, "*Oui, monsieur*. I am going to repair one of the Langlois commodes. Some idiot has bumped into it and damaged it."

"Oh, I see."

"Allow me to present myself. I am Pierre Dominique Jean, son-in-law of Pierre Langlois, the cabinet maker. I am known as Dominique."

John knew the name. "How do you do, sir? I am Jo —" He caught himself just in time. "Fintan O'Hare," he continued. "You are a cabinet maker also?"

Dominique shook his head. "No, I am a water gilder. In other words I design and make ormolu mounts for furniture, amongst other things."

"So what's gone wrong in West Wycombe House?"

"Some idiot knocked over one of the commodes, indeed must have given it a hearty shove, and has displaced two of the feet. Sir Francis wants me to repair it as soon as possible."

"I see."

"I'm going to assess the damage and see if I can mend it on the spot or whether I must take the commode back to the workshop."

"How are you going to manage that?" asked John, staring at the horse.

"My dear *monsieur*, I have a coach which has lost a wheel and is awaiting repair in Maidenhead. I usually call on Sir Francis in my best clothes but, alas, they are in my trunk. So he must take me as I am."

"He's not there," John answered. "He's coming back tomorrow."

The Frenchman looked relieved. "That's as well. Lady Dashwood does not deign to notice what I am wearing."

"Where are you staying?" the Apothecary asked.

"In the George and Dragon. The coachman will bring my equipage to the inn when the repair is done."

"Well, sir, it would be an honour for me to buy you a drink there this evening."

"And I would be honoured to accept it. And now I must be on my way."

The Frenchman swept his hat from his head, dislodging the well-used wig slightly. "*Au revoir, monsieur*."

"Until tonight."

"Indeed."

The last sight John had of him was going hell for leather up the drive towards West Wycombe House.

Samuel was waiting for him outside the gates of the east drive, sitting on the ground and reading a book. He looked up as John approached.

"Success, my friend?"

"More than I could have bargained for." And John dismounted and walked back to the inn recounting to Samuel all the extraordinary events that had happened that day. Samuel's face took on the strange expression which meant that he was thinking deep thoughts.

"And how did you feel seeing Coralie again after all this time?"

"To be honest, Samuel, I felt somewhat frozen. As if I were in a dream. In fact, even now, I can't really believe that I saw her."

"Well you did." Samuel's eyes glinted. "How would you feel if . . ."

"If what, my friend?"

"Oh, never mind," the Goldsmith replied hastily.

"I think you were going to say how would I feel if she had still been single?"

Samuel gave a sheepish grin.

"I don't know is the answer. Our love affair was a long time ago and a great deal has happened to both of us in the interim. Her husband, by the way, is a complete wastrel. He was sick all over me — hence these extraordinary garments — and looks wrecked into the bargain. As a matter of fact I don't think he has long for this world."

"Then there's hope!"

"Samuel, really," John said impatiently. "I cannot cut out the past as if it never happened and neither can Coralie. We are two entirely different people. And that is truly all I have to say on the matter. Please let it rest."

"I was only conjecturing," said Sam, somewhat hurt.

"I'm sure you were. Anyway, here's the inn. I'm going to have a drink. I feel as if I've earned one."

They were joined an hour later by Dominique Jean, grinning all over his face at the sight of them.

"This is my manservant," said John hastily. "His name is Samuel O'Swann. He and I often share a jug of ale together."

Dominique raised his eyebrows but made no comment and sat down happily enough, raising his glass of claret to John.

"To you, *monsieur. Merci.*"

"How did you get on up at the big house?"

Dominique frowned. "Let me explain to you about the two commodes that my late father-in-law made. They are not to be confused with those smelly close stools which were used in the past for lavatorial purposes. No, they are small cabinets for storage made by a master craftsman. You have not yet seen them, *monsieur*, but when you do please note the *bombe* form of the pieces and the exquisite use of marquetry. Furthermore, the great Pierre Langlois crowned their tops with specimen marbles imported from Florence." The little bird-like man kissed his fingers.

"Pierre Langlois, eh?" said Samuel, forgetting his Irish accent. "He was a well known craftsman. Did you say he was your father-in-law, sir?"

"Indeed he was. As you know, gentlemen, he died recently, which was a great loss to us all."

"May I address you as Dominique?" said John.

"Please do so, *monsieur*."

"Tell me, how was Lord Arundel when you left?"

"I did not see him," Dominique answered, sipping his wine. "His wife came and spoke to me when I examined the commode."

John felt a thrill of interest. "Oh really?"

"Yes. She seemed very guilty about the whole affair. I imagined it was either her husband or her daughter who fell over it in the first place."

"How bad is the damage?"

"Reasonable. I can do the repair on site, though it will probably take a day or two."

"What about your tools?"

"They are in my coach which, with luck, should be here this evening."

"I have been invited to dine there tomorrow, you know."

"Then no doubt I may well see you."

"Tell me, my friend," John asked, liking this Frenchman and feeling that his opinion would be worth consideration, "what is Sir Francis really like?"

Dominique barked a laugh. "He is one of the most colourful characters of the age. He is utterly ruled by his prick, if you'll forgive my being so forthright. He loves women and drinking above everything else. Do you know what Bubb Doddington said about him?"

"No," answered Samuel, leaning forward.

"I heard this from my father-in-law who overheard the conversation in another room. He — that's Doddington — said that Dashwood was like a public reservoir, laying his cock in every private family that has any place fit to receive it."

John laughed but Samuel guffawed joyously.

"Oh, John," he said, "you're going to be hard put to it tomorrow."

"Indeed I am," the Apothecary answered.

Dominique looked surprised. "You obviously get on very well with your servant, *monsieur*."

"Yes," said John, calming down, "I most certainly do."

CHAPTER
EIGHT

The following night, John Rawlings dressed very finely in a creation of succulent damson taffeta with a silver waistcoat embroidered with a million little stars in a shade of ripe plum. He set forth at exactly three-forty in the coach belonging to Pierre Langlois, currently in the ownership of his son-in-law. It had arrived on the previous evening — much to the delight of Dominique — and had gone round to the stableyard of the inn. But early the following morning the water gilder had set off in it carrying a long apron together with the tools of his trade. On his face he had had the most determined expression. He had returned, looking somewhat sour, at exactly half past three.

"What's the matter?" John had asked as he had met him in the downstairs lobby.

"That bastard Arundel, he is a *salaud*."

"Why? What has he done?"

"He owes me £700 for work I have carried out on his behalf. I have sent him bill after bill but all I get is vague promises and when I press him he becomes the noble aristocrat, too high and mighty to settle up. Furthermore he terrifies that child of his. She is scared out of her wits by him."

"Really? What gives you that impression?"

"Something I overheard today. I'll tell you of it another time. Now you must make haste."

John stepped into the coach gratefully, glad that Dominique had offered to lend it to him, delighted that he was not going to have to ride in his most elegant night clothes.

He was set down at the front door in the colonnaded entrance, already lit with flaming torches set in sconces along the wall; all this despite the brightness of the day. He pealed the bell which was answered immediately by a footman.

"Sir Francis is expecting you, sir. If you would follow me."

The servant led the way across the hall to a room directly opposite. Throwing it open he said, "The Honourable Fintan O'Hare, my Lord," in an extremely adenoidal voice.

John stepped inside and hardly knew where to look first, so fine and splendid was everything about him. Immediately opposite where he was standing were three mighty arched windows giving splendid views of the lake and its little wooded islands. Above his head the ceiling was painted with a fresco depicting a meeting of the gods, the males with pieces of flowing cloak or discreetly raised knees hiding their genitalia, the women with arms draped decorously over their breasts. He was still gazing at it when a voice from a deep and comfortable chair said, "Good afternoon, sir."

The Apothecary dragged his attention back and gave a florid bow before saying, "Good afternoon, my Lord."

"You may call me Sir Francis," replied the other with a growl of a laugh. "Everybody does."

John focused his eyes and found himself looking down into an extraordinary face the colour of a rich royal ruby, adorned by a long and large shining nose that spoke volumes of its owner's addiction to fleshly pleasures. Above the nose were two deep-set eyes, dark as chestnuts and equally fierce in their aspect. But the lips were those of a worldly libertine, the bottom one being full and demanding, the upper scarcely visible. In his hand Sir Francis held a glass of red wine and while he scrutinised John from top to toe he sipped at it continuously.

"You're very finely arrayed if I may say so, sir. Who's your tailor?"

The Apothecary was on the point of telling him and then remembered his pose. "Oh, I don't suppose you'll have heard of him, sir. 'Tis a wee fellow from Dublin. My father swears by him."

Sir Francis got to his feet, moving athletically for a man of his build. "Let's have a good look at you." He studied John's face in the light streaming through the three windows. "Oh, it's quite a handsome lad that the Earl of Cavan produced. It was the Earl of Cavan you said, wasn't it?"

"Yes, sir."

John prayed silently that if such a man existed then Sir Francis would have no particular knowledge of him.

"I don't know much about the Irish peerage," the other man said reassuringly. "In fact all I know about that country is that I am thinking of introducing some sort of postal system at some time in the future. A good plan, don't you agree?"

"Oh yes, Sir Francis," John replied enthusiastically. "It is high time that we were organised in that regard."

"Um, well I'll remember your words if ever the time comes. Now, my boy, to more serious matters. What would you like to drink?"

"A glass of claret would go down well, thank you."

Sir Francis crossed to a sideboard, poured out a glass of deep-red wine from a sparkling crystal decanter, then motioned John to a seat, and returned to his own chair opposite.

"My wife tells me that you want to interview me with regard to writing something or other in an Irish journal."

"That's correct, Sir Francis. Any views you have about the postal system or anything else for that matter would be greatly appreciated."

"I see. Well, now is not the time. Perhaps later in the week."

John was just starting his torrent of effusive thanks when there were footsteps in the hall outside and then the door was flung open. Arundel stood in the entrance, swaying very slightly.

"Ah come in, Charles. I was wondering where you had got to. Allow me to present to you the Honourable Fintan O'Hare, son of the Earl of Cavan."

"How dee do?" said Lord Arundel, extending a long white hand before making a perfunctory bow.

"How do you do, my Lord?"

John echoed his bow but made his a little deeper. It was perfectly clear from the expression on Charles Arundel's face that he had no recollection whatsoever of their previous meeting.

"A glass of wine, Charles? You just have time before we sit down to dine."

"That would be splendid, Francis. I slept this afternoon so I've recovered from this morning."

John shot him a glance from under his lashes. Lord Arundel was thin, indeed almost gaunt, and wore a brilliant white wig which accentuated his *beau monde maquillage*. He looked to the Apothecary as if he suffered from anaemia and was covering it up by wearing a white foundation and powder. His lips, which he had not carmined however, appeared bloodless and drawn, and John thought him a most unattractive specimen. He wondered what could possibly have possessed Coralie Clive to marry such a creature and could only conjecture that he must have been handsome in the days when she first knew him.

"Cavan?" said Lord Arundel, wrinkling his nose very slightly. "Is that an Irish title?"

"Yes, my Lord," John answered politely.

"I see." And Charles put a great deal of meaning into those two words.

John found himself disliking the fellow, partly because he had ruined the green velvet coat of which the Apothecary had been particularly fond.

"Are you feeling better?" he asked spitefully.

"Than when?" said Arundel, peering down the length of his thinly sculpted nose.

"Than yesterday, sir. I was the person who helped you to your room." John smiled disarmingly.

"Were you, by Jove? Then I owe you my heartfelt thanks." Despite the warmth of the words Charles contrived to say them with a chill in his tone.

John was just beginning to get annoyed when a footman threw open the door and intoned that dinner was served. At this Sarah, Lady Dashwood, accompanied by Coralie Clive appeared and were escorted in to dine by their husbands with the Apothecary following somewhat lamely behind.

Once in the dining room, he was again struck by the beauty of the ceiling which carried a huge painting of the Triumph of Bacchus and Ariadne. Indeed the theme of the room was definitely bacchanalian and John, looking at the sideboard loaded with decanters, felt that he was in for a definite feast. Mentally he girded himself for the fray. His eye wandered to a plaster statue of the Venus de' Medici standing in a niche in the right-hand wall. She seemed to preside over the room and John could not help but contrast her voluptuous curves, scarcely concealed by her judiciously placed hands, with the flat and forbidding figure of Sir Francis's wife, who sat looking grim as ever on her husband's right. Coralie, on the other hand, looked beautiful, though greatly changed, in deepest red.

John studied her. Her figure was much the same, perhaps an inch or so fuller, though still admirable. Her hair, black as midnight, had just a hint of frosting, yet her emerald eyes were clear and fresh despite the little lines round them. He looked at her hands, one toying with the stem of her wine glass, and was filled with a longing to hold one.

She must have caught his gaze because she said with a certain amount of amusement, "And how was your father when you last saw him, Mr O'Hare?"

He answered, with Sir Gabriel Kent in mind, "Still well despite his great age, thank you, ma'am. He spends much time in reading these days but is most delighted when he is visited by my daughter."

Lady Dashwood looked up. "You have a daughter! I did not realise you were even married, sir." She said the words like an accusation.

"I was married some years ago, my Lady, but unfortunately my wife . . . died."

"I'm sorry to hear that," she replied in her usual stiff way.

But Coralie said in an undertone, "How unhappy you must have been."

"I was indeed, madam. I was wounded to the heart for more than one reason."

Sir Francis called from the end of the table, "Mr O'Hare, I'm sorry for your personal tragedy but we do not have sad people around us for long. So drink and be merry. I would like to propose a toast. To the Earl of Cavan and his many sons."

"I'll drink to that and gladly," John answered and rose to his feet as did the other men present.

"And now," said the host, beaming geniality, "let us eat."

It was an excellent meal of several courses into which John tucked heartily. However, he could not help but notice that Charles picked at his food, moving it round his plate with his fork, yet drinking heavily all the while. He came to the conclusion that there was something wrong with the man though he couldn't as yet identify what it was.

It was a strange sensation, sitting next to Coralie, wondering what she was thinking, almost as if the clocks had been turned back and the intervening years with all their spent passions and terrible dramas had not taken place. But they had and there could be no denying them. John decided that there was only one thing to do and that was to get as merry as possible without reducing himself to the level of Charles Arundel, whom he already cordially disliked.

"Do you travel at all, Mr O'Hare?"

"Not a great deal, Sir Francis. But I hear that you are quite a voyager."

"Oh yes, indeed. When I was very young I went on the Grand Tour and the impression it left on me was remarkable. I also went on a visit to meet the Empress Anna Petrovna of Russia and I have made a journey to Greece and Asia Minor."

"I envy you that, sir."

"It was in Asia Minor that I met young Arundel's father."

"Really?"

John stole a glance at Charles and saw that a bright pink flush had now invaded his cheeks.

"Oh yes. I have been a friend of his ever since. He was a member of the Divan Club which is an organisation specifically for people who have visited the Ottoman Empire."

John's ears became alert, wondering if it was possible that this was the club to which Sir John Fielding had referred.

"How very interesting, sir. Does that club still function?"

"No, alas. It was difficult to find members with the right qualifications. But I am still friendly with several of the people concerned."

At this Dashwood gave rather a coarse laugh in which Charles joined. John was convinced that they were referring to something else and wondered if it could possibly be another club. He was just about to make some superficial comment when there came another ring at the front door.

Sir Francis looked up. "That will be James Avon-Nelthorpe. He is travelling from London and said he might be late." He turned to his wife. "You have no objection to him joining us I take it, my dear?"

She sighed a little and turning to a servant said, "Lay another cover, would you."

There was the sound of voices in the hall and then the door to the dining room was opened and a footman intoned, "The Honourable James Avon-Nelthorpe and Mrs Avon-Nelthorpe."

Every head turned to look and John, giving the couple who stood in the doorway a quick glance, formed the immediate impression that the Honourable

James had brought an ancient London whore with him. For the woman in his company was easily old enough to be his mother and was fat, short and wore far too much rouge. On top of her white-blonde mass of curls she had a pink hat with a whirl of pink feathers floating at the side, this matching her open robe which covered a very fussy white petticoat beneath. Dimly visible beneath this extraordinary outfit were a pair of pink top-boots, and pink gloves gave the finishing touch.

"Damme, James," said Sir Francis, rising. "You did not say you were bringing your wife."

"Oh, cooee!" exclaimed the newcomer. "Sorry to intrude, I'm sure. Do hope you'll forgive me, Lady Dashwood. It's just that James has hurt his back and he has no one to attend to it for him but his little wifey."

She grinned, displaying a row of small white teeth, sharp as blades.

"Oh, no trouble at all," Sarah answered in her monotonous voice. "Wilkins, lay two places."

"I don't think you know everyone," said Sir Francis, still standing. "Lady Arundel, may I present Mrs Avon-Nelthorpe?"

The fat lady bobbed a curtsey. "Pleased to meet you, I'm sure, Lady Arundel. The pleasure is entirely mine."

"How do you do, ma'am," said Coralie extending a gracious hand.

"And may I present the Honourable Fintan O'Hare to you, Mrs Avon-Nelthorpe?" Over him she ran a shrewd little eye, encased in pouches of fat, in quite one of the most penetrating glances he had ever seen; indeed he almost felt stripped bare so all-consuming was it.

John rose and bowed fulsomely. "How nice," was all he could think of saying.

The Honourable James meanwhile stood shuffling from foot to foot, blushing violently. He was an extraordinary young man with bright hair, the colour of carrots, which he wore tied back in a queue. In contrast with his wife he had a lanky frame with hardly an ounce of superfluous flesh on it and wore his clothes with a certain natural inelegance, rather as if they were the first thing he could find to put on. His skin was fair and covered with freckles and he was only saved from being rather ugly by a fine pair of eyes, topaz in colour, which gleamed as he looked round the assembled company.

"Sorry indeed, Lady Dashwood, to be a dashed bore but the fact is that Betsy and I had a most appalling journey from London, don't you know. We hardly stopped at all."

"Except for comfort," Betsy said predictably.

"Quite," said Sir Francis. "Do please sit down. Mrs Avon-Nelthorpe, if you would sit next to Lord Arundel and James next to Lady Arundel."

She took her place at once and gave His Lordship a nudge in the ribs. "Hello, Charles," she said and flashed one of her sharp-toothed smiles.

He looked slightly discomfited. "How are you, Betsy? Well, I trust."

"Yes, thank you. I am in good health." She turned her attention to John. "I'm sorry I didn't quite catch your name."

"Fintan, ma'am. Fintan O'Hare. I am Irish."

"Are you now? How delightful. I think them a most amusing race."

John smiled and nodded as she rambled on in this vein, wondering all the while about her origins. She was, he could have sworn, a lady of the night who had somehow — his mind reeled away from going down this path — inveigled a respectable young man into marrying her. His gaze turned on the husband. A plain creature when all was said and done with only his eyes to redeem him.

James looked up at this point and, fleetingly, the Apothecary saw something beneath the workaday surface; something quite molten and alarming. But almost instantly it was gone, leaving John with the impression that he had imagined it, that the carroty-haired young man was ordinary in the extreme. Yet had that notion been deliberately foisted upon him?

Betsy was holding forth. "I do find coaches so uncomfortable these days. La, but they make my bum ache."

"Really?" said Coralie, icily polite.

"Ah well," put in Sir Francis jovially, "you'll find the beds here really restful. A good night's sleep will soon put you at your ease."

This remark was completely harmless in itself, but at that particular moment John glanced up and this time caught an extremely lewd wink given by the host to

94

Arundel, who returned it with an elegant shrug of his shoulders.

The Apothecary decided to enter the conversation, saying, "How do you manage to amuse yourselves, here in the heart of the country?"

Lady Dashwood said boringly, "Oh well, we enjoy country pursuits."

"Such as?" John persisted.

"Of an evening we play chess, or have music and singing, or we might even dance."

"Oh come now, Mr O'Hare, you live in the country in Cavan. Surely you must know what people get up to in the evenings," said Coralie, turning to regard John with her wonderful green eyes.

"I think I have some idea, ma'am," answered John, innocently enough, but at that moment catching Sir Francis's nut-brown gaze.

"We find plenty to do with ourselves, young fellow, don't you worry."

"Oh no, sir, I'm quite sure you do. I'm not worried at all," John answered insouciantly, and looking straight at his host raised his eyebrows in a question.

CHAPTER
NINE

"And what happened then?" asked Samuel, brimming with ale and jolliness.

"I watched like a somewhat drunken hawk and felt sure that at least two of them — I refer to the men of course — were hiding something," John answered.

"What?"

"That I am not certain about."

"Well I am," said Dominique, slurring his words very slightly. "What you refer to is the Hellfire Club."

"Ah! Tell me, does it still exist?"

"Of course it does. But it doesn't meet at West Wycombe. Oh no, they're far too clever for that."

"Then where?"

"At a place called Medmenham Abbey, not far from here. At least that is what my father-in-law told me and he overheard much during his days at the big house."

John gave a subdued shout and several lingering customers turned to look at him. "As I thought," he said.

The dinner party had gone on for rather a long time, during which he had become more and more convinced that Sir Francis and Lord Arundel were sharing some sort of secret. Eventually, though, he had managed to escape, bowing to everyone and thanking Sir Francis and Lady Dashwood profusely. Then he had hurried back in the Langlois coach to the George and Dragon to find, much as he had expected and hoped, that both Samuel and Dominique were in the taproom and drinking merrily. Samuel in his guise of manservant had stuck to ale, which had made him both excited and sweaty, while Dominique, a Frenchman to his fingertips, had ordered a good wine and had already consumed a whole bottle.

John, feeling positively sober in comparison, took a sip and said, "Tell me, Dominique, was your father-in-law ever invited to any of these meetings?"

Dominique snorted. "Not he, sir. He was considered trade."

The Apothecary looked at him levelly. "I am trade too."

The water gilder stared at him. "But I thought . . ."

"I'm afraid I lied to you. The fact is that I am by profession an apothecary and I have a shop in Shug Lane, Piccadilly. At the moment I am working for Sir John Fielding . . ."

"You mean the Magistrate?"

"Yes, I do. To cut a long story short he asked me to investigate this club because he believes it might be subversive. At one time that wretched man Wilkes was a member and Sir John is anxious to know who belongs to the organisation and exactly what they get up to."

"Go on."

"Well, I agreed to investigate it for him but I had to have a cover so I pretended to be a remote member of the peerage. So I invented the Honourable Fintan O'Hare and his redoubtable servant Samuel."

"I had thought the two of you were rather familiar but I had put it down to your Irish ways."

"No," said John, cuffing Sam in a friendly manner, "my friend is actually a well-respected goldsmith and we have known each other nearly all our lives."

"So you see," said Samuel, laughing robustly, "I am in trade too."

"A toast," said Dominique Jean, leaping to his feet. "'Ere is to trade."

"To trade," chorused the other two, and drained their glasses.

After they had settled down again Samuel put on his serious face which did not sit easily with his generally hot and happy appearance.

"So when are you seeing Sir Francis again, John?"

"Tomorrow morning. I am to conduct an interview with him about the postal system."

"Do you know anything about it?"

"No more than you do I dare say."

"Then that should be amusing."

"Indeed, indeed."

They looked across at the little Frenchman and saw that he had fallen fast asleep in his chair. "Sam, I'm going to bed. I'll leave you to deal with our friend from France."

"Sleep well, John. I hope you don't dream about that child again."

The Apothecary paused in the doorway. "Do you know I had almost forgotten about her. Dominique said that she was frightened of her father and promised to tell me something he had seen."

"Well, you'll have to ask him in the morning."

"The morning it is."

As he approached West Wycombe House on the next day John was struck once more by the place's intense beauty. Yet again he reined in his horse in order to have a better look and was gazing at the sun reflecting on the lake when he heard the sound of hooves behind him. Turning he saw Coralie's daughter, young Georgiana, riding her pony fast, coming towards him.

"Good day to you, Lady Georgiana," he called.

She ignored him, riding as if all the devils in hell were behind her. As she drew alongside, John had a close look at her. Georgiana was as pale as a cloud and, with her mop of yellow hair streaming out behind her, looked quite other-worldly. She reminded him at that moment of a demonic angel. He got the distinct impression that she was — for all the fact that she was only ten years old — tormented.

"Slow down," he called in a voice that to his ears sounded unnatural. "I'd like to ride with you."

She shot him a glance, a glance that appeared to go right through him, almost as if she couldn't see him. Yet all the while she did not ease her pace but just kept on, thundering towards the house as if her very life depended on it. John did the only thing possible. As she hurtled past him he joined in hot pursuit.

The pony was showing some signs of distress as the child shot round to the stables where a groom, hearing the clatter, rushed out to see what was happening. Georgiana was half out of the saddle and he only just caught her in time as she slithered towards the ground. A second or two later John careered into view and hurried to dismount. But he was not fast enough to catch the child who, again without speaking, rushed towards the house. The Apothecary was left with no option but to run after her. He caught her up just as she reached the colonnaded entrance.

"My dear girl," he panted, "where are you going at such a rate?"

"Leave me alone," she answered. "I promised my father I would see him at ten o'clock and I dare not be late."

"Why?" John said. "What will happen if you are?"

She gave him a strange look. "Nothing. It's just that I said I would be there."

"Well that doesn't seem a very good reason to half kill your pony and not speak to anyone who enquires."

The child was clearly about to make some retort but at that moment the door opened and a footman said, "Ah, there you are, Lady Georgiana. Your father awaits you. Good morning, sir, Sir Francis is in the red drawing room."

John would have answered but his attention was arrested by a vision descending the great staircase. It was the Marquess of Arundel clad in a crimson night-rail and white turban, his face without make-up but deadly pale for all that. His eyebrows, the Apothecary noticed, had been plucked into high black arches and on his hand he wore a great dark ring. He looked down at the pair of them, John and Georgiana, and said in a voice which trembled with some hidden inner excitement, "Ah, good morning, Mr O'Hare. I see you have brought my child to me. And where was the little wretch?"

Before John could reply the girl said, "I went for an early ride, Papa. But I got back in time, didn't I?"

"Yes, my dear, so you did. Well, now you can come and read to your old father. Poor old soul that he is."

He laughed loudly at this remark and after a second or two the child giggled. But to John her laughter sounded false and put on for the listener's benefit. And it was at that moment that Coralie appeared, sweeping down the stairs behind Charles, who turned at the sound of her.

"My dear, I didn't know that you were up."

"Did you not?" she replied coolly. She moved her gaze to take in her daughter. "Why, there you are, sweetheart. I've been looking everywhere for you. Come with Mama and have some breakfast."

The little girl looked from one parent to the other.

"I can give her some food," drawled Charles, turning to look at Coralie better.

"Nonsense," she said firmly, coming down to draw level with him. "I haven't seen my daughter alone for quite some time. And you know how I delight in her company. She shall come with me and there's an end to it."

All this was said in a light bantering tone but underneath, John, who knew Coralie almost as well as he knew himself, could detect steel. Walking down the stairs with a firm tread, she took Georgiana by the hand and led her off in the direction of the breakfast room. Acting entirely on impulse he hurried after them.

"Sweetheart," he heard Coralie say, "you are to eat as much as you can and then we shall have a talk, you and I."

But to eavesdrop further was impossible. A heavy tread behind him announced the arrival of Sir Francis. Bowing deeply, John appeared confused.

"Oh, forgive me, Sir Francis. I must have mistaken the rooms. Where was I meant to go?"

"To the study. Follow me, young man."

Once again John found himself in a chamber with an exquisitely painted ceiling which he would have liked to observe were it not for the fact that Sir Francis was motioning him towards a chair.

"Take a seat, young fellow. Now ask me all you want about the postal system."

John gulped and launched forth, having found a few key questions in an old copy of *The Tatler* which he had been fortunate enough to come across in one of the public rooms of the inn. Having committed to memory as much as he could, he managed to converse in a fairly meaningful manner until eventually the older man said, "Enough. You've plenty there to write your wretched articles. Let me press you to a sherry, a far more enjoyable pastime wouldn't you say?"

"Yes, indeed I would. But allow me to thank you, Sir Francis, for spending your valuable time with me."

"Nonsense. I reckon it to be part of my duty."

He sipped deep and as he did so John took the opportunity to have a very good look at him in the brightness of day. It was the face of a libertine, there was no doubting that. Red of texture, chinned voluminously, the dark brown eyes looked at the world with an expression of worldly knowledge that the Apothecary had rarely encountered before. And beneath all his tremendous joviality John sensed something wicked and wayward, as if life had been an experiment which Sir Francis had probed to the maximum. He looked down into his glass as he felt those eyes which had surely never been youthful turn in his direction.

"You've been a married man I take it?" asked the rich velvet voice.

"Yes, Sir Francis, I have."

"So now you're a sad young widower?"

"Yes," John answered shortly.

"Oh well, bad luck. But one can't dwell in the past, you know. Off with the old, on with the new and all that. Have another sherry."

John held out his glass and realised that he was being scrutinised closely. Not feeling altogether comfortable he turned his attention to the window and the beautiful vista outside.

"Fine place you have here," he said somewhat lamely.

"Yes. Do you want a look round?"

"I'd like that very much."

"Come then," said Sir Francis, and heaving himself to his feet led the way from the room.

It was good to be outside again, breathing the fresh air from the lake, which this morning lay like a sheet of glass beneath a vivid sky. Beautiful though the house was it seemed to John that it was a place of secrets, of dark whispers and strange events, and he was glad to be away from it and striding downhill towards the water. A pair of peacocks strolled past, followed by a couple of pure white ones. As it moved away from them one of the males displayed its tail feathers and the Apothecary drew breath at such brilliant splendour.

On the largest of the three islands there was some sign of building work, though a little slow and desultory as far as John could see. He stopped walking and shaded his eyes with his hand, the better to look.

"What's happening there, Sir Francis?"

"I'm building a little music temple. I plan to have concerts, musical entertainments, that kind of thing."

"How very nice. But how will the audience get there?"

"By boat. I can think of nothing more pleasant on a summer's evening than to cross the water and listen to the strains of music." He gave a deep laugh. "Actually I can think of one thing better."

"What's that?"

"To make love, long and deep, in the open air."

Fractionally startled, John said, "I can see your point, Sir Francis."

"Can you, by Jove? A man after my own heart, eh?"

Something told the Apothecary to play along with the way the conversation was running. "Very much so, I imagine."

Sir Francis turned to look at him, his eyes holding an unreadable glint. "We must talk more on this subject, I believe. Tell me, would you care to dine this afternoon?"

"I couldn't impose, sir."

"Nonsense. It would be my pleasure. And afterwards we can chat privately."

John bowed. "Nothing would give me greater satisfaction."

"Nothing?" said Sir Francis, and gave John an extremely lewd wink.

John was far away in thought as he walked round to the stables at the end of his tour. He felt sure that he was on the point of discovering exactly what it was that Sir Francis got up to in his spare time, indeed had a feeling that he — John — might soon be invited to attend some sort of orgy. With a consequent spring in his step at having wormed his way in, he made his way towards the loose boxes then paused as he heard the sound of a workman tapping gently within. The noise was coming from one of the larger outbuildings. He took a shrewd guess that it was Dominique repairing one of the Langlois commodes and promptly made his way inside. The Frenchman looked up at the sound of someone approaching and wiped his hands on his apron.

"Ah, *bonjour, mon ami. Comment ça va?*"

"Very well, at least I think so. Dominique, I have been asked back to dine and I have the strongest feeling that my respected host is going to tell me more of this club of his."

"That is good. But I don't know if I can lend you the coach. I have decided to work late and get the job done. I don't know what time I will be back at the George and Dragon."

"Never mind. I'll ride up if necessary. But I wanted to ask you one thing before I left."

"Which is?"

"You promised to tell me about Arundel and his daughter. You said you saw something strange."

Dominique bent his head to his task. "It was disgusting. A horrible thing to have to see."

"Tell me about it."

"Well, I was in the house and was examining the damage to this piece. I was working silently and I don't think they realised that I was in the room. Anyway, Arundel came in with his arms wound round the girl — tight they were — and she was weeping. Not boo-hooing but crying without sound, the tears pouring down her face. And as for him, his hands were caressing her — and I mean properly, like a man does a woman. Then I made a noise and he jumped and swore at me and left the room again. It left me with a ghastly impression."

"You surely don't think . . .?"

"Child molestation? I'm not sure. But the sight of it made me feel sick. I have a young daughter and I swear to you that I would never touch her in that way. Never."

John stood stock still and felt a cold sweat break out on him. He had heard this kind of story many times, knew the depraved and terrible things that people did to the young. But he had never come across a case of it

106

quite so close. Then his mind leapt to Coralie. Surely, before God, she could not know the truth. Then he got a grip on himself. Perhaps Dominique was exaggerating. Perhaps he was mistaken in what he had seen. But whatever the answer John felt sure that there was something odd about Lord Arundel and swore that come what may he would keep a close eye on any future developments.

CHAPTER
TEN

Fortunately, John — loving high fashion as he did — had brought another set of night clothes with him and this time set off for the big house adorned in scarlet and silver, his waistcoat heavily embroidered with little flowers the colour of jet. He rode carefully in order not to spoil or crease anything and dismounted with equal caution. As the groom led his horse away he could hear the sounds of faint tapping coming from the outbuildings and knew that Dominique was still at work, which for some reason John found vaguely reassuring.

He entered the house as usual, this time some twenty minutes before the hour to dine, and was ushered immediately into the red drawing room. It was empty and John crossed to the window to gaze out once more on that perfect view, then he spun round as a voice spoke behind him.

"Good afternoon, sir."

He turned and regarded the woman who stood in the doorway. She seemed almost like a phantom, clad in deepest black as she was. A pair of chilly, arctic blue eyes stared at him and John could not help but notice that her hair, swathed in a head-dress of black gauze, was white as ice from that frozen country. Wearing no cosmetics, her colourless lips did not move as he answered, "Good afternoon, ma'am," and gave a polite bow.

She bobbed the slightest curtsey. "I am Lady Juliana Bravo, sister of the Marquess of Arundel."

The Apothecary stood silently for a moment, wondering who she was talking about. Then he realised that Bravo must be the family name of the Dukes of Sussex and that Lord Arundel was her brother. The thought that this cold creature was sister-in-law to Coralie fundamentally shocked him.

He tried gallantly to make conversation. "A pleasant afternoon, is it not?"

"Very. And who did you say you were, sir?"

John felt totally embarrassed. "Forgive me, madam. I forgot to tell you. I am the Honourable Fintan O'Hare, fourth son of the Earl of Cavan."

"Irish," was Juliana's only comment, and taking a seat she picked up a newspaper that someone had left lying about.

John felt suddenly annoyed. If she had known who he really was she presumably wouldn't have addressed him at all. But he curbed the sudden rush of irritation and said, "Yes, my family is Irish. I presume that yours came over with the Conqueror."

She glanced up at him. "Yes, that is correct. The Dukes of Sussex are an ancient family."

At that moment the door opened and the child Georgiana stood in the entrance. She curtseyed. "Aunt Juliana! When did you arrive?"

The woman's face lit up from within. "Georgiana, my dearest girl. About an hour ago. Come, give your aunt a kiss."

The child walked sedately towards the chair but at the last minute broke into a little run and was scooped up into Lady Juliana's arms with a great show of affection.

"I'm so glad you're here," Georgiana continued. "I always feel at ease when you are present."

The woman held the child at arm's length and looked at her. "At ease? What a strange phrase to use."

"But it's true, ma'am," Georgiana answered. "I know that you will look after me."

"You are a quaint little creature," her aunt replied, but John thought that her voice held a certain thoughtfulness.

It was at that moment that Coralie entered the room and stood hovering in the doorway a moment, taking in the scene of her sister-in-law and her daughter conversing. Both females, the old and the young, turned to look at her. Great actress that she was, it was only John who could tell that her smile was forced.

"My dear Juliana," she said, coming forward, hands outstretched, "how very nice to see you. Are you staying long?"

Juliana rose to her feet and gave Coralie an icy kiss on the cheek. "A few days. You know I am still in mourning for our sister Harriet."

"Yes, of course. I'm afraid that Charles has left off his dark clothes."

"He was never a one for following convention."

"No, indeed," Coralie answered, and John thought he could detect a certain bitterness in her voice.

But the conversation got no further. Lady Dashwood, accompanied by a grinning Betsy Avon-Nelthorpe entered the room. She stopped short on seeing Juliana.

"My dear Lady Juliana, welcome to my home."

"Thank you."

"May I present Mrs Avon-Nelthorpe?"

The look of disgust on Milady's face was almost comical but fortunately Betsy appeared not to notice. She dropped a wobbling curtsey and said, "Charmed, your Ladyship. I am a great friend of your brother's."

"Really?" came the frosty reply.

Lady Dashwood went on in her boring voice. "Lady Juliana, this is Betsy Avon-Nelthorpe, wife of James Avon-Nelthorpe."

"How dee do?" Juliana replied and turned away.

The little girl spoke up, addressing her remarks to Coralie. "Mama, may I dine with you? I do not wish to go upstairs at present. I should so enjoy it if you said yes."

Coralie turned to Lady Dashwood. "My dear Sarah, would it be possible? The child has been very good and she loves her aunt so much."

How anybody could be fond of that formidable creature clad in mourning was beyond the Apothecary's comprehension. But then he reckoned that the only tenderness he had seen Juliana exhibit had been towards her young niece. He stood silently awaiting the hostess's verdict.

"Very well. Georgiana may dine with us. She can sit next to Mr O'Hare."

"That will be my pleasure," John answered gravely, and made a bow to the child. He caught Coralie's eye at that moment and read in it a look of gratitude. He made another small bow in her direction.

Sir Francis appeared with Lord Arundel at that second, followed by the carroty-haired James, who stood, very pink in the cheeks and swaying slightly. John guessed that they had been at the decanter before coming to escort the ladies in to dine. He offered his arm to the little girl who took it with an adult precocity and followed the procession going in to the dining room.

The meal was memorable for two things. Firstly came the downright lack of any kind of good breeding exhibited by Betsy, who chortled and giggled and nudged her dining companions, and bared her dagger teeth when she burst into gales of laughter. Secondly was the reaction of Georgiana to her father's display of affection. Indeed she noticeably shuddered when Charles Arundel leaned across the table and covered one of her hands with his. John's suspicions about his unnatural attachment to the child were doubled.

Eventually, though, Lady Dashwood stood up and led the other females out of the room at which Sir Francis passed the port and leant towards John.

"My dear Mr O'Hare," he said, "I've been having a chat with my two companions here and we think you look a likely type."

John raised his glass and saluted them, allowing a merry twinkle to appear in his eye. "Thank you, gentlemen."

"And we have therefore," continued his Lordship, leering at the other two, "decided to ask you to join us tomorrow."

"I would be honoured, Sir Francis. But to do what?"

"To come with us to Medmenham Abbey, which is a place I have some few miles away."

"And what happens there?" asked John politely.

There was a low laugh from the other three.

"I run a club," said Sir Francis. "It is called the Knights of St Francis of Wycombe — at least that is its official title. But it is better known as the Hellfire Club."

"Really? How interesting. What is its purpose?"

"Mainly whoring," said Sir Francis, and laughed a laugh so rich in humour that John could not help but join in. "So are you game to come along to a chapter meeting?"

"Count me in, Sir Francis. I'm ready for anything."

"Good boy. You'll have to put aside your Catholic sympathies however."

For a second John was startled and then remembered that Fintan O'Hare, the Irishman, would undoubtedly belong to that particular religion.

"Why is that, sir?"

"We indulge in a little religious ceremony before we get down to work."

"And who are the ladies might I ask?"

"They come from London, from Covent Garden mostly, nearly all brothel girls. Mind you, we have one or two better class of women as well. What we require is females of a generally cheerful disposition. And they must be discreet. Which reminds me that you must swear an oath that binds you to silence before you are admitted to the Order."

"Of course. May I ask how the ladies get there?"

"Some come by coach, others by water. Others . . ." He gave a deferential cough. ". . . make their own way."

Highly intrigued as to the identity of these women, John looked suitably impressed.

"And so, my friend," Sir Francis continued, "the three of us decided that a young widower like yourself could do with a little cheering up. Were we right?"

"Utterly. It is quite some time since I attended a maiden in her bower, as it were."

Sir Francis growled a laugh. "You can take your pick tomorrow night." His voice changed rapidly at the sound of footsteps crossing the hall. "No, as I was saying, it seems you have quite a good social life in the city of Dublin."

"An excellent social life, Sir Francis." John winked his eye at his host. "Truly excellent indeed."

They had joined the ladies and were now sitting in the Portico Room listening to Coralie playing the harpsichord. John, leaning back in a chair close to the fire — which had been lit despite the heat of the day — realised with a shock that he had never heard her play before and that she was reasonably talented. But then how could she be anything else, he thought, with her great career on the stage and her undoubted touch of genius. His mind wandered back to his first meeting with her — had it really been all those years ago in Vauxhall Gardens? — and he smiled fondly at the thought that she had been a friend of his ever since. Except, of course, for the time when they had broken up and had not spoken to each other for some years.

By natural progression his thoughts turned to Emilia and how sweet she had been. A perfect wife for him, whereas he and Coralie would never have made a match. And now, he considered with a sigh, he had recently loved that black-haired tempestuous woman, Elizabeth di Lorenzi. So warm and passionate in his embrace yet so capable of turning him down on a whim. He wondered where she was and how the world was using her, for he had heard nothing from her since their last meeting in Cornwall two months ago.

His eyes slid round to Charles, Marquess of Arundel, and John thought he had never seen such a pale and desolate looking man. Tonight Milord wore full cosmetics, even having rouged his mouth slightly, and as a result appeared thoroughly debauched and terrible. Had he once been fine and upright so that Coralie, dedicated to the theatre, had fallen in love with him and given him her heart? Or had it simply been the temptation of the title and money that had finally wooed her away from the stage? And what was the relationship between him and his daughter? John could not help but wonder whether Dominique Jean had read more into what he had seen than was actually there. Yet he himself had quite definitely noticed a type of feverish preoccupation with the little girl. John made up his mind that somehow, however delicate the matter might be, he must speak to Coralie.

The music stopped and he applauded politely. Sir Francis rose to his feet and it was a signal for the party to break up.

"Come and have a final port with me," he breathed into John's ear.

As he left the room John noticed that Arundel had gone upstairs while Coralie remained below talking to Betsy and Lady Juliana, who retained her usual icy composure. Lady Dashwood had wandered from the room to speak to the servants, or so she said. This left John and James Avon-Nelthorpe to slip off quietly into a small dressing room which led from an imposing bedroom with an equally splendid bed in it. Sir Francis made a gesture in the bed's direction.

"Don't get much activity in there," he said, giving a large grin. "But we'll see some sport tomorrow." He turned to James. "Is Betsy coming?"

"She would not miss it for the world," came the totally surprising answer.

So John had been right. She had obviously done her stuff in Covent Garden before marrying well. But he still couldn't help being totally astonished by the whole situation, for James, when all was said and done, obviously came from the upper echelons of society.

A quarter of an hour later John left the house, his horse ready and waiting by the front door. Sir Francis had insisted on a servant accompanying him bearing a lanthorn, and the two of them set off, taking a different pathway which ran through the grounds in the direction of the church, that was visible — along with the mausoleum — high above them. John looked up and once more shivered as he saw that nightmarish outline. Then he intook breath rapidly as a light appeared up there, bobbing its way round the various arches.

"What's that?" he asked the servant.

There was a low laugh. "That's old Bubb Doddington, Baron of Melcombe Regis. He left the money to have the place built. It's his ghost wanders up there."

"Oh, good heavens! What nonsense."

"No, sir, that it ain't. They say he still wants to go to the Hellfire Club like he used to when he was alive."

"My goodness, such determination."

At that moment the lanthorn dimmed in the mausoleum, then suddenly went out. Filled with sudden curiosity, John felt an overwhelming urge to search the place.

"I'm going up there," he said.

"Oh, sir, I beg you don't. There's some things best left alone."

"Nonsense, man. It's probably a poacher. You can stay here if you like."

"No, sir. If I do that Sir Francis will give me notice. Oh, my God!"

They left the path and started the steep, almost perpendicular, climb up through the trees and coarse scrubby bushes that decked the hillside. Looking upwards John saw that the mausoleum was now in total darkness and began to wonder whether he were on a fool's errand, whether the quarry had flown. Beside him he could hear the groom's teeth chattering.

Eventually they reached the top, the church looming like a dark shadow, the golden ball on its spire pale and almost luminescent in the moonlight. With a certain amount of trepidation John dismounted and entered the confines of that strangely shaped place of the dead.

"Is there anybody there?" he called out, his voice reverberating oddly in the emptiness.

There was total silence. And then the moon came out fully and he saw that something white was nestling in the far corner. Seizing his courage, the Apothecary walked towards it and then his heart nearly stopped as he drew close. Pale as a ghost indeed, her head drooping downwards, her arms woven tightly round her knees, was the figure of Georgiana Arundel. The daughter of Coralie Clive had left West Wycombe House and was hiding alone in the darkness.

CHAPTER
ELEVEN

John bent down till his face was on a level with Georgiana's, then he spoke very softly.

"Georgiana, what are you doing here?"

She kept her head averted and would not look at him. Very gently John put his fingers under her chin and raised it so that she could not avoid his gaze. She immediately closed her eyes.

"Hawkes," he called over his shoulder to the groom. "Bring the lanthorn here. There's no ghost — it's Lady Georgiana."

The servant approached cautiously, swinging the light high, and at that moment the moon appeared from behind a lacy black cloud so that John had a good view of the little figure before him. Her shoes and stockings were green with grass stains and wringing wet from the dew. She was also trembling violently in the chill night air. He immediately removed his scarlet coat and placed it round her thin and somehow anxious shoulders.

"Georgiana," he said coaxingly, "won't you speak to me?"

She shook her head and remained silent. John stood up and addressed the servant.

"We'll have to take her back, Hawkes. We can't leave the child sitting out here all night."

"No, sir. She should be tucked up in bed. Whatever caused her to run away and hide herself amongst the dead folk?"

"I've no idea," John lied expediently. He crouched down to Georgiana once more. "Come along, my dear," he said, "it's getting very cold. Won't you let me take you home?"

Once again she shook her head mutely and before his eyes seemed to shrink, drawing her arms and legs close to her body in a gesture of despair.

"Come now," he whispered. "I promise to put you into the care of your mother and let no one else at all go near you. How does that sound?"

She started to weep, very quietly, almost silently, the tears rolling down from beneath her closed lids like a sudden summer shower. John felt every paternal instinct in him rise.

"Don't cry, little girl," he said gently, "I assure you that I will take care of you."

It was as if she fainted, suddenly going limp and allowing him to lift her from the ground and carry her out of the mausoleum to where the horses waited.

"Whatever ails the child, sir?" Hawkes asked.

"I must speak to her mother," John answered slowly as he carefully lifted Georgiana up into the saddle then swiftly mounted behind her.

"I think you should indeed, sir," Hawkes answered as he, too, got onto his horse.

John's mind raced as he set off in the direction of the house. He must see Coralie and have a private conversation with her, hand the little girl into her care and make sure that she was warned about her husband. Yet what proof had he that Arundel was doing anything wrong? Something seen by Dominique Jean; his own observations? Could they just not have been the expressions of an over-zealous parent's love? The more he thought about the problem he had to face, the more difficult it became to know how to solve it. Every instinct in him longed to protect Coralie's daughter, of whom, if fate's cards had been dealt differently, he could have been the father. Very conscious of the seriousness of what lay ahead of him, John and Hawkes approached the house from the back and while the Apothecary lifted Georgiana down, Hawkes went into the servants' quarters. After a few minutes he returned with a very flustered looking nursery maid.

"Lady Georgiana . . ." she started to remonstrate, but John stepped in.

"Please be silent, I beg you. The child ran away for a prank. The last thing you should do is be angry with her. Now, be good enough to fetch Lady Arundel to the door. At once."

She shot him a furious glance but disappeared into the depths of the house. John, alone with Coralie's daughter, stroked her hair, rather as he would that of a cat. But some instinct together with his professional judgement told him not to hold the child close, as he would have done Rose, but just to let her rest quietly, leaning against him.

Coralie appeared about five minutes later and John stood looking at her, vividly reminded of how lovely she was and how much he once had loved her. She caught sight of Georgiana and ran to the child, gathering her into her arms. Over the top of her head, she gazed at the Apothecary.

"John, what's this? What has happened? Why is Georgiana out here and not in bed?"

For answer he said, "Can you trust that nursemaid not to leave her? Not even for a second?"

"Yes, of course I can. Stokes has been with me for some years."

"Well, tell her to stay with the child and refuse to take anyone else's orders but yours."

Coralie turned to the servant. "You heard what Mr O'Hare said, Stokes. You are to stay with Georgiana until I come."

"Very good, my Lady. Come, my dear."

They watched in silence as the pathetic little creature was led away into the house. As soon as she was out of earshot Coralie turned to John.

"For God's sake, what is going on? Where did you find her?"

"I'll tell you in a moment, Coralie. Can we go anywhere where we can be private?"

She shook her head. "Only the stables."

"Well, let's go there then."

They entered the dimly lit building and immediately were consumed by the sweet smell of straw. Making their way to the harness room, full of brushes and polishing cloths and scented saddle soap, they sat down side-by-side on a wooden bench.

"John, what is happening? Why did Georgiana run away?"

"I don't know," he answered honestly, "but I have my strong suspicions."

"What do you mean? What are you trying to say?"

He paused, then said, "That your husband might well be perverted and that your daughter is possibly the object of his longing."

She gave a hiss like a snake and turned on him furiously. "That is a terrible thing to say about the man I married. How dare you?"

John sighed deeply. "I am only telling you for the sake of the child. Believe me, I hate having to do so."

She rose to her feet, her skirt rustling as she did so. "Damn you, John Rawlings. I will not listen to another word. For all his faults Arundel is a good father."

John stood up. "Coralie, I beg you to watch out. That is all I ask."

She did not reply but turned her back on him and walked rapidly away, leaving John standing — as she had so often in the past — wretched and helpless. With a hopeless gesture he walked out to where his horse was waiting, only to see Dominique Jean emerging from one of the outhouses.

"Dominique, what are you doing here? I thought you had finished long since."

"No, my friend, I decided to work on until my eyes gave up on me. They just have." He pulled a wry grin and rubbed his hands over them.

"Are you leaving now?"

"Certainly. Can I give you a lift?"

"No, but I'll follow your coach if I may. It's a dark, lonely road else."

"Of course. You look as if you have a great deal to tell me."

"I most certainly have," John answered as he put his foot in the stirrup.

An hour later, in the warm confines of a private snug, he sat with Dominique and Samuel, relating the stories of the night to them, all three relaxed by alcohol and a feeling of camaraderie. A fire had been lit in the grate but had recently gone out and now the scents of the night air stole in whenever anyone from the taproom went in or out. It was a drowsy sensation, the smell of roses combined with the pungent stink of urine of both horses and men, blending somehow into a soporific odour. The Apothecary leant back in his chair.

"So that was it. She did not heed my words. She turned her back on me and walked out into the night."

"Then 'eaven 'elp the child," said Dominique, his French accent growing more pronounced when he was tired.

"Yes, indeed," answered Samuel heavily.

"I simply can't understand why Coralie married that terrible rake in the first place. What was she after? Was it money or the title? Or both?"

"Perhaps," said Samuel, "she genuinely loved him. The human race is hardly responsible for its actions when you regard the people we fall in love with."

"You're right," John answered quietly, "she probably did love him. God help her."

"Why are you using the word 'did'?" asked Dominique. "Does it not occur to you that she loves him still and that your words, John, upset her deeply? Perhaps, even now, she is sitting in her bedroom with her whole life in ruins."

The Apothecary's eyes brimmed with tears, he could not help himself. In his anxiety to help the child he had ridden roughshod over the mother's feelings. He turned his head away to hide the fact that he was weeping.

Samuel, as ever attuned to his friend's emotions, said, "It's late. I think we could all do with a good night's sleep."

John looked at him gratefully. "Yes, I'm very tired. Besides I have a long and interesting day ahead tomorrow." He wiped his eyes with his handkerchief. "Will you forgive me?"

"Of course," said Dominique. "By the way, I find that I have a day's work at West Wycombe left. His Lordship has found several other items for me to repair."

"Not made by your father-in-law surely?" asked Samuel, surprised.

"Alas, no," answered the Frenchman, and pulled a face.

All night long John was haunted by the haggard and hunted expression on Coralie's face as the meaning of his words had sunk into her mind. Then he had thought of Dominique's question: Why are you saying *did* love him? Perhaps she still does. Eventually he had fallen asleep as dawn began to break and had woken three hours later, feeling less than ready for the day ahead. Despite this he had risen, washed well in hot water, shaved, then dressed himself carefully.

He came downstairs to find Dominique had already left and Samuel kicking the cobbles.

"Can't I come with you, John? I feel so utterly useless here. I've nothing to do all day but wonder what time you will be returning. I am really finding it a total bore."

John, still jaded after his bad night, immediately relented. "Of course you can. Get yourself a horse and come with me. I leave in ten minutes."

"Right. I'll go to the stables immediately."

"Good. I could do with your expert eye taking a look round."

Poor Samuel hurried off busily and when John went down the yard to collect his mount found him in earnest conversation with an hostler.

"This'll be the mount for 'ee, gaffer."

"It's rather a fat brute."

"Ah well, sir, the bigger the rider the bigger the horse, if you take my meaning."

"I take it very well indeed," Samuel answered huffily, and clinked a coin into the hostler's outstretched fingers. "Damnable cheek," he added as soon as they were out of earshot.

"Never mind, Sam. The man's just a bucolic," John said, humouring his old friend who clearly did not like any reference to his ever-spreading waistline.

126

"Um," came the reply, and after that Samuel relapsed into silence until they had proceeded halfway up the east drive and the sight of the lake, complete with ship, and the stunning facade of the house came into view.

"Hare and hounds!" he exclaimed. "What a palace."

"I take it you are impressed?"

"I'll say I am. I hadn't expected anything quite so grand."

They rode round to the main door where they both dismounted, John allowing Samuel to peal the bell. The usual footman replied.

"The Honourable Fintan O'Hare by appointment with Sir Francis Dashwood," Sam said in an Irish accent so broad that one could have stood on it.

"If Mr O'Hare would like to step inside." John obliged. "And you may go round to the servants' quarters," the servant added, and pointed to the back of the house.

"To the stables first, Samuel, if you please," the Apothecary said loudly. He added in an undertone, "You'll find Dominique Jean working in one of the outhouses. Talk to him. But when Sir Francis and his cronies come for their horses I want you to follow at a discreet distance. Can you do that?"

"Of course I can," Samuel answered with a note of irritation in his voice.

John laid his hand on Sam's arm. "Please don't be seen. I think it is vitally important that you are not."

"I shall be a shadow," the Goldsmith answered.

"And when we get to our destination creep around and observe all you can."

"Leave it to me," Sam said solemnly.

Shown into the saloon, John almost reeled back at the fine company assembled there. For as well as the usual crowd of cronies he saw Lord Sandwich, First Lord of the Admiralty, together with Sir Henry Vansittart, the Governor of Bengal. A third man also stood by the window, a man whose features John could hardly recognise.

This morning Charles Arundel looked ghastly, his face having been carefully painted as white as a cloud. He — or his servant — had rouged his cheeks, carmined his lips and blackened his brows so that the man appeared like a travesty of his sex. John thought of Coralie's attitude on the previous evening and felt momentarily sick.

Sir Francis Dashwood looked up. "Ah, O'Hare, here you are. Allow me to present you to the others. Lord Sandwich . . ."

John gave his very best bow.

". . . Sir Henry Vansittart and Paul Whitehead the poet. Gentlemen, this is the Honourable Fintan O'Hare, son of the Earl of Cavan."

John was still bowing as the other men murmured a greeting.

"And now, my friends, let us to horse. It is a fine day and I am sure we will all make haste when we think of the pleasures awaiting us."

In the stables their mounts stood waiting, Samuel solemnly holding the bridle of Rufus. John was given a leg-up and once in the saddle he gave Sam a wink and mouthed the word "Follow". His friend nodded his head silently.

It was a pleasant ride through the countryside following the course of the meandering river. John, being new to the group, rode slightly behind and occasionally looked over his shoulder for any sign of Samuel. But there was nothing and he came to the conclusion that Sam had either got lost or had mastered the art of shadowing to a fine degree.

It was one of the most beautiful days of the year; late July and already destined to be hot. The cornfields glowed in the early warmth and the scent of wild flowers blew on a minute breeze, filling his nostrils with delight as their perfume hung in the barely stirred air. Barley, long-whiskered and gentle, swayed down by the water and over their heads the sky was as bright a blue as a stained glass window. John, not a religious man, found himself thanking the Creator for all this glory, all this splendour, and wondered what he was doing heading for such a sordid gathering. And yet he could not deny some hidden excitement, some lustful urge, working its way towards the surface of his mind.

About five miles from West Wycombe a narrow bridge appeared before them which they crossed, riding in pairs over its stone surface. The sound of the horses' hooves was magnified by the high sides of the edifice and momentarily John felt trapped. He looked round in a panic and caught the gaze of his companion, Paul Whitehead, whose long face and nose and unsmiling rat-trap mouth did nothing to reassure him. As they left the bridge and hastened through the meadows on the far side John thought he could hear the distant sounds of a horse in pursuit but turning his head again could see nothing.

A mile further on and Medmenham Abbey came into view, a gracious building built by the river's edge. A cloister with soaring arches had been constructed next to an ivy-mantled tower which gave the place a slightly mysterious and melancholy air. Above these cloisters stood windows with pointed decorations above, while on the top of the roof there was a large and imposing chimney. Sir Francis dismounted.

"Well, here we are again." He rubbed his hands in anticipation. "Allow me to escort our guest first."

There was a murmur of approval and John was led toward a front door like that of a church. His eye wandered upward. Over the arch were written the words *Fais ce que tu voudras*, which he translated as "Do as you wish".

"The slogan of the club," said Sir Francis, and his voice was molten.

John stepped into the house and looked about him. He stood in a fine hallway with various rooms leading off it. But it was to the fireplace that his eye was drawn, for there, repeated in French, was the club's motto once again.

"This is a very fine building, sir," he said to his host. "It obviously has been designed with care."

"It was my idea entirely," Sir Francis answered. "I bought the place as a ruin and had it totally restored. Come, let me show you around."

He led John to a large room situated behind the cloister. Here there were signs of pictures having been recently removed for the marks where they had hung were clearly visible.

Sir Francis, seeing the direction of John's eye said, "Security, old chap. You never know who might come snooping."

"Indeed not," the Apothecary answered, and looked urbane.

They stepped out into the cloister and Sir Francis gave a laugh. "Allow me to show you the monks' cells. You'll be sleeping in one of these tonight."

"I see."

They were very small but all had the necessary wooden cot required for the amorous dalliances which the ladies of London were more than willing to provide.

Off the chapter or common room led the refectory, large enough to seat a very goodly gathering. At one end stood the statue of an Egyptian god and at the other end a goddess.

"Who are they?" John asked.

"Harpocrates, the god of silence, and his female counterpart, Angerona. That the same duty might be enjoined to both sexes," said Sir Francis, and gave a lewd wink.

His whole manner had changed since he had entered the Abbey for he seemed barely able to contain his excitement. And when the others caught up with him the Apothecary could not help but notice that they all seemed volatile. As if to underline this fact Sir Francis rang a small bell and when a servant answered ordered some wine.

"And now, gentlemen, the first ceremony," he said, and reaching in his pocket removed a bottle of pills. Solemnly he handed one to Lord Sandwich, Sir Henry Vansittart, Lord Arundel, Paul Whitehead and the Apothecary.

"What are they?" John asked curiously.

"They help us be fine, upstanding gentlemen," Whitehead said in a toneless voice.

John sniffed the aphrodisiac and assessed it as being relatively harmless. He swallowed it.

"We take a great many of these during the proceedings," said Sir Francis, and swallowed his down with a great glass of wine and another of his laughs, in the depths of which was a slightly unpleasant tone.

CHAPTER
TWELVE

The women from London had arrived and the proceedings were in full swing, everyone having been called together at six o'clock. Prior to that there had been a great deal of time spent strolling in the grounds which were, in John's estimation, amongst the most erotic he had ever seen. In one place he had read the words *Ici mourut de joie des mortels le plus heureux* inscribed over a grassy bank. And had seen one young monk doing his best to obey the sentiments expressed therein, namely, "Here the happiest of mortals died of joy". Over a couch of flowers had been written *Mourut un amant sur le sein de sa dame*, which John translated as "A lover died on the bosom of his lady". Against a sturdy oak where upright love-making was clearly practised was a stone banner which read *Hic Satyrum Naias victorem victa subegit*, which meant "Here the vanquished naiad overcame the conquering satyr". But as far as the Apothecary was concerned the absolute winner was at the entrance to a cave, in which Venus was bent over pulling a thorn from her foot. Over the cheeks of her behind were inscribed some words which translated read, "Here is the place where the way divides into two: this on the right is our route to

Heaven; but the left-hand path exacts punishment from the wicked, and sends them to pitiless Hell".

John, a washable condom in his pocket, had been standing, reading it, when a voice behind him said, "Pray, what does that mean, sir?"

He had turned to see one of the sauciest little packages it had been his pleasure to set his eyes on in a long time. She was masked, as were all the women present, but that could not hide her natural assets of hair, a glorious shade of rich red, a tipped up cheeky nose, a full mouth with a most attractive underlip, and a pair of pert and pretty breasts which were almost breaking free of their constraining garments. Whether it was the recently swallowed aphrodisiac or the general eroticism of his surroundings but John felt instantly attracted to her.

He bowed and said, "I'm not sure," then picked up her hand and kissed it slowly.

She gave him an amused glance and said, "Shall we go into the cave and see if there is anything written in there?"

He knew perfectly well what she meant but was more than happy to comply. "Come on then," he said, and taking her hand led her inside.

Within the atmosphere was highly charged, for there was a mossy couch made for love with probably the most explicit inscription of all written above. For John, reading in Latin, saw, "Go into action, you youngsters; put everything you've got into it together, both of you; let not doves outdo your cooings, nor ivy your embraces, nor oysters your kisses".

"I wonder what this one says?" she asked teasingly, obviously having had it translated for her many times before.

"It exhorts us to go into action," John answered.

"Like this?" she said, and putting her arms round his neck gave him a voluptuous kiss.

"Or, even better, like this," the Apothecary replied, and leading her to the couch, lay down beside her.

Vaguely he heard a couple come into the cave, say "Sorry," and leave again. But John was past caring, indeed was having such a pleasurable time that the whole world could have walked through the cavernous entrance as far as he was concerned.

The little whore, who had remained masked throughout, grinned at him impudently. "I think you had a good time, young sir."

"I had one of the best times ever."

"Oh, you men. You all say the same."

"And you? Did you enjoy yourself?"

"Not completely," she answered truthfully. "It'll take a bit of practice."

John grinned and wiped his brow. "Madam, I am entirely at your disposal."

She sat upright. "Oh, it don't go like that. The Abbot has first choice of all the women. And then the men file past us for inspection. That's in case a lady's husband should be present, or an acquaintance for that matter."

"Not very likely I would have thought."

"Oh, you'd be surprised. We have a mix of females of quality amongst our number, here for the sport, like. And they enter into it with as much enthusiasm as any

Covent Garden doxy. Anyway, if they should see anyone they know they have permission to retire without revealing themselves. But if all goes well, when every man has passed us by we unmask and that is how we remain."

"I see. So how are the women picked?"

"By the gentlemen present, as you would imagine. But once they have taken one of us we become their lawful wives during our stay here. So, sir, if I please you and the Abbot doesn't want me, then I am yours for the asking."

"And ask I will," John replied with enthusiasm.

And now it was evening and the men had walked past their prospective "brides" and the Abbot — Sir Francis Dashwood himself — had made his choice. Somewhat to the Apothecary's surprise he had picked for his escort an extremely buxom blonde lady who John thought he recognised as Betsy. There had also been a slight mishap as John had seen her standing amongst the whores and ladies. He had wondered for a moment whether she would withdraw but instead she had given him a cheerful grin as he had gone past her. So her husband didn't pick her, John thought, or was this part of a little game they played in order to keep their marriage alive?

"Brother monks," the Abbot said rising, "you have seen the ladies and I have made my choice. Now you must make yours."

The assembled company, all designated monks for the next few days, sallied forward, and John hurried to where his pretty little whore stood waiting.

136

"Well, sir, do you choose me as your wife?" she asked, smiling at him.

"Will you do me the honour, ma'am?"

"Gladly, sir," and she curtseyed.

"By the way, what is your name?"

"Teresa, sir. Sometimes known as Tracey."

"I think I shall stick to the old-fashioned version."

"If that pleases you."

She really was quite the most fascinating young creature the Apothecary had seen for some while and now, aided by yet another aphrodisiac, he sat in a bemused state of high excitement while dinner was served. It seemed part of the ceremony that every member present should introduce his lady and the Abbot now rose to his feet.

"Brothers, I pray you to look upon my fair Betsy who is the flower of her art and has taught many a young monk the rites of initiation."

There was a rumble of laughter and one or two whistles. John, looking round, saw the lady's husband, James Avon-Nelthorpe, sitting with an experienced-looking harridan of the older variety and thought that was obviously where his tastes lay.

"Now, brothers, it is up to you to introduce your ladies to us."

A member of the company sitting at the far end of the table rose and gave his woman's name and there was much general hilarity when one or two had to consult the lady before he stood up. It came to John's turn and he got to his feet.

"Brothers, I want to thank you all for including me in your company. So far I have found it to be one of the most pleasant and enjoyable times of my life. Allow me to present to you my wife, the beautiful Teresa."

Just for a minute the effects of the drug wore off and looking round he saw dissipated young rakehells and raddled old men; whores and hard-faced ladies of society; a gathering of people intent on an orgiastic pursuit of pleasure. But then he took himself to task. He had never been a saintly figure, had lived his life to the full, so why not take part now that he was here?

"I thank you," he said, and sat down amidst applause.

And it was then, just as he was taking his seat, that he saw the faintest hint of a movement behind one of the columns, several of which filled the apertures leading from the anteroom. John stared and saw the briefest flash of a brown coat. So Samuel had not got lost but had followed and was now faithfully observing.

Wine was being poured from silver cups fashioned in the form of female breasts and John noticed several of the older men downing yet more pills. Running his eye amongst the women he definitely recognised several ladies of high society and realised that they were included amongst the gathering in order to have secret rendezvous with their lovers, for sitting beside them were certain high-born gentlemen whose faces were also familiar to him. For a moment he thought of the enormity of the whole concept, then a pressure on his knee brought him back to reality.

"What are you thinking, eh, pretty boy?" said Teresa.

"I was thinking about you," lied John.

But he was silenced as another brother got to his feet. "A toast, brothers and sisters. Here's to shaving. I see a look of alarm on the sisters' faces. I refer of course to chins only, nothing below."

There was a titter and several ladies raised their fans and hid their cheeks. Naturally they knew they were not blushing but were aware that the movement showed their eyes to advantage. The brothers, however, rose to their feet and drank, chorusing, "To shaving."

Sir Francis stood up. "To those of us who must stand . . ." His hand briefly went to his privy parts so that no one could doubt his meaning. ". . . May Venus give us strength. To those beauteous receptacles, may Bacchus grant them be ever open."

"Here, here," came the general chorus and once again the brothers rose and drank. Eventually after much toasting the food was served and John, realising that he was extremely hungry, tucked in heartily. Teresa, he could not help but notice, ate delicately, and he was suddenly and vividly reminded of Emilia and how much he had loved her. He recalled times when she too had picked at her food and how he had chided her for doing so.

He turned to the girl. "Are you not hungry?" he asked.

"Usually, yes. But these Abbey meetings quite put me off my food."

"Why so?"

"I don't really know. Perhaps it is the crowd."

John looked round at the sixty or so present, evenly divided between the sexes, and asked, "Are there more people here than usual? Or is this about average?"

"About normal. Don't tell anyone, will you, but I find it rather intimidating."

"Do you?" He took her hand suddenly wanting to protect her against the vicissitudes of life. "Shall we slip away when the meal is done?"

"Yes, please. By then the Abbot and the apostles will be at their private devotions."

"Really? And where do they take place?"

"In the chapel upstairs. Nobody is allowed in but themselves."

"Good gracious. I wonder what goes on."

The girl giggled. "I don't know but I reckon it is devil worship."

"Do you now?"

"Yes, I do. And I'll tell you a tale of that. You've heard of John Wilkes? The one who has been banished?"

"Yes, of course I have."

"Well, he used to be a member here and one night . . ." Teresa put her hand over her mouth to stifle a laugh. ". . . he got the Abbey's mascot, which is a baboon, and dressed it up in phantasmic garb and conveyed it to the chapel. Then he hid it in a large chest which is used to hold the ornaments and utensils of the Order when everybody is away."

"What happened then?"

"Wilkes attached a cord to the spring of the lock, then hid it under the carpet and drew it through to his own seat. Well, later that night during the proceedings he jerked the cord and the baboon leapt out and landed on the shoulders of Lord Sandwich. My Lord went mad and thought Satan had come to claim him, and screams and hollers that he is not really a sinner, that he hasn't committed a thousandth part of the vices he has boasted of. He tells the Devil to go and fetch those who really deserve it. Have you ever heard anything like it?"

John laughed at the mental picture. "No, I haven't. What did they do to Wilkes when they found out?"

"Lord Sandwich, who is probably the most lecherous man alive, hated him from that moment on and set out to ruin him."

"Which he has succeeded in doing."

Teresa wrinkled her nose. "Apparently. But it would never surprise me to see him come back into politics one day."

John looked at Lord Sandwich, who had his arm round an amply built girl, his hand inside her top, openly fingering her breasts. Then his gaze moved on to Coralie's husband who sat, pale and withdrawn, next to the woman of his choice. He had not chosen a Covent Garden girl but had picked a member of the aristocracy. John stared at her, fairly certain that she was none other than the youthful Countess of Orpington, yet not completely sure because the lady had remained masked.

"What you looking at?" asked Teresa.

"Lord Arundel. He's the one wearing —"

But Teresa interrupted him. "I know who he is. 'Tis said amongst the girls that he has the French pox, you know."

John gazed at her in astonishment. "He has? Are you sure?"

"He's never picked me, thank God. So I've no direct proof. But it is certainly rumoured about that he has it."

John thought of Coralie and he wondered if she, too, had contracted the disease. His mind shied away from conjecturing about the little girl.

"You're looking horrified. Why?"

"I know his wife. I can't bear to think of her with such a complaint."

"Well," said Teresa philosophically, "if she has, she has. There's little you can do about it."

But further conversation was made impossible, for it was at this juncture, the meal being over, that Sir Francis rose to his feet once more.

"I call the apostles to the ceremony," he said in a thrilling voice. "For those of you who are attending for the first time, this is a totally private rite and takes place in the chapel. The rest of you brother monks, go to your pleasures with a will."

John turned to Teresa.

"Await me in my cell, my dear. I have one small errand to run then I promise to come to you."

She gave him an inquisitive look but did not ask any questions, while John, seeing nearly everyone leave the room strolled out into the anteroom and gazed around him.

142

"Sam," he said in a whisper.

Something stirred in the shadows and a voice murmured back, "Here."

John crossed the space between them. "Well done, my friend. I thought we'd lost you on the way but you tailed us beautifully."

"I had a job to follow you. There were times when I thought I'd been seen. But I made it safely and have been lurking round ever since."

"What do you think of the place?"

"Well it's a novel form of brothel, I'll say that for it. But tell me about the women, John. I'll swear that I saw the Countess of Orpington amongst the strumpets from Covent Garden."

"You did, Sam. And there are other ladies from the *beau monde* present as well."

"I suppose they do it for the sexual freedom it must bring," said Samuel gloomily.

"They might well. But the consequences could be dire. It is rumoured amongst the whores that Arundel has got the pox."

"'Zounds! Has Coralie been infected?"

"I've no idea and I'm not likely to find out. She is no longer speaking to me."

Samuel groaned, quite loudly, and John raised a warning hand. "Quiet. Someone might hear you."

"I'll be careful, I promise."

"Where are you going to spend the night, Sam?"

"Probably in the grounds."

"I think they'll be alive with copulating couples."

"In that case I might go to a local hostelry and creep back early in the morning."

"I wish we could get a look in the chapel. The Abbot and the apostles are celebrating something or other up there."

"I can try."

"No, Sam, it's too dangerous. If anybody goes it will have to be me."

"Then good luck, John. But be very careful."

"Yes, I will."

They parted company, Samuel tiptoeing out into the cloisters, John standing hesitantly for a few minutes. It was Sir John Fielding's brief that he should find out as much as he possibly could. Yet he knew that if he were discovered prying into the Chapter's secrets he would be asked to leave West Wycombe and probably be told never to return. Was it worth the gamble? Eventually he made up his mind that it was and squaring his shoulders he walked up the deserted staircase to the chapel above.

CHAPTER
THIRTEEN

The stairs were dimly lit by candles, a chandelier in the hall below throwing some light, more being provided by another hanging from the ceiling on the landing above. Moving silently, John climbed upward, uncertain which direction to take. But as he ascended he could faintly hear the sound of chanting coming from his left and knew that this is where the chapel must be situated. Creeping along in the dimness, the Apothecary quietly approached a small flight of steps leading downward, then stopped short before two heavy oaken church doors. He had clearly arrived at the place in which the rituals were held.

He paused irresolutely, not at all certain what he should do next. To go in would be tantamount to instant ejection from the Abbey, but on the other hand there were instructions from Sir John Fielding to discover all he could. In the end John knelt down, put his eye to the keyhole and peered through, only to discover that somebody had had the foresight to seal it up, allowing him no vision whatsoever.

It was at that moment that he heard footsteps coming up the stairs and stood petrified, knowing that he must hide but not knowing where. He stood up and looked round. In front of him were the doors to the chapel, behind him the flight of stairs, and to his left a few more steps leading to more of the corridor. John hurried up them and followed the passageway which obviously led to further rooms. Fate was with him for he spotted a large oaken chest standing against the wall. Without hesitation he lifted the lid and dived in on top of a mass of linen which lay inside it. Then he lay very still, listening.

The footsteps, which were heavy and measured, passed the entrance to the chapel and made for the corridor in which he lay hidden. John trembled slightly, wondering if for some devilish reason of his own the owner of the steps was going to open the chest. Then, to his horror, he heard fingers scrabbling with the lid. His worst fears had been realised.

The lid was pulled back and the servant — that much was obvious from the man's apparel — gave a gasp as John, scrambling to his feet, leapt out and fled down the corridor as fast as he could, only to hear the sound of those measured feet pursuing him as soon as the servant had recovered from his fright. If he was caught the Apothecary knew that the game was up. Consequently he fled to the top of the stairs which he descended two at a time.

As he hastened away he could hear the servant yelling, "Stop! Intruder! Come here, you wretch!"

John hurried as if his life depended on it — which in a way it did — and did not stop until he reached the cloisters, where he turned right and found the row of monk's cells. Diving into one which he mistakenly thought was his own, he discovered a young couple fully engaged. They did not even notice him and he hurried out, somewhat embarrassed. The next cell was his and he raced through the door, which he leant on, panting.

"Whatever is the matter?" said Teresa, somewhat sleepily.

"I was nearly caught," he gasped.

"Did they see you?"

"A servant did but only in the half-light. I doubt he could identify me."

"Then you've nothing to worry about. Come in . . ." she giggled, ". . . husband." And she held the bedclothes open invitingly.

John jumped in beside her, stripping off his clothes in the same movement and they were lying in each other's arms when they heard the sound of heavy footsteps patrolling up and down the cloisters.

"Don't worry, you're safe," Teresa whispered, close to his ear.

"I sincerely hope so," John answered, and fell asleep.

At midnight they rose, all being quiet, and strolled, dressed negligently, in the grounds. It was moonlight and as John had suspected there were many couples up and about. The aphrodisiacs he had taken had entirely worn off and walking thus, hand in hand with his chosen friend, John felt a wave of revulsion that such a beautiful spot should have been turned over to an orgy of sexual activity. But then, as a man of medicine, he thought how frail humans were, indeed, how needy. He turned to look at Teresa.

"Do you enjoy your life?" he asked, then regretted the words, realising he must have sounded harsh and rude.

"When I meet someone like you," she answered. "But can you imagine being stuck for these few days with a creature with bad breath and projecting teeth?"

"Only too vividly. I don't know how you stand it."

"We must all earn our living, however differently the ways," she said simply, and smiled at him in the moonlight.

The next morning there were few at breakfast, only John and a handful of others, one of whom, surprisingly, was Charles Arundel. He looked even more ghastly than usual — almost an impossibility the Apothecary found himself thinking. Paler than white, his eyes lined with black, he peered at John blearily.

"Good morning, O'Hare. Did you sleep well?"

"Soundly," lied John cheerfully.

"I have not been to bed at all. Apparently there was a prowler round last night."

John put on his honest citizen face. "Good gracious. Did you catch the wretched fellow?"

"No. One of the servants found him near the chapel. But he escaped and despite a night of looking for him he got away."

"How dreadful. Did you search personally?"

A rictus smile crossed his Lordship's features. "No, I had too fine a lady to pleasure. But the servants spent most of the night looking for the blackguard."

"I expect it was a curious monk anxious to see the rituals," said John, digging in to a slice of beef.

"Possibly." Arundel took a sip of coffee and pulled a face. "This is disgusting." He gestured to a footman. "Fetch me a brandy, would you."

"Certainly, my Lord."

"Starting early," said John innocently.

"Why not?" Arundel answered, and shrugged his bony shoulders.

He was enormously thin, the Apothecary thought, looking at the fellow critically. Yet again the thought of what Coralie could have seen in the man came to plague him. One day he felt he would know the answer but at the moment he could not think of any reason other than the title and the money.

John tried another tack. "Your daughter is a handsome child, sir. One day she will be as beautiful as her mother, I feel."

Charles looked at him with an unreadable glance. "She reminds me of what Miss Clive was like when I first met her. Young and fresh, despite her apparent worldliness."

John looked at him closely. Was there perhaps just a hint of wistfulness in the way his Lordship was speaking?

"And now?" he said quietly.

"Now my wife is a woman of the world, a lady of fashion."

"Do you still love her?"

"Of course," Arundel replied, but the twist of his lip and the curve of his nostril denoted a certain cynicism.

So at least Charles's attitude to Coralie was clear but his obsession with his child remained as big a mystery. John decided to ask no more questions.

Later that morning, strolling in the gardens alone — Teresa having gone with some of her younger friends to gossip about the standards of the men present — John caught a glimpse of Samuel hiding amongst the trees by the riverside. Making his way towards him, the Apothecary noticed that his friend looked pale.

"My dear fellow, you look terrible. What is the matter?"

"Oh, John, I can hardly speak. I spent last night in an hostelry, as I told you. But this morning, making my way here, I was spotted and mistaken for a man who had come in to clean out the privies."

The Apothecary felt a wild desire to laugh but the expression on Samuel's face forbad any such thing.

"Oh, you poor soul. Was it ghastly?"

"Ghastly." The Goldsmith clutched his guts. "And that, my dear, is an understatement. They were in an indescribably terrible condition."

"I think I would rather not know."

"Oh, but you must. I refuse to suffer this on my own."

And Samuel went into colourful detail of the various things he had found and what he had been forced to do to them. In the end John silenced him.

"Enough! I have heard as much as I can stand. All I can say, Sam, is that the experience will make you a better person."

From pallid, Samuel flushed the colour of a poppy. "Why should it? Why should I have to endure such hell? I do it for the sake of our friendship, that's why."

"Come on, my good old comrade. Brace up. It's a beautiful day and I need to talk to you. Let's take a boat out."

There was a small jetty close by with several craft moored to it. Between them the two friends managed to launch one and John, in charge of the oars, rowed away from Medmenham Abbey and over towards the opposite bank. There, hidden by the overhanging branches of a willow tree, he told Samuel his experiences of the previous night.

"So what do you think goes on at those rituals?"

"Your guess is as good as mine. Somebody had blocked off the keyhole."

"Do you think it is devil worship?"

"My friend, it could easily be so. I could not see a thing. They may well have been sacrificing someone or drinking children's blood for all I know."

Despite the warmth of the day, Samuel shivered. "I hope to God you're wrong."

"So do I, my dear. So do I."

And with that they had to be content.

The next day Samuel set off by horse for the village of West Wycombe, having done as much as he could in the way of spying and still angry over his grim experience in the privies. And John, growing slightly bored with the decadent way of life, was glad to hear Sir Francis announce at dinner that tonight the monks must bid farewell to their wives. The Order was breaking up until the next meeting.

Teresa wept a little in private.

"I wish you weren't going."

"Nonsense. I've just been another client after all."

"Will you come and see me in London?"

"Yes, if you'll tell me where I can find you."

She gave him the address of the brothel at which she worked and John committed it to memory, then they went for a final stroll in the grounds. But they had hardly taken more than a dozen steps when they encountered a female figure lying amongst the grasses, face downwards. All the Apothecary's training came to the fore and he hurried to pick the woman up. Turning her over he found himself staring into the large blue eyes of the Countess of Orpington. Close to, she looked little more than a girl and John found himself calculating her age as sixteen or so.

"Oh, Sir Monk, I am sorry. I must have fainted. I cannot think why."

A strawberry blush had crept into her cheeks and she sniffed like a child.

"Do I have the honour of addressing the Countess of Orpington?" John asked formally.

She struggled to sit up. "I am just a sister here, sir. I have no title."

"Forgive me, madam. I had no wish to intrude."

But it was definitely her. The girl chosen by Charles Arundel to be his "wife" for the few days of his stay.

Helping her to her feet, the Apothecary bowed. "Allow me to escort you back to the Abbey."

"No. No, thank you. I am waiting for someone. I shall just sit here quietly until they arrive."

John bowed again. "As you wish, madam."

As soon as they were out of earshot Teresa said, "Who does she think she is? She may be a countess but she's as ready as the next one to do the feather-bed jig."

"You're right, of course."

"Anyway she's been tied up neat with Lord Arundel so no doubt she's caught the pox by now."

John shook his head. "Poor little girl. I pity her."

"Well I don't," Teresa answered defiantly. "She's nothing but a troublesome miss, mark my words."

"You're not jealous of her?"

"No, I ain't. She may be prettier than I am, she may have married a fancy old earl, she may have as many silk gowns as I have hot dinners, but she'll end up in the powdering-tub and for that reason I would rather have my life."

John shuddered at the thought, thinking of the sweat pit used in some hospitals to try to cure the pox. He put his hand on Teresa's arm.

"Be very careful, my dear. I wouldn't like to think of you in similar circumstances."

"I'll take great caution, sir, I promise you."

And she smiled at him in the warmth of that summer's evening. But for some reason John was not reassured, as that strange feeling that all was not well, a cold presentiment of something being wrong, clutched at his heart and made him shiver despite the fineness of the night.

CHAPTER
FOURTEEN

Throughout the ride back to West Wycombe Place, John had the strangest feeling that they were being followed. Yet logic told him that he must be mistaken. Samuel had left early on the previous day and must be safely back by now. Despite this he kept glancing over his shoulder but never to see a sign of anyone in pursuit. Still the certainty persisted and he was almost relieved when Sir Francis trotted up beside him.

He looked as if he had not slept at all, his face red and heavily lined, his nose like a bonfire. Thoughts of the state of other parts of Milord's anatomy put an unintentional grin on John's features and he laughed to himself.

"What's so amusing, young man?" asked Sir Francis.

"Nothing, sir. It's just such a beautiful day and I was thinking of all that happened," John replied convincingly.

"Yes, indeed. And did you like your little doxy?"

"Very much. The whole concept of Medmenham Abbey is one of immense pleasure."

It was Sir Francis's turn to laugh robustly. "Entirely my creation, I assure you." He suddenly looked angry.

154

"My one regret is that we didn't catch that blackguard who tried to spy on our ceremonies."

"No, that was an unfortunate business."

"I'll say. The rituals practised by the inner wheel are strictly private, as you will have gathered."

"Indeed, sir. I feel you have a traitor in your midst."

And the Apothecary pulled a face that bore an almost saintly expression. Sir Francis gave him a surprised glance, clearly not at all convinced.

"Yes, quite so. Glad to have your opinion." He trotted off again.

John caught up with Lord Arundel, who had his usual air of being fit for nothing.

"Good morning, sir," he said loudly. "I hope I find you well on this excellent day."

Arundel visibly shuddered. "Not so hearty, if you please. I had something of a time of it last night."

"Oh?"

"Yes. The Countess of Orpington protested at my leaving her. She has some girlish notion of running away with me to France. I had to dissuade her and left her weeping, alas."

John thought of Teresa's unhappy face and wondered whether many of the meetings of the Order ended so miserably.

"I'm sorry to hear that."

"Not a word to my wife, mind. Of course I see the wretched girl in London from time to time. Her husband is incredibly ancient, by the way. It was an arranged marriage."

"You may trust me to be discreet, sir. But how old is the Earl?"

"Sixty to her sixteen. He has been married before and has children older than she is."

"I see."

"And now if you'll forgive me, I'll end our conversation. Good day to you, Mr O'Hare."

Yet again that feeling of things being awry came over John. But he bowed politely enough to his Lordship and proceeded to ride on alone.

Lord Sandwich and Sir Henry Vansittart had left the party, having proceeded direct to London. Paul Whitehead had remained behind to oversee the shutting down of the Abbey. Thus it was just the three men who proceeded through the sunshine towards West Wycombe. John deliberately hung back so that he rode last and once more felt himself overwhelmed by the feeling that they were being followed. But, as before, nobody was visible and he supposed the idea was a product of his over-active imagination.

Overhead the sky began to darken and he wondered whether they were going to be subjected to a summer storm. And they had not proceeded very much further when there was a distant rumble of thunder and the rain began to pour. The riders drew in beneath some sheltering trees.

"I say we make a dash for it," Sir Francis said, looking about him. "We're only about a mile away."

"We'll get soaked to the skin," Arundel answered petulantly.

They both turned to John. "I agree with Sir Francis. Let's make haste," he said.

Pushing their horses hard they raced through the digging rain until eventually they saw the house from the top of the hill, lying below them.

"Back to respectability," shouted Sir Francis, and led the rush downwards.

Ten minutes later they were dismounting from their dripping mounts, Arundel being practically lifted from the saddle by two grooms. As they swung him downwards he banged hard against the stirrup and let out a cry of pain. John instinctively went towards him.

"Are you all right?"

"No. I've hurt myself. I've an old wound, you know."

"Would you like me to look at it for you?"

"The devil with it — no I wouldn't. My wife can do that."

Remembering just in time that he was meant to be Fintan O'Hare from the bogs of Ireland John turned to go away, but Arundel's voice cut across.

"Sorry, O'Hare, I was a bit short with you. It was just the shock that made me so."

"Of course. I quite understand."

"If you would be so kind as to help me into the house."

With one arm round Arundel's waist, Charles was so close that the very essence of him filled John's nostrils. It was a smell of decay, of rot, of things better not spoken of. For the hundredth time the Apothecary's mind went to Coralie and he thought of her dressing the wound and wondered if she would vomit in disgust.

They reached the front door, Sir Francis striding on ahead and calling out, "I'm back, madam. Where are you?"

Lady Dashwood appeared from one of the inner rooms.

"I was just chatting to Mr Jean. He has been so useful to me and has mended practically everything in the house."

"The man's not a bloody carpenter," said Sir Francis, throwing down his riding whip. "Here, help me off with my boots."

Dominique appeared in the doorway. "Allow me, Sir Francis." And before his Lordship could refuse had neatly pulled both of them off.

Meanwhile a great deal of moaning was coming from Charles Arundel, who was clutching his side. The Apothecary, aware that he must continue to role-play but for all that anxious about the man, noticed that a very faint bloodstain had appeared through the material of his breeches.

"Let me help you upstairs, sir," he said. "I really think you should lie down."

"No, I'll be perfectly all . . ." Arundel let out another groan and stumbled.

"I insist," said John firmly, and taking the man in a firm grip propelled him upward.

"Where's my wife?" Charles asked, his head lolling so that his wig slipped slightly and showed a close cut of chick-yellow hair beneath.

"I don't know but I'll find her for you," the Apothecary answered shortly.

158

Below him in the hall he was aware of Sir Francis and Lady Dashwood, together with Dominique Jean, watching his slow progress upward, and it was at precisely that moment that there came a loud knocking at the door. John paused in his ascent and looked down as the footman went to answer it. Standing there, soaked to the bone, her violet eyes almost purple with fury, was the Countess of Orpington.

Everyone stared at her silently until she shouted at Sir Francis, "Well, aren't you going to ask me in?"

He collected himself. "Of course, madam. Perkins, show the lady inside at once." He stepped forward meanwhile and said with a certain irony, "I take it you lost your way, my Lady."

Beside him John heard Charles give a groan of recognition. "Take me to my chamber, please. I have no wish to speak to the wretched girl."

"I rather think she wants to speak to you."

"Tell her I am not well. In fact you can tell her anything you like but just keep her away from me."

But she had spied her quarry making his laborious way upstairs. "You bastard!" she yelled. "You downright rogue. How dare you play fast and loose with me."

She flew up the stairs, her damp clothes leaving a trail of moisture behind her. But John was too quick for her. Pushing Arundel behind him he whirled round and barred her way, flinging both his arms out.

"Madam, I insist that you leave Lord Arundel alone. He has wounded himself and is bleeding. His wife . . ." he put particular emphasis on those two words,

". . . awaits him upstairs. Be so kind as to restrain yourself."

At this Dominique Jean, moving very swiftly, came up and seized Milady's arm. "Come with me, madam," he said, his charming French voice flowing over her like a gentle waterfall. "You are overtired and overwrought by your terrible journey."

The poor child burst into tears, leaning against his shoulder. "I am so miserable," she said between sobs.

"There, there," soothed Dominique, leaving John feeling quite awestruck. "Come and have some refreshment. Everything will feel much better when you have had something to drink and removed your wet things."

Lady Dashwood gave her husband a dirty look but nonetheless came forward and prepared to act as hostess.

"Come along, madam. You must get into something dry. Do you have luggage with you?"

"No, I sent that on to London," the girl snivelled.

"Well, we shall find something for you. Walk this way."

And she led the Countess off into an inner sanctum. Charles lolled his head against John.

"Thank you, my friend. You've done me a great service."

Gritting his teeth, the Apothecary eventually managed to find his Lordship's bedroom and there laid Lord Arundel down on the huge four-poster bed.

"Now, sir, I am going to look at that wound."

"No," protested the other.

160

"I'm sorry. I insist."

"What right have you?"

"The right that I am an apothecary," John answered, blowing caution to the breezes.

And before there could be any further protests he stripped off Charles's coat and shirt and looked for the wound. It was not there and, peering closely, John could see blood seeping through from lower down. He undid the top of his Lordship's breeches. And there was a chancre, the small soft swelling which occurred in the early stages of syphilis. It was close to the testes, very much as John had imagined. It had also had the top knocked off it and was bleeding.

"My dear fellow, this is indeed serious. You must get this wound dressed," he said. "Unfortunately I do not have my medical bag with me or I would do it for you."

Charles was looking at him beadily. "So you're an apothecary, are you?"

"Yes, sir. Trained in Dublin. I told you my father wanted all his boys to have a trade."

"I don't believe a word you're saying. I think your whole pretence of being Fintan O'Hare is utterly false."

"You can believe what you damn well like," John retorted sharply. "I shall go and ask Lady Dashwood where she keeps her medicines and herbs and I shall return."

It was at that moment that the door opened and Coralie stood framed in the entrance. She looked both beautiful and deadly, her skin very white against the dark blue of her gown.

"Charles," she said, ignoring John, "what is this I hear about you not being well?"

He made to cover the chancre but could not pull his breeches up in time. She looked at it with distaste.

"I see," she said. "I shall get a dressing."

John, suddenly annoyed with the pair of them, gave her a sweeping bow and said, "Madam, I will do that, if you have no objection."

She gave him a look and just for a second he read everything in her eyes; all her pain, all the suffering she had been forced to endure for the sake of her child.

"Of course," she said, and added low, "you are an apothecary after all."

Pacified, he snatched her hand to his lips, then bowed again. "If you could get your husband a drink," he said, and left the room.

Downstairs he found Dominique Jean, just following Sir Francis into the saloon. "Milord has asked me to stay the night because the weather is so terrible," he said to John.

"Absolutely yes. You too, O'Hare. I think we should have a few drinks to celebrate the last few days."

"How kind of you, sir. I will certainly accept your offer unless the weather improves. But first of all I must have a word with your wife if that is convenient."

Sir Francis nodded brusquely. "She is in the saloon with Lady Orpington. Go to her by all means."

John went into the grand room to see a very grey aspect from its commanding windows. The lake had turned the colour of slate and the sky was full of threat. Everything looked dismal in this light and he saw that

162

despite the fact it was only early afternoon Lady Dashwood had ordered the candles to be lit. He also saw that the poor woman sat alone, working on some rather unappetising embroidery. Of Lady Orpington there was no sign.

The Apothecary bowed and came straight to the point. "Madam, I need to dress a wound which Lord Arundel has incurred. Would you be so kind as to direct me to your medicines."

She laid down her sewing and stood up. "I shall attend him personally. There is no need to bother you, Mr O'Hare."

"There is every need, my Lady. The wound is of a personal nature and not fit for a woman's eyes."

She actually went white. "Oh, I'm sorry. I had no idea. Please do come with me, sir."

She led John out of the saloon and down a passageway until they came to a back staircase. This in turn led to the kitchens and beyond them a store room. Here Lady Dashwood opened a cupboard and said, "This is where I keep the household medicaments. I hope you will find what you need."

It was amply stocked with everyday physicks and even contained some suppositories which John looked at with curiosity. He sifted through a jar of ointment of Kidneywort for painful piles or swelling in the testicles, a decoction of the seeds of Fenugreek for women to sit upon in order to relieve hardness of the matrix, an infusion of Mugwort to help bring down the courses. Though these were of interest there was nothing which could really help Lord Arundel. Then he saw an ointment made of Mezereon Spurge and wondered if this were used in fact by Sir Francis. Seizing the jar John hurried up the back stairs and eventually found himself on the first floor. Going into Charles's bedroom he saw that Coralie was there, leaning over her husband with a glass of water in her hand. She turned on hearing someone enter.

"Oh, it's you," she said. "Have you found anything?"

"Yes, something very suitable."

He said no more but spread the ointment on a piece of bandage and placed it carefully on the wound which still bled slightly.

Charles opened his eyes. "Thank you, my friend. I trust that you will not speak of this to anyone in the house."

"You can trust me to keep quiet, I can assure you." The Apothecary straightened up and went to wash his hands, pouring some water from a ewer. Over his shoulder he said, "May I speak with you privately, Lady Arundel?"

"Yes," she answered, gliding towards him silently.

"Outside," he mouthed, and she nodded her head to show that she had understood.

They went onto the landing and she turned to John immediately. "My husband has the pox, you know that?"

"Yes." He looked at her earnestly. "Have you been infected?"

She shook her head. "No. I haven't slept with him for a year. It was at that time that he picked up some wretched creature who gave him the disease. I found

164

out and refused to have anything further to do with him."

"And Georgiana?"

"She is clear."

John thought of the story that Dominique had told him and wondered privately if the child had been corrupted by the father. He turned to look at Coralie, taking hold of one of her arms in his anxiety.

"Why did you marry him, Coralie? I beg you to tell me."

She turned her head away and said softly, "Because I felt sorry for him."

"Sorry?"

"Yes. He once was young and gauche, even inclined to be spotty. He saw me acting in some play or other and came after me in hot pursuit. At first he bored me but eventually his vulnerability became so obvious that I felt myself softening towards him."

"So it wasn't for the title or the money?"

She laughed scornfully. "How could you think that of me? You, who once loved me? Do you regard me as so base that I would do such a thing? I had plenty of money of my own; a title means nothing to me. To me it is up to each individual to make the best of themselves, and those are the only people that I admire and respect. But Charles was like a child; a pathetic, needy child. That is why I married him. Because he had need of me."

"And I did not?" said John with immense sadness.

She gave a bitter laugh. "No, you never did. You were always so independent, so self-assured. You and Sir

John Fielding were a unit that it was impossible to break."

"And did you want to break it?"

"Of course not. But I could have done with more attention."

"I asked you to marry me, Coralie."

She opened her mouth to reply but the words never came. Running down the corridor, wearing a night-rail several sizes too large for her, her feet bare and her hair down, came the Countess of Orpington.

"Where is Charles?" she said to the Apothecary pleadingly. "I've got to see him. I must speak with him."

"Madam," said John, extremely formally, "may I present to you Lady Arundel, the gentleman in question's wife."

CHAPTER
FIFTEEN

Lady Orpington barely swept Coralie a curtsey, in fact she did not even look at her. John felt rather than saw the actress's annoyance.

"I must see Charlie," the girl babbled on. "If he is ill I must go to him."

"How do you do, Lady Orpington," Coralie answered icily. "I trust I find you well. I'm afraid my husband is resting at present and cannot be disturbed."

"But he will see me," the Countess said. Then, raising her voice, shouted, "Charlie, Charlie, forgive me. I love you. I want to see you, my darling."

"Oh, for heaven's sake," snapped Coralie, losing her temper and her patience simultaneously, "go away, you meddlesome creature. You are welcome to have my husband at any time you wish but not when the poor devil is trying to get some sleep. Now be off with you."

At that moment, running up the main staircase, clearly alarmed by the shouting, came Dominique. He bowed to Coralie.

"My dear madam, what is happening?"

"The Countess of Orpington is behaving very badly," said the actress, not mincing her words. "If you could remove her, Monsieur Jean, you would be doing us all a great favour."

"It will be my pleasure to attempt to do so, madam." Very gently he took hold of Lady Orpington's arm. "Would it be possible, my dear lady, to know your first name?" His voice had adopted an almost hypnotic quality, much aided by his wonderful French accent. "That is if you have no objection to telling me."

She looked at him through tears, though whether they were being wept because of genuine sorrow for her lover or just plain frustration it was difficult to tell.

"It is Arabella," she replied coldly.

Dominique kissed his fingertips and gave her a deep look. "How charming. What a delight."

"But only intimate friends use it . . ."

"Like Charlie," Coralie interrupted sarcastically.

Lady Orpington gave her a chilly look but made no response.

"Would it also be in order for you to accompany me downstairs," Dominique continued blandly, "because Sir Francis Dashwood is most anxious for you to rejoin him."

"I shall go down," the girl replied with dignity, "because you wish me to and I have no desire to make a scene in a strange house . . ."

A little late for that, thought John.

". . . but I shall return later and look in on the Marquess of Arundel."

And with that she turned on her heel and stalked downstairs, Dominique following calmly behind her.

★　★　★

Dinner that early evening was one of the most strained occasions that John had ever attended. Little Georgiana was there, her hair flowing round her shoulders like a cascade. She sat in silence, looking at her plate, not catching the eye of any of the adults. Coralie, her mother, sat opposite her, beautiful but drawn, her face almost a mask that even John, who knew her better than any other at the table, could not penetrate. Beside him, wearing one of Lady Dashwood's gowns which ill became her, was the young Countess of Orpington. She had got a grip on herself and was putting up a creditable performance, though Sir Francis kept shooting glances at her and winking his eye, which glistened in his rubicund face like a jewel. Dominique was also at table, looking very different from when he was arrayed for work in a smart suit of clothes, discreetly but effectively embroidered with silver thread. John could not help but wonder how poor, sick Charles Arundel, whose future looked grim indeed, could be faring.

As if reading his thoughts, Lady Dashwood said, "I shall get some soup sent up to poor Lord Arundel."

She sat at the right of Sir Francis, trying desperately to make small talk, and the Apothecary felt his heart go out to her. Nobody was in the mood for conversation, except for the host who was enjoying his wine and his recent memories. But the rest sat in silence, the sound of cutlery banging on plates enhanced, the noise of the rain beating down outside like that of distant drums. John felt himself getting more and more depressed and longed to be back at the George and Dragon, recounting everything to Samuel, who would sit listening to him, large-eyed and faithful as ever. Yet he knew that to set off in these conditions would be disastrous. Then an idea struck him. He turned to Dominique.

"Is your carriage not here, my friend?"

"Alas, no. It is being repaired in the village. Today I paid regard to my health and walked here and I am rewarded by a thunderstorm."

He rolled his eyes and looked terribly Gallic and John smiled.

At the sound of their voices the others tried to make desultory conversation and Lady Orpington said, "I was heading for Oxford, don't you know, but I lost my way and ended up here. I do trust you will forgive my intrusion, Lady Dashwood."

Sir Francis boomed a laugh. "Yes, strange how one road can look like another. Strange, too, how signposts are often turned to point in the wrong direction. I mean to say, Oxford is rather difficult to find, what?"

He exploded with mirth, a laugh in which nobody else joined at all.

"Quite so," said his wife in her dull tones. "I think it was most unfortunate for you, my dear, to lose your direction on such a terrible day. Never mind. It will probably rain itself out overnight and you will be able to leave in the morning."

The Countess nodded and said, "I hope so," in a voice that utterly lacked conviction.

Coralie looked up. "So we are all to stay here overnight?"

"Indeed yes," answered Lady Dashwood. "Mr Jean, if you would not mind having a spare bed in the servants' wing."

"Me, I sleep anywhere. Of course I do not mind."

"And you, Mr O'Hare, will be in the small guest bedroom at the eastern end of the house."

"Thank you, Lady Dashwood," John answered solemnly. He turned to look at Georgiana, who so far had sat absolutely mute. "Well, my dear, have you had a pleasant day?"

She regarded him, her face pale and almost haggard looking. "I went riding this morning but after it started to rain I did painting in my room."

"How interesting," he found himself saying. "I would like to see some of your pictures."

"I will show you," she answered and ceased to look at him, clearly indicating that the conversation was at an end.

Yet again John wondered that such a silent child could be the product of that most vocal of women, Coralie Clive. Then he thought of Georgiana's history, of the strong possibility of molestation at the hands of her father, and regretted his thoughts.

Lady Dashwood was making a move to rise. "Ladies, if you would like to follow me we will withdraw."

Coralie got up and took her daughter firmly by the hand; the Countess of Orpington, looking terribly young, came up behind them.

As soon as the door closed behind them, Sir Francis said, "Now, lads, let's get down to some serious drinking."

John could only marvel at the stamina of the man. He was no youngster yet he had ridden back from Medmenham Abbey after a night, no doubt, of total debauchery. And he had then proceeded to cope with the unexpected arrival of the Countess, the sickness of Charles Arundel, whilst simultaneously getting comfortably drunk. And here he was instructing Dominique and John to join him in serious drinking. It was Dominique who, after finishing one glass of port, stood up.

"Forgive me, sir, but I have worked hard today and I am feeling tired. If you would be kind enough to excuse me. I shall, of course, say goodnight to your wife."

John made this his moment. "I, too, am exhausted, Sir Francis. Will you forgive me if I leave you also?"

"I don't know what it is with you youngsters. You've got water in your veins, not blood. I'd have taken you for a drinking man, O'Hare."

The Apothecary winked an eye. "Forgive me, sir. I would normally have joined you but the excesses of last night are catching up with me. I really must to my bed. I, too, will bid your wife —"

But here his words were stopped for once more there came a thunderous knocking on the front door.

"God's wounds, whoever can that be?" exclaimed Sir Francis, signing the other two to be silent while he listened for sounds from the hall.

There was the noise of the door being opened and then a man's voice said, "Is Sir Francis Dashwood at home?"

"I shall see, sir."

172

"Don't give me that, you rogue. Out of my way, damn you."

There was the sound of confusion and the next minute the door of the dining room flew open and a red-faced man of aristocratic mien stood in the entrance.

"I'm the Earl of Orpington," he announced angrily, "and I have reason to believe that my wife is at present hiding under your roof."

Sitting up in bed an hour later, John thought that it had been Dominique who had saved the day. He had risen to his feet, bowed, and said in a pronounced French accent, "*Monsieur le Duc . . .*" an oversight which could be forgiven in the circumstances, ". . . *votre bonne femme est ici.* Ze poor lady lost 'er way and 'aving knowledge of Sir Francis's house she came 'ere for protection."

"A likely story," her husband had fumed.

He was an unattractive creature to say the very least. Extremely red in the face with swinging, swaying jowls, he had large yellow teeth which gnashed as he spoke. His figure, too, was not of the best, skinny legs and a big stomach topped by a pair of sloping shoulders. Knowing that one should not judge people by appearances alone, John had nonetheless taken a dislike to the man on sight.

"Where is she?" the Earl had gone on. "I demand to see her."

"Demand away, sir." This from Sir Francis. "The lady has withdrawn from the table in the company of my wife and Lady Arundel."

"Then I'll go to her and sift her. She's up to no good and I know it."

John, eating an apple before he cleaned his teeth, reflected on what had happened next. The Earl had gone storming into the hall, closely followed by the other three men, and had tried every door until eventually he found the one to the drawing room to which the ladies had withdrawn. This he had flung open and had stood in the doorway, one trembling finger pointing at his wife.

"So, madam, I have found you at last."

The poor girl had jumped to her feet, thoroughly startled, and had promptly erupted into a wild tempest of tears.

"Oh, Husband, I beg you don't be angry. I was on my way to visit Aunt Dorothea in Oxford and I lost my way. Oh forgive me, do."

The Earl had stood silently, staring at Lady Dashwood and his girl-wife, for Coralie had disappeared with the child, presumably to bed her down for the night. John imagined that while the man remained quiet he had been working out the best strategy and had decided that to make even more of a public scene would not be in his best interests.

He said gruffly, "Forgive my tone of voice, Lady Dashwood. I've been near apoplexy over the disappearance of my wife. You could have written to me, you little wretch."

She started to wheedle, getting up and quite literally stroking herself round him like a cat at feeding time.

174

"But, my dearest, I left you a note. Did you not see it? Aunt Dorothea was taken poorly and I felt it my duty to wait upon her. Surely you must have read that?"

"One of the servants must have removed it. I saw nothing."

"Oh, how could they be so careless?" She had by that stage been actually stropping herself round his frame. "Poor, dear Husband. No wonder you were in such a fury."

John and Dominique had stood watching, Sir Francis a step or two in front of them, and the Apothecary had thought to himself what buffoons men were. For here was this angry old man actually being soothed by his little wife's cat-like performance. John had seen at a glance how Arabella had got the old idiot eating out of her hand. But for how much longer? he wondered.

Dominique had murmured to him, "I think I've seen enough. I'm travelling back to London day after tomorrow and I need all the sleep I can get."

"I'm off too. I've had my fill of it."

The Frenchman had given him a wry grin. "There's no fool like an old fool, so they say."

"How true."

And now John was eating his apple and thinking about returning to London himself. He had seen the sexual activities of the Hellfire Club and could report back to Sir John Fielding that there was nothing of political danger, nothing that could harm the state at least. His task was done. Besides he was longing to see

Rose, to find out whether she and Miss Octavia da Costa had become as close as he had hoped.

With a sigh John rose swiftly and cleaned his teeth, then blew out the candle. He was vaguely aware of several sets of footsteps going past his door but eventually the whole house grew quiet and he fell asleep, wondering whether the Earl and Countess of Orpington had finally been reunited.

CHAPTER
SIXTEEN

John slept fitfully, dreaming that people were walking past his room all night. He finally woke completely just as dawn was breaking and got out of bed, crossing to the window. Pulling back the curtains he saw that it had indeed rained itself out during the night and the morning lay crisp and fine before him. Not stopping to wash or shave, John pulled on a pair of riding breeches and a shirt and crept out of the house, glimpsing only a handful of servants as he did so.

The morning was as green and fresh as any he had ever seen. The lake, refreshed and revitalised by the heavy rain of the day and night before, glittered and dazzled, while the boat on it stood tranquil, its perfect reflection in the water below. John left the house by the door in the east entrance and stood at the top of the steps, looking about him.

As far as the eye could see there was beauty and harmony everywhere. Velvet lawns swept down to the water's edge and up to the hill beyond; the church, its golden dome glimmering in the early dawn light, and that frightening mausoleum standing menacingly by. Shrubs and trees were prolific, planted to give the best advantage to the line of sight; peacocks swept past to present an added flash of splendour.

The Apothecary fell to thinking about the character of Sir Francis Dashwood. A truly indecent old man who had difficulty in restraining himself sexually, who could hardly keep his cock in his breeches, yet who had dreamt up this vision of loveliness and who had dammed the River Wye to make the lake and the lower lake, joined together by the cascade. He seemed to John at that moment to be two different people inhabiting one body. And then it occurred to him that Sir Francis worshipped beauty in all its forms and he could not help a half-smile crossing his face. Quickening his pace, John headed down to the lake.

This morning it looked alive, gleaming in the dawning, the waters temporarily taking on the colour of a rose. John set off to walk round it, determined to have a good look at the grounds without interruption. It was soothing, surveying the great waterway from close to, and he found himself enjoying the exercise enormously. His glance went to the frigate, on which a lazy figure had appeared, yawning and stretching, still wearing a nightshirt, but for all that appreciating the morning. John waved at him and the figure waved back.

He had reached the point where the waterway narrowed, prior to going downward through the cascade. Here there was a grass walkway and John set out to look at the statue close to. And then something caught his attention. Bobbing in the water below the cascade was a light blue object, its identity obscured by the distance. Suddenly he knew that familiar feeling of danger, of all being not well. Running round from the walkway he scrambled down the drop until he had gained the riverbank.

The thing was floating midstream and John still could not see what it was. But a small wave from somewhere moved the object slightly inshore. John stared and saw that it was a blue nightshirt partially covering a man floating face down in the water. Without hesitation he kicked off his shoes and threw his jacket to the ground, then he dived in.

It was not pleasant bringing a corpse to the shore. He had heard the expression "dead weight" and now the true meaning of the words was borne in on him as he floundered to the water's edge. John stood shivering in the early sunshine as he turned the body over and looked into the dead face of the heir to the Duke of Sussex, Charles, Marquess of Arundel.

He did the only thing possible. Leaving the body where it was he sprinted round the side of the lake to where the little frigate lay moored.

"Help," he called, cupping his hands round his mouth. "Help. There's a man dead here."

The figure reappeared on deck, emptying a pail of slops into the water. "What?" it shouted.

"Somebody has been drowned. Can you help me?"

"Drowned, you say?"

John nodded.

"Right ho, sir. Coming."

The man climbed down a short ladder into a little rowing boat and set out for the shore at a swift pace. As he drew alongside John was able to get a close look at him. Typical of his type, he was dark, swarthy and fully bearded. He was also still in his nightshirt with nothing on beneath.

"You did say someone had drowned, sir?"

"Well, he's dead certainly. But whether he was drowned or fell in after death is anybody's guess at the moment."

"Well, let's take a look at him."

They proceeded on, slithering down the slope once more, to where Lord Arundel lay inertly on the ground, a large swan stretching its neck curiously towards him.

"Shoo!" said John, and was hissed at for his effort.

He knelt down by the body and raised it up, looking down into the face. In death Charles seemed younger, the lines of dissipation and illness smoothed out. His eyes, John noticed, were shut.

"Poor bugger," said the Captain. "Who is he? Do you know?"

"He's the Marquess of Arundel, heir to the Duke of Sussex."

"Well, the Duke'll have to find another heir now, won't he?"

"He certainly will. Listen, Captain . . .?"

"Hughes, sir."

". . . Captain Hughes, I wonder if I can leave you to guard the body while I rush back to the house and break the news to Sir Francis."

"You certainly can, sir. It's not the first body I've seen and I doubt it'll be the last."

"Well said. I'll go."

John ran fast, feeling as if his heart would burst by the time he arrived back at the house. Clattering in past the servants, he demanded to know where everyone was.

"Sir Francis is still asleep, sir. Lady Dashwood is up, however. She is in the saloon having a cup of chocolate but I don't know that she would wish to be disturbed."

"Why not?"

"She is not yet dressed."

John made an impatient gesture. "And what about the rest? Has anybody risen?"

"I believe Lady Arundel is stirring, sir."

The Apothecary mounted the stairs and hurried to the room in which he had last seen the dead man. Giving a peremptory knock he entered, then stopped short. Someone who had been missing from dinner last night, Lady Juliana Bravo, stood by the window, gazing out. She was fully dressed but so far her maid had not done her hair and she had not a scrap of paint on her face. She turned and stared at John with those cold blue eyes of hers.

He bowed. "Forgive me, madam, I was hoping to find Lady Arundel."

"She is in the room next to this one. She is sharing it with her daughter."

"I see." He hesitated, then said, "Lady Juliana, I am afraid that I have some very bad news for you."

"And what might that be?" she asked, totally composed.

"I'm sorry to tell you that your brother is dead," he said.

She stared at him uncomprehendingly. "What do you mean?"

"I mean that Lord Arundel is dead; drowned apparently. I found him below the cascade while on an early morning walk. The captain of the frigate is guarding the body and I have come back in order to raise the alarm."

Her hands flew to her throat. "Oh God's wounds, I must go to him."

"Wait a moment, madam, I beg of you. I must inform Lady Arundel and Sir Francis Dashwood before you do so." He looked at her kindly. "Believe me, there is nothing you can do for him."

She gave him a glassy-eyed stare. "How dare you order me about? I shall go to my brother now." And with that she ran from the room, her hair flying round her head.

A door opened and Coralie stood there, clad in her sleeping gown. John was suddenly filled with memories of how many times he had seen her like that, how charming he had thought she looked.

"What is it?" she said. "What's all the noise about?"

He went up to her. "Coralie, my dear . . ."

She turned on him a whimsical smile. "You have not called me that for a long time."

"Have I not?"

"No." She suddenly sensed the tension in him. "John, what's happened?" Her glance went to the bed. "Where is Charles? Is something wrong?"

"Yes, I'm afraid it is. Sweetheart, be brave. I'm sorry to have to inform you that your husband is dead."

She sat down on the bed. "Dead? How? What are you saying?"

He sat down beside her. "He appears to have drowned."

"What does that mean — appears?"

"I found him earlier this morning when I was out walking. He was in the River Wye, just below the cascade. But how he got there is a mystery."

"Poor Charles," she said, her face full of sudden pity. "As I said to you recently, he was such a sweet and vulnerable youth."

"Tell me again how he caught the Great Pox?"

"From some little doxy or other."

"And there is no chance that you . . .?"

"Quite definitely not. As I told you I stopped sleeping with him as soon as he began having affairs. Our married life in that sense of the word was over."

"Why did you not leave him?"

"To go where? Admittedly I could have returned to the stage but the truth is that I am getting older, John. There are many aspiring actresses more than willing to step into my shoes. Besides, I have my child to consider."

"How are you going to tell her?"

"I don't know yet. At the moment she is asleep and I don't intend to wake her."

John stood up. "I shall leave you to dress. I must go and rouse Sir Francis."

"Yes, you must." She turned to him and laid a hand on his arm. "I am sorry I was rude to you the other evening."

"Think nothing of it."

Sir Francis Dashwood slept in a vast bedroom on the ground floor of the house and it was to this that John now hurried. Fortunately his host, magnificently arrayed in a satin turban and a long flowing robe, appeared in the doorway just as the Apothecary was going to risk knocking.

"O'Hare," Sir Francis exclaimed in some surprise. "Whatever gets you up and about so early?"

"Sir, I am sorry to have to inform you that there has been a tragic accident. Lord Arundel is dead and it looks as though he may have drowned."

"Good God! Drowned, you say?"

"Yes. I went for an early stroll, just as dawn was breaking. I saw something in the water below the cascade. I dived in and brought it to the bank and saw that it was poor wretched Arundel."

"Where is he now?"

"Still there. Captain Hughes is guarding him. Unfortunately Lady Juliana has gone down to see for herself. I just hope she won't interfere with him too much."

"I'd better go at once. Come with me, my boy."

What a motley crew they must have looked, John thought. He dressed like a countryman, Sir Francis arrayed as would befit some Eastern potentate. Behind them, running along as best they could, came a host of servants, grooms and stable boys, carrying between them a large plank of wood. Behind *them*, presumably woken by the noise was the figure of Dominique, scantily clad. Had the circumstances been any different

John would have guffawed but as it was he was debating whether to reveal himself to Sir Francis as being an associate of Sir John Fielding or whether to continue his pose as Fintan O'Hare. In the end he decided to remain anonymous.

They reached the riverbank to discover Lady Juliana, pale and weeping and wringing her hands, seated on the ground beside the body of her brother. John noticed that she had pulled his nightgown round him respectably. Captain Hughes had disappeared, presumably to get dressed.

Sir Francis approached, pulling her to her feet. "There, there, Juliana. What a sad business to be sure. Poor Charles. He must have gone for a walk and accidentally fallen in. Tragic affair. Tragic!"

John knelt down beside the body and did something he should have done earlier. He raised the nightshirt and quickly examined the chancre. The dressing was no longer on there, having clearly floated away in the water. Of the paste he had placed on it during the previous evening there was no sign.

Seeing him, Juliana called out, "What are you doing, you Irish rogue? Give my poor brother some decency if you please."

The Apothecary rose and said, "I am an apothecary, madam. I was merely examining a wound your brother had."

"What's all this?" asked Sir Francis. "Are you a medical man, O'Hare?"

"I am indeed, sir. My father insisted on all his younger sons getting a training."

"Remarkable. And they say the Irish are a lazy lot of bastards."

"I don't believe a word he says," shrieked Juliana hysterically. "I think the man is a phoney and a fraud."

"Don't answer, O'Hare," Sir Francis muttered. "The woman doesn't know what she is saying."

By this time Dominique had caught them up as had the stable lads and servants. The Frenchman surveyed the body with a somewhat shocked expression.

"Poor soul. What a way to die."

"It may have been a mercy," John muttered.

"Why? What do you mean?"

"The man had the Great Pox," John whispered to Dominique.

"Are you certain?"

"Positive."

The Frenchman crossed himself. "Then it was heaven-sent."

They watched in silence as the stable lads hefted the body onto the plank and covered it with a cloth. Then they started their dismal procession back to the house. But they were only halfway there when a solemn figure joined them. It was Coralie, clad from head to foot in dark colours. John thought he had never seen her look more dignified and the thought shot through his mind that this was one of her most magnificent performances. She approached them dramatically, moving at a steady pace, and as the sad party neared her it slowed right down till she had drawn alongside. Bending down, Coralie moved back the cloth and stared into Charles's dead face. She shook her head several times, then said quietly, "Poor Charlie," before placing the covering back again.

Juliana, who seemed to be temporarily crazed, shouted out, "What, not a tear? Do you not weep for my poor dead brother, you heartless creature?"

Coralie merely smiled at her, quite distantly, then went walking on down to the lake. John made to join her but she looked at him and said, "Please, no. If you don't mind I would prefer to be solitary."

He gave a little bow. "As you wish, madam."

Hurrying, he caught up with Sir Francis, who was shaking his head and saying, "Where to put the poor devil? That's the question."

"Don't you have a cool outhouse somewhere?"

"Nowhere's very cool at this time of year."

"Well, there must be somewhere."

Eventually they decided on a small shed close to the icehouse and having placed the body therein, Sir Francis locked the door.

"I need a drink," he said heavily.

John and Dominique followed the man into the red drawing room and accepted the brandy that he offered them.

"What's to be done?" he said, emptying his glass and pouring himself another one.

John thought rapidly, wondering what it was about the death that made him feel that all was not well. It was quite plausible, surely, that Lord Arundel had risen in the night and gone for a walk in the grounds. Yet two things were against that idea. One was that the poor wretch was still wearing his nightshirt, the other that the weather had been so bad. Making a mental note to find out from someone at what time it had stopped raining, John sipped his drink.

Lady Dashwood came into the room. "So it's true?" she said to her husband.

He sighed heavily. "I'm afraid so."

"I'll get some women to lay him out. We can't just leave him as he is."

"If you don't mind, madam, I would like to have a final look at the body before you do so."

She stared at John in astonishment and Dashwood — who by now was on his third glass of brandy — said, "Turns out that O'Hare is an apothecary. Apparently the Irish train their younger sons to do things."

"But why should you want to look at poor Lord Arundel?"

"To see there are no marks of foul play."

They stared at him in astonishment. "Foul play?" Sir Francis repeated, looking dazed.

"I feel it is my duty to do so," John answered pompously.

"But who . . .?"

"That, Sir Francis, would remain to be seen."

"But surely it might involve one of us."

"If I find anything, yes it would."

"Must you take this course of action?" This from Lady Dashwood.

"I am afraid I must," John said portentously.

CHAPTER
SEVENTEEN

John let himself into the outhouse with a strange sense of inadequacy. For how to prove the actual cause of the Marquess of Arundel's death? Steeling himself, John pulled back the covers and saw that the body had started to bloat, swelling up to twice its size after its time in the water. Despite this, the Apothecary set to, pulling up the nightshirt till Charles lay as good as naked.

There were no marks of blows anywhere which could only lead John to think that the man had fallen in the lake quite naturally. Indeed, the only blemish anywhere was the chancre, which looked ghastly, swollen as it was, with its open wound on top. Again, John examined it but there was nothing to indicate any interference with the gash. There could be little doubt that death had been caused by drowning.

And yet the same two questions nagged in the Apothecary's brain. Why had Charles, feeling ill as he was, gone for a walk in the darkness dressed only in his sleeping clothes? And why, if it was pouring hard with rain, had he even ventured outdoors? There was no question that Lord Arundel had gone out in the dawning because that was when he — John — had ventured forth and there had been no sign of anyone else around. It was vital that he find out from somebody or other at precisely what time it had ceased to rain during the previous night.

He finished his examination and covered the swollen body up decently. Then he made his way, deep in thought, to the house. As his knock was answered he saw that the Earl and Countess of Orpington were making their way downstairs. She was wrapped round him, literally, and had a sweet seraphic smile on her face. While he, stupid old fool, looked large and loving. Glancing at them, John felt certain that as yet they had not heard the news. But at that moment a door opened and Sir Francis Dashwood, fully dressed and wearing the most serious expression John had seen on him to date, came out.

"Lord Orpington," he said briefly. "Did you sleep well?"

"Like the dead," came the reply, and he ran his hand caressingly over his wife's buttocks.

"An unfortunate simile," Sir Francis answered unsmilingly.

"Why?" asked the older man, picking up something in the atmosphere.

"Because I have grave news, sir. Lord Arundel died last night."

"What?" the Earl exclaimed, while his wife let out a scream then put a hand over her mouth.

"True enough. He wandered out in the night and drowned in the lower lake, that narrow part of the River Wye below the cascade."

190

At this the Countess was suddenly overcome with hysterical weeping and Lord Orpington's piggy eyes narrowed as he gazed at her.

"What's the matter, my dear? Surely you were barely acquainted with the man."

She tried to recover herself but could not help the tears pouring down her face. "Oh no, I hardly knew him. But it's just so horrid to think of somebody dying like that."

"I see," the Earl answered, looking decidedly as if he saw no such thing.

Noticing the Apothecary, Sir Francis approached him. "Have you examined him?" he asked.

"Yes, sir, I have."

"And?"

"Nothing. There's not a mark on him save for that slight injury he incurred last night."

"I don't remember that."

"As he was being helped from the saddle a stirrup caught him and hurt him."

"Oh, yes. But surely that was merely a pinprick."

"In a way, yes."

The expression in the Apothecary's eyes prevented Sir Francis from asking any further questions. Meanwhile the Countess of Orpington had gone pale and consequently been forced to sit down on an uncomfortable-looking chair. Her husband, instead of tending to her, was glaring at her with suspicion. Into this uncomfortable ménage walked Georgiana, child of the dead man, hand in hand with her aunt, Lady Juliana, who seemed to have composed herself.

"Your mama is out walking, dearest," she was saying, but stopped short on seeing the assembled company.

"Are you quite recovered, madam?" enquired Sir Francis pointedly.

"As much as I can be in the circumstances," she answered with a certain acidity.

"Oh, merciful heaven," sobbed Lady Orpington. "What a tragedy it is."

John, watching them all carefully, wondered just how much emotion was real and how much was purely pretence for the sake of the others. He went up to the weeping young woman.

"Head between your knees," he said cheerfully, "and take a good sniff of these."

He produced his salts from an inner pocket and thrust them beneath her nose. She sniffed suspiciously.

"Ugh!" she said, eyeing him with a narrowed eye.

"Mr O'Hare is an apothecary," announced Sir Francis, looking as if he would countenance no trouble from anyone.

"I see," she answered meekly, and took another cautious sniff.

Lady Dashwood appeared and said in her dreary voice, "Breakfast is served for those who would like it."

"Well I, for one, am going to have some," responded her husband. "This sad business has made me extremely hungry."

"Me too," said John.

"I could eat a horse," announced the Earl of Orpington. "Wife, you can sit and wail to your heart's content. If you want me, I shall be in the breakfast room."

Georgiana piped up. "I know that Papa has been drowned but I still would like to eat something."

"And so you shall, dear heart," her aunt answered, and led the way into the room in which the repast had been laid. John, walking behind her, thought her one of the most extraordinary women he had ever met. She had now transformed herself into a quiet, serious creature, loving of her niece and acting like a mother. Remembering her earlier, screaming abuse at poor Coralie, John could hardly believe it.

The only person who did not join them for the meal was Lady Orpington. John, feeling slightly guilty about her, stepped into the hall with a cup of tea to find that the woman in question had vanished, presumably to go upstairs and fling herself down on her bed, enjoying the luxury of an uninhibited cry. He was just about to return to the breakfast room when Coralie appeared, walking through a side door.

"My dear," he said, putting the cup down on a window sill, "how are you feeling?"

She looked at him quite calmly. "I think we had better talk outside," she answered.

For the second time that morning John walked out of the east portico, only this time he was accompanied by the woman who for many years he had adored. Looking at her sideways he was struck, as if for the very first occasion, by the timelessness of her beauty.

"You're lovely," he said.

She cast him a look in the depths of which was just a hint of amusement. "I was once," she answered.

John decided to be utterly honest with her. "Coralie, your husband drowned, there can be no doubt about that. But two things puzzle me about his death."

"Which are?" Was there just the hint of a quaver in her voice?

"Firstly, why did he go for a walk wearing only his nightshirt? And secondly, why did he go out in the pouring rain?"

"How do you know that he did?"

"Because I left the house at dawn, dressed roughly but for all that dressed. It wasn't raining then but it looked as if it had only stopped about half an hour since."

"How could you tell?"

"Because the lawn and trees were dripping wet."

Coralie smiled. "It stopped raining at half past four. I know because I woke up and looked at the clock and I heard the last of the downpour die away."

"I would say that he had been in the river at least an hour. So he must have gone out in the inclement weather."

"There's one question that you haven't asked, John," she said quietly.

"Oh? And what is that?"

"Did somebody push him in?"

"I see. Do you have any suspicions?"

Coralie shook her head. "It could be anyone in this house. There are several people present who had cause

194

to dislike if not hate him." She gave a humourless smile. "Including me."

John gave her a deep look. "Did you force him into the river, Coralie?"

"No. There is a small part of me that still loves him. I can't think why."

As soon as she spoke, he wondered whether she was telling him the truth. If she had found out about the supposed abuse of her daughter. And yet he felt base for even suspecting her. John had a sudden longing to get back to the George and Dragon and discuss the entire matter with Samuel.

They had been walking down the lawn while they spoke and now they saw Dominique coming towards them. As soon as he recognised Coralie he hurried up to her and kissed her hand.

"Madam, may I offer you my profound condolences. I cannot tell you how sorry I feel."

Coralie nodded. "Thank you, Monsieur Jean. It is kind of you to say so."

"I mean it, madam. Now if you will excuse me I must get back to the stable block. I finish the last of my work today."

"I am sure you will be glad to return home," said Coralie, keeping up a show of courtesy. She turned back to the house. "Forgive me, gentlemen, I will leave you. My daughter will be needing me I feel certain. Good day to you."

And she was gone, leaving the two men to stare after her retreating figure.

"So how many suspects are there?" asked Samuel, eyes round as the full moon.

"Many," answered John, ticking them off on his fingers. "First of all there's Sir Francis Dashwood."

"Motive?"

"Unknown. But it could be some private business, particularly something connected to the Hellfire Club."

"What about Lady Dashwood?"

"Again, unknown. But they are connected through that endless chain of relatives that the nobility seem to have. Maybe she secretly hates the man."

John leaned back comfortably. He was sitting in The Ram, a private snug contained within the George and Dragon, and was on his second pint of ale, despite the earliness of the hour.

Samuel leaned forward. "Go on. Who else?"

"There's Coralie of course," John answered somewhat reluctantly. "She has plenty of motive. Her husband had contracted syphilis several months ago. It's all right," he said to Samuel's stricken expression. "She gave up sleeping with him before he became infected. But she could have killed him to protect her child who — according to Dominique Jean — was being molested by the man."

"Sounds as if the bastard deserved drowning and more," Samuel stated robustly.

"He did actually. This is one killer I can sympathise with, they appear to have done the world a good service. Then there comes that idiotic child, Arabella, Countess of Orpington. She is sixteen years old, thinks she's clever but is actually as stupid as they make them. Either of those two could easily have committed the murder."

"And you're quite sure it *was* murder."

"No, that's the devil of it, Sam, I'm not. The only two clues are the ones I've already told you. Why did the man leave his sickbed and go wandering round in the middle of a terrible storm?"

"That's certainly odd, I must say."

"It's more than odd. It's highly suspicious. The feeling in my gut tells me that it was not by chance and that Arundel was deliberately killed."

"Are there any other suspects?"

"Plenty. There's his sister — a cold-faced bitch if ever I saw one — and, I suppose — though I am reluctant even to say it — his daughter."

"But she's only a child."

"I have known children kill before," said John, and sighed deeply.

"Anyone else?"

"Strangely enough, Dominique Jean. He is apparently owed £700 by the late Lord Arundel and feels particularly bitter about it."

"And that's the entire crew?"

"All of 'em, unless the murder was done by somebody outside. All those people spent the night under Sir Francis's roof. At least I presume they did. The Lady Juliana Bravo — Lord Arundel's sister — went out and apparently came back late."

"And you?" Samuel asked. "What time did you go to bed?"

"Early. I felt exhausted."

Samuel's face underwent a change, an expression of boyish mischief taking over his features. "Tell me, John, what actually goes on at that Hellfire Club?"

"A lot of sex, my friend. A lot of arrant fornication. That's all everybody seems to do all the time."

"By Jove, I wish I'd been included."

"A happily married man like you, Samuel? Come, come! I find myself totally surprised."

The Goldsmith actually blushed. "I just meant for the experience. I would not have participated."

"Then more fool you." And putting out his hand, John ruffled his friend's hair.

It was at that somewhat amusing moment that Dominique entered the snug. "'Ello, you two," he called cheerily. "I've been looking for you."

"Well now you've found us. Come and have a drink."

"Gladly." Dominique sat down and ordered a jug of ale. He looked at John over its rim. "How are you getting on, my friend?"

John put down his tankard and assumed a serious face. "I am treating the death of Lord Arundel as one of murder," he said.

Dominique gulped noisily. "Oh, my goodness. Why?"

"Because it strikes me that no one would have gone out on such a night wearing only his nightshirt."

"Is that the only reason?"

"No, there are others," John answered mysteriously.

Dominique took a deep swallow and said, "Tell me."

"I'm afraid I can't reveal too much about my theories — Sir John Fielding's orders and all that." John waved an airy hand. "But you slept in the house last night, Dominique. Tell me, did you hear anything?"

"Yes. I found it rather a noisy place, for despite the fact that I was tired out I still couldn't get off to sleep. Round about midnight, give or take an hour, I heard someone walking along the corridor. I had just been dozing off but I awoke and listened."

"What happened?" asked Samuel, his eyes huge.

"Well, I could have sworn that whoever it was went into Lord Arundel's room — I was sleeping almost directly opposite him and —"

"I thought you were put in the servants' quarters," John interrupted.

"Yes, I was to have slept there but at the last moment Lady Dashwood remembered a little boxroom over the eaves and put me in it."

"Go on."

"Well, I thought someone went in there and shortly afterwards there was a funny little noise, like a subdued scream, and I heard the feet coming out again, moving quite fast."

"Was it a man or a woman, could you tell?"

Dominique shook his head. "I truly am not certain. All I know is that I heard the clatter of shoes on the wooden floor."

"And then?"

"After that I must have dropped off to sleep because the next thing I knew it was three o'clock and there was another disturbance."

"What?"

"Somebody else came shuffling along the corridor."

"Why do you use that word? Shuffling?"

"Because that is what they were doing. I heard it quite distinctly."

"And you were sure it was three?"

"Yes, I looked at the clock. Anyway, the sound ceased, almost abruptly, and after that I went back to sleep and was woken by the noises of people in the grounds below."

John nodded. "Yes, I remember you joining in the group."

Dominique nodded. "Who would have thought it, *mon ami*? Who could possibly have wanted Lord Arundel dead?"

"Well," said John, smiling broadly but watching Dominique intently, "you might have done for a start."

CHAPTER
EIGHTEEN

The Frenchman's eyebrows shot up and his jaw tightened but to his credit he maintained his equilibrium. He took a sip of ale and said, "Really? And what makes you say that?"

John, silently admiring the man's poise, answered, "Because the wretched fellow owed you money. You told me so yourself."

Dominique shrugged. "Everyone owes me money. It is one of the risks I take. But to be honest, in this instance it was my late father-in-law Pierre Langlois who was the creditor. I am hardly likely to commit a murder on his behalf."

He smiled disarmingly and John found himself half believing him.

"True enough," he said.

Samuel put in, "I should say not."

"And now, sir, if you have finished quizzing me I think I will go and make myself presentable before I return to the big house to say farewell. I have an early start tomorrow morning."

John wished at that moment that he had the power to instruct Dominique to wait, that he could order him to stay until the mystery had been cleared up, but knew

201

that such an act would be treated with contempt. Instead he rose to his feet and bowed to the Frenchman.

"My dear sir, we shall miss your company. But I am sure that you will be glad to return to London."

"I am going on to Rousham Park to see about an order first, so I will not be completely out of your way yet awhile."

"I see. So who is running your business now that Pierre Langlois is dead?"

"His widow, my mother-in-law, Tracey Langlois. A formidable woman indeed."

John smiled, remembering another more recent girl of the same name, though admittedly she had called herself Teresa.

"So if we need you we can write to you at Rousham Park?"

The Frenchman flashed him a brilliant grin. "Yes, if you want to accuse me of the murder. I shall be there three days or so. After that you can contact me at the business in Tottenham Court Road."

And with that somewhat daunting remark he bowed politely to John and Samuel and left the room. As soon as he was gone the Goldsmith turned to his friend.

"Well, what do you think? Was that just a good performance?"

"It could have been but, if so, it was polished to the hilt."

"Ah, but what else could you expect. After all he's French," Samuel replied, and there the matter was laid to rest.

★　★　★

At midday John and Samuel rode on horseback to West Wycombe Park, the Goldsmith full of admiration for the beauty of the place. They went in by the eastern entrance and in this way passed the River Wye, the cascade and the lake itself. Hidden by trees as they were, John dismounted and led Samuel to the actual spot where he had discovered Lord Arundel. Perhaps it was his imagination but now the river had a forlorn and somehow desolate air, even the waters — usually so bright and sparkling — looked seal grey. The Apothecary gazed around him, wishing that the trees could speak. For what could have induced Charles Bravo, Marquess of Arundel, to come blundering out of the house and down to the lake on a night when even a cat would wish to be indoors? It must have been almost as if something had driven the man. Thoughts of demonic possession swept through John's mind but were as rapidly dismissed.

Samuel meanwhile was busy walking up and down the river bank, presumably searching for clues. Then suddenly he bent down and scooped something up.

"What have you got there?" John asked.

"A button. Come and have a look at it."

The Apothecary scrambled down the slope and stared at the object lying in Sam's square hand. It was a very small button, pale blue, and could have belonged to either sex. As John looked at it he had a short burst of memory but it was too brief for him to form any cohesive ideas. The idea literally came into his head and left it again with equal speed. He turned to Sam who was looking at him with a somewhat anxious expression on his face.

"Do you think it is useful?"

"It could be. Keep it carefully."

They proceeded on to the house, walking their horses slowly side-by-side, to discover as they entered through the front door — which, for once, stood open — that a melee of sorts had broken out. Juliana Bravo was physically attacking her sister-in-law, Coralie, aided and abetted by that obnoxious brat, Lady Orpington. Lady Dashwood was making an enfeebled effort to intercede, watched by her husband who was clearly enjoying the spectacle, while the child, Georgiana, was howling her head off, occasionally swinging a small arm into the air. Meanwhile the Earl of Orpington had collapsed into a chair, looking as if he were about to have a heart attack, while the servants stood helplessly nearby waiting for a command from their master.

John did not hesitate but swept himself into the fight, pushing Juliana, who was shrieking, "Murderess, murderess!" out of the way and standing firmly by Coralie's side. Samuel promptly picked Lady Juliana up — receiving a violent kick in the shins for his pains — and carried her to the other end of the hall, where she beat him about the head with her hands. At that moment Dominique Jean appeared in the doorway and rushing up to the throng seized Arabella Orpington hard round the waist, knocking the wind out of her.

"Oh, John," said Coralie, her eyes full of tears, her icy facade totally shattered, "I can't stand much more of this."

204

He turned to her, then was astonished to feel something wrap itself round his leg. Looking down he saw that Georgiana, her face wet and her nose running, had caught him in an octopus-like hold.

"Help my mama," she bleated.

"Oh, my little angel," said Coralie, and, weeping, picked the child up.

"Well, here's a how d'you do!" exclaimed Sir Francis. "Women fighting. Whatever next. Control yourself, madam, do."

He addressed this remark to Lady Juliana, still struggling with Samuel who now held her at arm's length away from him. At the sound of his commanding voice she ceased to kick and Sam lowered her to the floor.

"I'm sorry, Sir Francis," she said breathlessly. "It is just that I cannot look at that woman, that *actress*, without feeling hatred rise like bile in my throat. She only married my brother for the title and money. She is nothing but a schemer and a bitch. And now to add to all her other crimes she has committed murder."

John, particularly furious because he had at one stage harboured many of the same thoughts, turned on Juliana like a whip.

"Have a care, madam. There is such a thing as the law of slander and you have most certainly just committed it, in front of witnesses too."

At this there was a wheeze from Arabella, who lay on the floor, purple in the face and gasping for breath. Everyone ignored her.

Sir Francis looked at John. "I would suggest, sir, you being an apothecary and all, that you sort some of these wounded women out."

John gave a crooked grin. "Certainly, Sir Francis, but I think I'll start with the child." He picked Georgiana up and said, "Come, my girl, I think it is high time that you and I had a little talk." He looked at Coralie. "I would prefer it if you were present, Lady Arundel."

Her face had once more become expressionless but she nodded her head. "Shall we go somewhere more private?" she asked in an undertone.

"Indeed. Madam, have you a quiet place where I may minister to this child?" he asked Lady Dashwood.

"Perhaps you should take her up to her room, Mr O'Hare. She certainly could do with a wash and brush up."

In silence Coralie and John, he carrying the child who was still sobbing loudly, went up the stairs, watched by everyone, particularly Lady Orpington, who was just starting to regain her breath and regarded them with as malevolent an eye as she could manage in the circumstances.

They reached the landing and saw the door to Charles's room had been left open. Coralie clutched at John's arm.

"Poor fellow," she said beneath her breath, "I hope that he did not suffer."

The Apothecary could not answer, merely shooting her a troubled glance in which she read his reply. Aware that the atmosphere between them had suddenly become fraught they walked on to the room which last night Georgiana had shared with Coralie because of the unusual number of house guests.

As soon as he had set her on her feet, the child ran to her mother and buried her face among Coralie's skirts.

"Oh, Mama, is my father really dead?" she said in a tired, strained little voice.

"Yes, darling. I'm afraid he is."

"Good," answered the child. "I am pleased." And she suddenly let out a burst of laughter which shocked John to the core.

"What are you saying?" said Coralie, bending over and seizing Georgiana by the arms, then giving her a thoroughly good shake.

"Don't be too hard on her, Coralie. I think she has her reasons."

Over the child's head the actress's eyes met John's. "What are you saying exactly?"

He opened his mouth to speak, suddenly tired of all this pretence and determined to tell his former mistress the truth, when the child burst out with, "He frightened me, Mama. He used to come to me at night, or even send for me during the day, and make me take my clothes off . . ."

John saw Coralie go white with horror.

". . . and then he would take all his things off too."

"And what would happen then?" Coralie asked in a deep low voice that even John could not recognise.

"Nothing, Mama. He just used to put his arms round me and go to sleep. He told me I was better than any sleeping draught in the world. But I hated it, I hated it! I hated lying next to him and seeing his skin so close to mine. It made me want to kill him."

There was a shocked silence into which John said quietly, "Did you, Georgiana? Did you push him into the river to drown?"

"No," answered the little girl, looking up at him and regarding him with her blazing blue eyes, "I just stood there and watched him die."

CHAPTER
NINETEEN

There was total silence while both adults stood looking at the child, an expression of horror on Coralie's face, on John's one of acute interest. Georgiana, gazing from one to the other, seemed to realise the full import of what she had just said, for she cried out suddenly, "I didn't kill him, Mama. And I couldn't pull him out. I promise I couldn't."

The actress sat down on the bed, saying not a word, staring at her daughter, her lips moving soundlessly. Georgiana, either not understanding or perhaps understanding too well, became hysterical.

"Please, Mama, I beg you not to look at me like that. I am telling you the truth. I swear I am."

John interceded. "For God's sake, Coralie, she is only a child. I don't believe for a minute that she killed Arundel."

Out of that white mask of a face, a voice came. "By Christ's holy wounds that is not what ails me. It is just that I am shocked beyond all reason by realising what the man was. A creature who molests children is not fit to live. I thank God that my husband is dead." She looked up. "Had I known I would not have hesitated to have put him down myself."

John said quietly, "Are you trying to tell me that you had no idea?"

She looked at him and he saw that she was drained of emotion, was now utterly calm in what she said.

"Recently I had begun to suspect something, knew that he was preoccupied with Georgiana but thought it was just an excess of paternal feeling. What a fool I have been." She looked down at the sobbing child who had curled herself into a ball round Coralie's feet, then picked her up and cuddled her. "You poor little girl. How can you ever forgive me? What future can life hold for you?"

John crouched down so that his face was on a level with the woman he had once loved and for whom he still felt an enormous bond of affection.

"Listen to me, Coralie, and listen well. The child will be perfectly all right if you explain to her that her father was a very sick man; had an illness which made him cling to her in a not very pleasant manner. Then you must introduce her to the finer things of childhood, the playing with other children, the fresh air, the sea. Clear her mind of all the cobwebs that have been allowed to gather in it."

She turned on him a ravaged face. "But what of her when she grows older? When it is her turn to fall in love? Surely the canker of these early years will remain with her always?"

John shook his head, perplexed but attempting not to show it. "Let me speak to her. I promise you that I will do my best."

Coralie comforted the sobbing child. "Hush, sweetheart," she said in a gentle voice. "I know that you did not kill Papa. And I fully understand how you must have come to hate him. But let us forget all that now. Let us leave this place tomorrow and spend some time with your friends. Would you like that?"

Georgiana looked at her through a tangle of hair and nodded.

"But first of all Mr Rawlings, who has been a great friend of mine for many years, would like to have a talk with you."

The child stared at him suspiciously, her eyes full of sudden alarm.

"Don't worry, my dear," John reassured her. "I just wanted to ask you about your father's final moments. Did you see anybody else at the riverside?"

"No, sir."

"Even though it was dark. I mean, could someone have hidden themselves in the bushes?"

"I don't know. I suppose somebody might have been hiding. But I saw no one. Truly."

"Darling," said Coralie, brushing the top of Georgiana's head with her lips, "how did you come to be there in the first place?"

The child shot her an anxious look. "You're not cross are you?"

"Most certainly not. I just want to know."

"Well, I wondered why Papa hadn't sent for me to go to him and the thought made me lie awake. Then he appeared in the doorway of my room. You were asleep,

Mama, and didn't hear him." She paused and looked at John. "He stood there but he couldn't see me."

"Couldn't see you?" he repeated.

"He turned his head without seeing anything, as if he had suddenly gone blind. He just stood in the doorway, then went down that back staircase and out into the gardens. There was something peculiar about him."

"What?"

"I don't know."

"What do you mean, Georgiana?"

The brilliant blue eyes grew wild and she gazed at her mother in consternation. "I can't say what I mean. All I know is that he slipped on the stairs and kept bumping into things in the grounds. I followed him to see what he would do."

"And what happened the?"

"He staggered down to the cascade and stood for a moment, swaying. Then he fell in."

"And he was alone?"

"Yes. As I told you, there could have been someone hiding but I didn't see them."

"What did you feel as you saw him drown?" This from Coralie, said very quietly.

"I was glad," answered the little creature truthfully, "that it was all over." She turned to John. "Is there anything else you need to know, sir?"

"No," he answered, his mind teeming with thoughts, "I think you have described it very well, my dear. And now I suggest that you go and wash yourself and then you and your mother can go out for a ride. I will have a chat with you another time."

"Very well," Georgiana answered, and taking Coralie by the hand she led her into an adjoining chamber. She turned in the doorway and gave John Rawlings a look which was to haunt him for many days to come.

Downstairs calm had been restored. Lady Juliana had disappeared from sight, heaven knew where; the horrid little Lady Orpington had somehow managed to talk her aged husband round and was currently receiving a series of tickles and pinches from his podgy fingers; Samuel Swann and Dominique Jean had both very wisely vanished. Sir Francis Dashwood, meanwhile, sat in his saloon, the doors open to the hall beyond, and stared out moodily at the lake whilst sipping a glass of restorative canary. John gave a polite knock and entered.

"Peace has returned," said the nobleman, glancing up. "Would you like a drink, old chap?"

The Apothecary shook his head. "Thank you, no. I am really in search of my servant."

"Oh, he's in the stables somewhere or other. Monsieur Jean wanted to show him round."

"Thank you, sir. I'll go and find him."

John bowed politely and left, his brain teeming with what he had just heard. If Georgiana was telling the truth then the thought which occurred to him was that possibly Lord Arundel had been administered an irritant poison; a poison which had caused him to weave his way out into the grounds and fall into the lake, where the teeming cascade had seized him in its clutches and tossed him into the river below.

But if this wild theory were to prove correct then he was left with three big questions: who, how and when?

Outside the fine day continued, the late morning pearl-like in its beauty. John, gazing round him, thought to himself about the inhabitants of the house, about the fact that one of them had died in suspicious circumstances, about the grim reality of the man's terrible end. About how Lord Arundel's only child had watched her father die with a sense of relief.

His mind wandered to thoughts of Rose and just for a moment he let his imagination stray over how she, the jewel of his life, would react if he were to meet an untimely end. He felt then that, young as she was, she would do everything in her power — small though it might be — to try to rescue him. He decided to make a new will and leave her in the care and custody of Samuel and Jocasta Swann should such an eventuality occur.

This train of thinking led inevitably to Sir Gabriel and the man's great age. Surely it would not be possible for that most elegant of mortals, that exquisite being, to defy nature and continue much longer. And yet he had an air about him which made his adopted son feel that perhaps he would cheat the Grim Reaper for a while yet. John found himself half-praying that Sir Gabriel would last another ten years or so.

His mind switched back to the present and he thought about the body in the outhouse, lying there alone and friendless. Then he thought of the terrible death that awaited some victims of syphilis and considered that maybe Charles had been released from

214

such misery. John realised with a jolt that Lady Orpington, the child bride, had probably caught the disease and had no doubt infected her husband with it. He suddenly felt hugely thankful that Coralie and her difficult child had both escaped such a terrible fate.

From one of the outhouses near the stables he heard the sound of voices conversing cheerily and made his way there to discover Samuel and Dominique in the process of hefting a heavy piece of furniture up between them. On seeing him arrive they placed it down again and stood there panting.

"Ah, John," said Samuel, wiping the sweat from his forehead with his sleeve, "how are you proceeding?"

"Quite well."

He was longing to discuss the whole business with his friend but did not dare do so in front of Dominique who could quite easily be responsible for Lord Arundel's death.

"I have much to say to you," he continued, giving the Goldsmith a look which meant that the two of them should be alone before he did so.

"I guessed as much," Samuel replied cheerily. "Tell me all."

It was the Frenchman who realised that the Apothecary needed to be on his own with his friend and said, "If you will excuse me, gentlemen, I shall go and present my bill to Sir Francis."

"Will he pay you?" asked John.

"Eventually yes, yes he will."

"And what about the money owed you by Lord Arundel?"

"I shall give the reckoning to his widow."

"Coralie will meet that, you can rely on it."

"I am sure she will. Gentlemen, I take my leave of you. I shall buy you a drink tonight in the George and Dragon."

Dominique made a small bow and John and Samuel returned the compliment.

"What's that banging?" the Apothecary asked as the sounds of someone working came from a neighbouring outhouse.

"The coffin maker is here," the Frenchman replied, and gave them both a solemn look before he left them alone.

The two men wandered out of the stable block, beneath the arch and headed off into the park, out of sight of the house. They sat down on the lower slopes of the hill leading up to the mausoleum and John lit a pipe.

"Was the man murdered or was it an accident?" Samuel asked.

"I think he was definitely killed by some irritant poison." And John proceeded to relay to Samuel all that he had learned that morning.

"But can you trust the child?" Samuel asked.

"She seemed to me to be telling the truth."

"I wouldn't listen to her. I think she's demented."

"She was very frightened certainly."

"Frightened, my arse. I think she could do with a good wallop."

"Oh, come now," said John and would have gone further to placate his friend but at that moment they heard the sound of someone approaching. Motioning Samuel to be silent, they sat quietly waiting to see what would happen next.

Rounding the corner, arm-in-arm with her husband, behaving in quite the most kittenish manner and looking totally ridiculous as a result, came the Countess of Orpington, all moues and smiles. The old man was lumbering along beside her, grinning from ear to ear. John wondered if they were about to make love *al fresco*. He rapidly stood up.

"Good afternoon to you. A pleasant day is it not?"

"It certainly is, sir."

"I see you are recovered, Lady Orpington."

"From what?"

"The death of Lord Arundel."

She pulled a sad face. "Oh, that was a terrible shock." She fixed John with a deep stare and said, "Of course, I hardly knew the man. He was little more than an acquaintance."

The Apothecary nodded. "I see."

Arabella turned to her husband. "This is such a heavenly place, Drogo. Look around you. Is it not fine?"

"Very beautiful, my love." The Earl raised his hat politely. "Well, good day, gentlemen. We must continue our perambulation."

John and Samuel bowed politely. As soon as the couple were out of earshot the Apothecary said in an undertone, "She was Arundel's woman at the Hellfire Club. That speech was entirely for her husband's benefit."

"She's probably caught the grand pox then."

"Indubitably. And given it to the Earl to boot."

"And could she have murdered him to be revenged?"

"Very easily indeed."

Samuel looked grim. "I think we should get away from here and go somewhere where you can think."

"Good idea."

They started walking towards the stables but the sound of hooves made them stand aside to see Coralie and Georgiana riding fast in their direction. John waved as did Samuel, and the woman and child returned the salute.

Samuel stared after their retreating figures. "A fine looking girl is Coralie. Why don't you marry her at some time in the future?"

John laughed. "I'm a very different person from the man who fell in love with her. Life has soured me up."

Sam guffawed. "You? Soured up? I've never heard such rubbish. You're about as sour as a sugar tart."

"What a very unpleasant simile. Come on, old friend. How about a tour of the grounds before we depart?"

"A very good plan, sir. Shall we walk?"

"Indeed we shall. And as we go, I'll think aloud."

"That will be even better," Samuel answered, and they strolled off side-by-side. "By the way," Sam asked, "did Georgiana own that button we found?"

"No, I don't believe so," John answered thoughtfully. "You see, she was wearing her sleeping clothes."

"Then whose was it?"

"That," John said slowly, "remains to be seen."

CHAPTER
TWENTY

Their stroll through the grounds took them about an hour including a couple of occasions on which they sat down to rest. Eventually they found that they had walked halfway round the lake and stood facing the house across the water.

"What's that?" asked Samuel, pointing to a little domed building standing atop a high mound and lying just beyond a wooden bridge.

"One of Sir Francis's follies I imagine. Want to go and have a look?"

"I think perhaps we should," Samuel answered.

They crossed the bridge and approached the mound which looked innocent enough from the distance. The domed rotunda had a lead copy of the Venus de' Medici within and gave a classical appearance which was altogether pleasing. Other than for a representation of Leda being ravaged by a passion-crazed swan on the roof above, everything seemed pure. But as they got nearer this illusion was abruptly shattered. Beneath the temple, at the base of the hillock, lay a small grotto the imagery of which was far more explicit. The entrance to it was oval with curving walls on either side and it needed little imagination to see that it represented a vagina and a pair of wide-open legs. In front of this artificial *mons veneris* was a collection of small statues made of lead, most of them doing rather disgusting things, including one of a homosexual satyr in full action.

"Hare and hounds!" exclaimed Samuel. "I say!"

John laughed. "Sir Francis really is a dirty old man. Do you want to go and look inside?"

"Yes, I think I rather do."

They ducked their heads and entered the cave, eyes temporarily blinded by the change from broad daylight to semi-darkness. There was a mossy couch within and John, his sight restoring itself first, said, "Oh, I'm sorry," and turned to go.

"What's the matter?" whispered Samuel.

"There's somebody in here."

But the person lying on the couch did not move and John, partly motivated by curiosity, took a step forward to have a closer look.

She lay like a queen of ancient times, still and white, her hat removed, her hair spread around her like lace. Over the edge of the couch trailed one small, white hand, the fingers curling round like the stamens of a flower.

John went up to her and very gently shook her shoulder. "Are you all right, madam?" he said.

There was no reply and he bent his head to listen to the beat of her heart. There was silence and he turned to Sam with a stricken face.

"My God, Samuel, this woman is dead."

His friend took a step forward to see the pale figure that lay there so silently. "'Zounds, John, it's . . ."

But the Apothecary was already raising the poor creature up in his arms. Looking over his shoulder, he said urgently, "But we only saw her an hour ago. And where the hell is her husband?"

For the woman who lay so very still in his arms was none other than that little doll of a girl, the Countess of Orpington herself.

Leaving the body where it was John and Samuel did their best to run all the way back to the house. But neither of them was sixteen any more and the Goldsmith had definitely gained weight in the last few years. Eventually, panting and somewhat red in the face, the Apothecary arrived first and thundered on the door of the east portico. It was opened after a few minutes by a somewhat surprised-looking servant who looked even more astonished as John thundered past him shouting, "Where is Sir Francis? I must see him immediately."

"Sir Francis has gone out riding, sir."

"Damnation!"

"I'm sorry, sir. Can Lady Dashwood be of assistance?"

"No. Or maybe yes. May I see her please?"

"I will check whether she is able to receive you."

Just as he was being shown into the saloon, Samuel gasped his way into the house.

"I think you'd better come with me," John said quietly.

Samuel thumped his chest and nodded, quite unable to speak. And in this somewhat sorry state the pair walked into the room with its glorious view over the lake. Lady Dashwood was just removing her hat having clearly just come in from the grounds.

John gave a short bow. "Madam, I am sorry to have to inform you that we have just discovered the body of Lady Orpington and will require some assistance to bring it back to the house."

Lady Dashwood simply stared at him, slowly laying her hat on a small table. Eventually she spoke.

"Dead, you say? But how? I mean she is little more than a child."

John looked at her. "I have not had a chance to examine the body as yet. It is impossible at this stage to say what killed her."

"What do you mean? Are you saying her death was not natural?"

"I cannot tell, my Lady. I really don't know."

Lady Dashwood suddenly went very white and sat down abruptly. "But what a terrible thing. First Lord Arundel, now Lady Orpington. It is as if a curse has been put on this house."

Samuel gave a bow, having got his breath back. "That's fanciful talk, my Lady, if you'll pardon me saying so."

She looked at him icily. "I'll do no such thing. Since when have servants expressed their opinion?"

"Oh, Sam is more a friend than an employee, ma'am. He has served the O'Hares since I was a child."

222

She was obviously a woman who considered the working class beneath the dust for her frozen features did not melt at all.

"I see," she said coldly.

"Can you tell me where everyone else is at present?" John asked.

"They are all out in the grounds. I can assure you of that because I myself have just come within doors."

"Where is Lord Orpington? I must tell him the bad news."

"He has gone riding with Sir Francis. You will have to wait until his return, I fear."

"Then I shall go and look for Monsieur Jean. I think the three of us should be able to manage."

"He also went for a walk, having finished loading up his coach."

John bowed again, very politely. "Then if you will excuse me, madam, I will go and search for him."

She was still very pale but clearly a woman of great strength of character, which, thought John irreverently, she would have to be to put up with her husband and his smutty little ways.

"By all means," she said.

Samuel gave a deep bow, as befitted someone of the servant class, and left the room following John politely. Once outside he said, "Miserable old witch. How dare she be so rude."

"Come, come, Sam. We've got another death on our hands. Concentrate on that."

"I am. But I think she could do with a reprimand. I wouldn't work for her for a thousand guineas."

"But you might for two. Now, we've got to find Dominique Jean and find him quickly."

"Does it occur to you," asked Samuel solemnly, "that he might be responsible for Lord Arundel's death?"

"Of course it does. He may have held a grudge against the Marquess over the unpaid bill."

As they had been talking they had entered the stable yard where the coach — polished and smart — had been drawn up in readiness for departure. And even while they noticed it they saw its owner strolling round the corner. John went up to him.

"Dominique," he said urgently, "there's been another death and Samuel and I need your help."

The Frenchman stared at him, clearly not taking in what had just been said.

"What do you mean?" he asked. "Another death? What are you talking about?"

"Lady Orpington," said John briefly. "She is lying dead in Sir Francis's extremely rude folly. We are going to need some help to bring her up to the house."

The Frenchman continued to stare blankly and it crossed the Apothecary's mind that he might well be dealing with a brilliant actor.

"Well, are you coming to help us?"

"Yes, of course. But I was hoping to depart within the hour."

John looked at him. "I thought you offered to buy Sam and myself a drink tonight."

The Frenchman looked uncomfortable. "I did. I was going to leave you a note."

Why the hurry to be away? the Apothecary thought. Could Dominique Jean be as guilty as he was looking at this moment?

"Well, we could do with another pair of hands to carry her back."

"Why not ask the servants?"

"Because we preferred not to," John replied crisply. "Now, are you coming or aren't you?"

Dominique nodded, clearly put out, and walked with the other two men towards the lake.

The body lay as it had been left. The Apothecary stood silently for several minutes, committing a mental picture of Lady Orpington into his memory, then he turned and signalled to the other two who stood huddling in the doorway.

"I think we can lift her now."

Sam, strong as a buffalo, picked the poor little corpse up and laid it on the plank which John had found in the stables, wondering as he did so whether it had been the same piece of wood that had borne the remains of her lover back to West Wycombe. John covered the girl with a piece of cloth and the solemn procession made its way slowly back. But as luck would have it the sound of horses could be heard in the distance and a voice called, "What the devil? What's going on?" John turned and saw the large and highly coloured face of Sir Francis, with that of Lord Orpington close behind him.

"What have you got there, O'Hare?"

John, cursing his luck, answered, "I think you had better dismount, sir. And you too, Lord Orpington."

Dashwood swung out of the saddle quite lithely but Lord Orpington had to be helped down by a sweating Apothecary.

"What's going on, eh?" his Lordship asked petulantly.

"You must prepare yourself for a shock, my Lord."

"Shock? Why? What have you got there?"

And before anyone could stop him the old man had seized the piece of cloth and pulled it off the last mortal remains of his wife. He clutched his throat and let out a gurgling sound then he fell to the ground, red in the face and clutching his chest.

"Oh 'zounds," groaned the Apothecary, "I believe he's having a heart attack."

He knelt down beside the poor old chap and loosened his cravat, glancing round wildly for something to give the man but finding nothing.

Samuel crouched down beside him. "Good gracious! Is he really?"

"Yes, I think so."

"Then we'd best carry him back."

And without further ado Sam lifted Lady Orpington off the plank and put Lord Orpington on it in her place.

"But what are we going to do with his wife?" asked Dominique, totally bewildered by this latest turn of events. "I mean we can't just leave her."

"Somebody will have to carry her," answered the Apothecary grimly.

"*Mon Dieu*, not I, sir."

"I'd rather not, John."

Sir Francis intervened. "Put her over the saddle. It's the only way."

So the ghastly sight made its way towards the house. Samuel and Dominique, both having removed their coats and sweating profusely, carried Lord Orpington, groaning upon his piece of planking, up to the house, the Apothecary walking beside him ministering to the man as best he could. Sir Francis, grim-faced, walked in the rear leading both horses, one of which had its terrible burden, still covered by a cloth but from which one small hand protruded, swinging limply as the animal moved.

The Apothecary was in a quandary, racking his brains as to the best thing to give for a heart attack. And then a vague memory came to him. Many years ago, when he had been apprenticed to Master Richard Purefoy of Evans Row, a medical herbalist had come into the shop to discuss the properties of various herbs with him. John had been compounding in the back but had been called through by his master.

"Come here, my boy, and listen to this."

John, aged seventeen and thinking he knew it all, had been amazed by the other man's knowledge. He had also remembered that the herbalist had had a little girl with him who had gazed about her at all the amazing alembics that the shop contained.

Now, as he concentrated, the memory became clearer.

"I tell you, Master Purefoy," the man had said, "that I cured heart failure by the use of Digitalis Purpurea."

"But, Mr Jenkins, everybody knows that foxgloves heal wounds and purge the body, that is their sole usage."

"Nonetheless I can assure you that the physicians had failed with this patient and I brought him back from the grave by using an infusion made from their leaves."

Master Purefoy had stroked his chin. "And how did you administer it?"

"I infused them in boiling water and gave the liquid to the man in teaspoonfuls."

The little girl had interrupted at this point. "I am going to be a herbalist when I grow up and I am going to use foxgloves to treat people." She had turned to John. "Are you going to be an apothecary?"

"I hope so," he had answered.

There had been further discussion between the two men, John recalled, and then the herbalist had left the shop. One thing he did remember vividly: the little girl had turned in the doorway and winked at him.

Now John started looking frantically for some wild bunches of the beautiful flowers. Sir Francis, seeing him quicken his pace and search about, said, "What's up, O'Hare?"

"I need to find some foxgloves. I think I know a way to cure Lord Orpington's heart attack."

"There are some growing over on the hill leading to the mausoleum."

"Oh, God's life, that's miles. Nothing nearer?"

"I don't know, my boy. I simply don't know."

Samuel turned his head. "Anything wrong, John?"

"I've got to find some foxgloves. No, don't stare. I might be able to cure the old man's heart trouble."

"Then go and look. Any instructions for when we get him — them — in?"

"Yes, get his Lordship undressed and into bed. She'll have to go into one of the outhouses. I'll need to examine the body later."

"Right you are."

It took John ten minutes of frantic searching and then a flash of vivid colour caught his eye and his breath simultaneously. There was a huge clump of foxgloves growing in some sandy ground amongst the profusion of trees behind the house. Tearing them up he hurried indoors and went straight to the kitchens.

He knew that by rights the leaves should have been stored and dried but he had no time for such niceties. Ripping them from the stalks, he poured boiling water over them and let them infuse. The kitchen hands and the chef, meanwhile, were staring at him askance and John's assurances — stated over a shoulder while he continued to make his potion — did little to convince them that he was a genuine apothecary. Eventually one of them slipped away to ask Lady Dashwood and came back looking surprised and nodding.

John, meanwhile, was weighing up the odds as to whether he should finally tell the company that he was working for Sir John Fielding. If he did, he thought, he would not dare tell Sir Francis that he had been present for the explicit purpose of investigating the Hellfire Club. Better to gloss over that and say he was in the neighbourhood by chance. Which led him to the difficult question of whether he should announce his true identity and lay to rest, for good and for all, the persona of Fintan O'Hare.

It was all going to be extremely awkward but for the moment he had other things to concentrate on. The infusion was as ready as it would ever be. Taking a small spoon, John left the kitchen and hurried upstairs.

Lord Orpington was clearly in agony, grasping his chest and groaning. He was wet with sweat and was calling out, "Arabella, Arabella," in a feeble voice, at which Sir Francis, who was standing anxiously beside the bed, could only shake his head and mutter, "But she's dead." Clearly glad to see John arrive, he stood to one side and watched, his usual jovial countenance for once changed to one suitable for the occasion.

"So you really are an apothecary, O'Hare?" he said, a note of wonderment in his voice as John spooned a small amount of liquid down the patient's throat.

John turned to face him. "Yes, I am, sir. In fact, I am not Fintan O'Hare, as I told you. My name is John Rawlings and I have a shop in Shug Lane, Piccadilly. Furthermore, I occasionally work for Sir John Fielding, of whom no doubt you will have heard."

"You're not O'Hare!" Sir Francis repeated in an accusatory tone. "Then tell me, why are you here?"

"There's been a bit of trouble in the neighbourhood," John lied blithely. "I came down to investigate it."

"What trouble?" asked the other, his eyes narrowed and porcine. "I don't know of any."

At that moment the patient moaned and raised his lids. "Where is Arabella?" he said, gripping John tightly by the shirt.

"Rest now," answered John, disengaging himself.

"Where is she?"

"She'll come soon."

Behind him he heard Sir Francis clear his throat and John shot round. "Please don't tell him the truth. Not at this stage. It could literally kill him."

"It seems that you deal easily in lies, young man. I suggest you soon turn over a new leaf."

"I promise to tell you everything, Sir Francis, but meanwhile I beg you to be patient. If Lord Orpington is going to survive he is going to need all my nursing skills."

"Very well. But I want a full explanation just as soon as you see fit to leave him."

"You shall have it, sir, of that I can assure you."

And with those words John Rawlings turned back to the inert figure on the bed and poured another spoonful of liquid between Lord Orpington's lips.

CHAPTER
TWENTY-ONE

It was quiet in the outhouse. Outside Samuel stood on guard while Dominique, badly shaken — or doing a good impression of being so — sat in the workshop, his head in his hands. John, having seen Lord Orpington drop into a fitful sleep, had left the house and gone under the arch to the stableblock. Samuel had greeted him.

"How is his Lordship?"

"Sleeping at the moment. You know foxgloves can be highly toxic. That's why I only give him very small amounts of the infusion. Quite honestly, Sam, it's kill or cure."

"Oh dear. Well, I'm sure you know what you're doing."

"Has anyone been near?"

"Several people, though none have seen the body. Coralie and the child; Charles Arundel's sister, Juliana; even Lady Dashwood came round, gave me a look that would have slain a gorgon, and went back to the house."

Despite the grim task he was about to undertake, John had laughed.

"I can just see her. Anyway, whatever you do let nobody in while I examine her."

"You can rely on me," Samuel answered, and had looked menacing.

And now he watched outside while the Apothecary once more stood alone with death. It was a job that he never relished, in fact positively disliked, though he was well aware that he was the best qualified to do it. Yet still there was that slight hesitation as he first laid his hands on the corpse and gently began to look for the cause of death.

First he removed the shoes, gazing into each one to see if there had been any foreign body lodged therein. Then, hating it, he removed the white stockings and minutely examined the legs, looking for a sign, any sign, that something untoward had taken place. There was nothing. Next he raised her skirts to her waist and performed the most horrible task of all — looking to see if Lady Orpington had been sexually active recently and whether this could have caused her sudden and shocking demise. Somewhat to his surprise he discovered that she had not.

Undressing the top half of the dead girl he stopped for a moment to admire her childlike beauty, then put such thoughts from his mind as he concentrated on looking for some clue as to how she had died. There was nothing. As far as he could see the cause of death must have been a natural one. Still he went to the door and called to Samuel.

"Sam, come in here a moment."

Samuel's round face appeared anxiously in the opening. "Why? John, I'm not very good with bodies."

"I want you to lift her for me, turn her over so that I can examine her back."

"But that will mean touching her."

"Of course it will. Now come along, my friend. Think of it as a favour to me."

The Goldsmith took a cautious step inside and said, "You've undressed her," in an accusing tone.

"Not completely. Besides, I had to do so in order to examine her."

Samuel crept forward, each step tentative. John, watching him, said, "She can't hurt you, you know."

"I am aware of that. It's just that I have had little to do with corpses."

"You've seen a few with me, my dear."

"Yes, I suppose so. But somehow this seems different."

"Well, it isn't. Now come on."

Samuel stationed himself by the girl's feet, while John took hold of her shoulders.

"Right, now turn her to the right. Are you ready?"

Samuel nodded and they performed their macabre task in silence. John gently placed Lady Orpington's head to one side so that her face was not pressed into the wood of the table on which she lay.

"By the way," he said, as he started his examination, "where is her lover now?"

"He's coffined up and been taken back to the house to lie in state before his removal. We must go and pay our respects before we return to the inn."

234

"Yes, indeed," replied John absently.

He was concentrating on the girl's neck, having pulled her hair up and out of the way. Just above the line of her dress he could see a little red mark, like the bite of an insect. John bent down over it, examining it carefully. Then he called Samuel, who was still standing by the girl's feet, looking pale.

"Come and have a look at this."

Samuel reluctantly made his way and surveyed the wound closely.

"It's very small. Looks like a bee sting."

"But it's not. The sting is missing."

John put out a finger and very gently rubbed the mark, then he sniffed and carefully tasted the substance on his digit.

"Samuel, I'll swear that this girl has been poisoned, though exactly how it was administered defeats me at the moment."

"You mean that it went in through that little hole?"

"I do. But how? A knife would be too big and would leave a different wound. Even an arrowhead would be larger. God help me, I could be wrong, but I have a strange feeling about it." He straightened up. "We have to inform the constable, I fear."

Sam groaned. "Oh dear, we all know what they can be like."

"Indeed we do. Anyway, back to the matter in hand. Do you remember that Lady Orpington's hat was lying beside her?"

"Yes, I do. She had it clutched in her fingers as I recall."

"She must have had it on when she was poisoned so that her neck was free of hair. So who took it off?"

"And," Sam added enthusiastically, "who put her in that folly? For surely she did not go in there to die."

"Definitely not. Somebody must have carried her inside after she was poisoned."

"Which points to a man."

"Not necessarily. She was a tiny little thing. A strong woman could have managed her with ease." John braced his shoulders. "Come on, let us leave her in peace. I must brave the wrath of Sir Francis. He is after my blood full pelt having realised that Fintan O'Hare was a figment of imagination."

They stepped outside, locking the door behind them. Dominique Jean was in the stableyard, just climbing into his coach, and he looked across in their direction.

"Gentlemen," he called, "I have decided to spend one more night at the inn and I am making my way there now. I will buy you that drink after all."

"Glad to hear it," said John, and bowed to him as the coach rumbled past.

In the house there was an ominous silence. Indeed there was no one around that either man could see, let in as they were by a servant.

"Where is Sir Francis Dashwood?" John enquired.

"He is outdoors, sir. I do not know where."

"And Lady Dashwood?"

"As far as I know, my Lady is with him."

John turned to Samuel and was just about to say that perhaps they should seek him out when a door at the far end of the hall opened and Lady Juliana Bravo stood there.

"I hear that you have been here under false pretences," she said coldly.

"I am here, madam," John replied with dignity, "on behalf of Sir John Fielding, Principal Magistrate of London. He sent me to investigate the proceedings of the Hellfire Club, which he believed might be subversive. As it happened, I could find no evidence of this. But in the meantime two people have been murdered and I regard it as part of my duty to assist the constable in his enquiries."

She gaped at him, going very white. "What are you saying? That somebody murdered my brother and the Countess of Orpington?"

"Yes, precisely that."

"And what may I ask was the method used?"

"Poison for the lady," John said firmly. "Of what origin I am not yet certain."

Juliana drew breath and brought herself under some form of control. "And you are sending for the constable?"

"Not to do so, madam, would be to go against the law of the land. As soon as I have seen Sir Francis I shall go straight to the village and make enquiries as to the constable's identity."

She sat down rather suddenly. "I am thoroughly shocked by what you say." She paused a moment and looked thoughtful. "Of course Charles and the lady in question *were* very friendly, you know."

John looked at her. "Yes, I was aware."

"It occurs to me that she could have been so upset at his death that she committed suicide."

Thinking of that strange little hole in the back of Arabella's neck, John looked sceptical. "I very much doubt that."

"Why? Could she not have administered poison by her own hand?"

"Indeed, she could. But I do not think it likely."

Lady Juliana looked determined. "Well, I am quite prepared to tell the constable my theories. I believe that I might well have hit upon the truth."

John bowed. "You must do as you think best, my Lady."

Samuel said nothing till they got outside, but once there he stated, "But that's not possible, the suicide theory I mean. For who stabs themselves in the back of the neck?"

"An acrobat," John answered tersely, seeing Sir Francis Dashwood sitting on a bench in the sun and already preparing himself for a severe reprimand.

He approached quietly but saw one eye open. "So there you are," Sir Francis said.

"Yes, sir. I have examined the body of the Countess of Orpington and concluded that she was poisoned. I intend to go at once to inform the constable," John answered very formally.

"A moment before you do so, young man. You say that you work for John Fielding, who is a likeable enough fellow in his own way. Did he ask you to find out about the Hellfire Club?"

238

"Sir, I was instructed to discover any hint of subversion amongst its members. I found none."

"And why should Fielding think that, pray?"

"Because I believe at one time John Wilkes was a keen member of the organisation."

Sir Francis literally ground his teeth together in a crunching sound.

"Merciful heavens! Are we all to be tarred with that man's beastly brush? He may be a rabid rabble-rouser but that is a matter entirely for himself and does not mean that everyone associated with him is of like mind. As you know well, O'Hare — Rawlings — whatever your name is, we concentrate on one thing and one thing alone."

John grinned, he couldn't help it, a vivid memory of Teresa coming back to him.

"Working the pilgrim's staff till it's ready to fall off," Sir Francis continued robustly. "And the Lord help any domine-do-little who joins our merry throng."

The interview was far more civil than the Apothecary had imagined it could be and he decided to retreat before any more could be said. He bowed.

"It is gracious of you to be so kind about my deception, Sir Francis. I am afraid that those attached to the Public Office are sometimes forced to adopt disguises in order to achieve their objective. I am sure that as a Member of Parliament you will understand and tolerate this predicament in which we find ourselves."

Sir Francis decided to be munificent. "One appreciates what you fellows have to go through." He already seemed to have classified John as a Beak runner, pure and simple. "Nonetheless, it is not so funny when the deception is aimed at oneself. However, in the present grim and terrible circumstances we should, I suppose, be grateful that you are among us."

"I sincerely hope so, sir," said John, while Samuel — not to be left out — also muttered something appropriate.

"Now, what are you going to tell the constable?"

"Nothing about the Hellfire Club. That shall remain our secret. But I must inform him of the two deaths and let him make his own investigations. By the way, sir, do you know who he is?"

"Of course I do. His name is Zachary Flint and he farms nearby."

John's heart sank, as it often did when he considered the local village constable. A job much hated and despised, some citizens picked a deputy to act for them and those people were probably the worst of all. At least this one was in an honest profession.

"You'll find him at Five Oak Farm, near the entrance to the east drive. But he goes into the George and Dragon most evenings. You'll probably catch him there."

"Thank you, Sir Francis. I shall put in my report how very cooperative you have been. And now if you'll forgive me, I think Mr Swann and I should pay our respects to the late Lord Arundel."

As they made their way upstairs they were joined by Lady Dashwood, looking, if possible, more dreary than ever.

240

"Are you going to see poor Charles?" she asked tonelessly.

"Yes, madam, that was our intention."

"Then come with me."

She led them into the bedroom he had occupied until recently, the curtains drawn against the light, the place lit by large candles which she had dotted here and there.

"We are having some of the neighbours round tonight," she continued in the same colourless voice. "I must give instructions about the catering." And she immediately turned on her heel and left them.

"Ah well," said John, approaching the bed on which the poor fellow's coffin had been placed.

"He looks better than usual," commented Samuel.

And it was true. Somebody had been at work applying cosmetics to the dead man's swollen face, so that now he had high patches of colour in each cheek and carmined lips. His eyebrows, too, had been blackened and someone had applied a beauty spot to his brow.

"I think I preferred him as he was," John commented.

The coffin was lined with blue satin and the Marquess had been dressed in his best suit of clothes, which were a matching shade of blue. His hands were clasped on his stomach, his eyes closed. Yet somehow he did not look peaceful. There was about him a sense of disquiet which John could not explain to himself. He stood, staring down at the dead man, when suddenly something rustled in the corner. The Apothecary nearly shot out of his skin in fright, while Samuel swore a terrible oath.

"Who's there?" said John.

The child, Georgiana, detached herself from the shadows round the bedhead and came walking towards them.

"What the devil are you doing here?" John asked angrily.

"Keeping watch over my father," she answered, while Samuel muttered, "I told you she was weird."

Georgiana turned towards the corpse. "He looks splendid, doesn't he?"

"I don't think that is quite the right word," John answered with asperity. "And I don't think you should be in here on your own. You are a child, Georgiana, despite things that may have been done to encourage you to grow up. For the love of God, embrace your childhood while you still have it."

"I have never been young," she answered wretchedly.

"Yes, you have," the Apothecary said fiercely, determined to talk some sense into her. "Listen to me. How old were you when your father asked you to cuddle him with no clothes on?"

"About eight."

"Then think of those early years. Did you not enjoy them? Did you not have fun with other children?"

The child nodded without speaking.

"Then they are what you must concentrate on. Do not let your father ruin the rest of your life for you. And think of your mother. Think of how grieved she must be by your plight."

242

"That had not occurred to me."

John wanted to shout at her for being a thoughtless little girl but he knew that Georgiana had suffered in silence for some years and must be treated with respect as a result.

"Well, it is a fact. She cares for you deeply and, if I were you, I would try to return that love with the same intensity."

"Poor Mama," the child said sadly.

"Poor Mama, indeed. Georgiana, if I may make a suggestion, be determined to put the past behind you and start afresh."

She gave him a look that made him grow cold. "Sometimes it is not possible to bury the past," she said. "You see, it can have a way of coming back to haunt you."

And with that she walked from the room with never a backward glance.

"There's your murderer," said Samuel, pointing at where Georgiana had just been. "She did it. It's obvious."

"What, Lady Orpington as well?"

"Both of 'em. I tell you, she's not right in the head."

"Oh, come on. She's suffered greatly. She'll settle down in time."

"She'll always be mad," Samuel pronounced with an air of finality. "Come on, we've said our farewells to her father. Let's go and have a drink."

"A good plan," John answered. "I need to emulate Joe Jago and make a list."

CHAPTER
TWENTY-TWO

The air in the taproom of the George and Dragon was thick with tobacco smoke, mixed with the stinks created by the mass of humanity who heaved within. First there was the pungent note of unwashed flesh — not entirely unpleasant as most of it was honest sweat — mixed with a general sharp smell given off by the press of people. To add a piquant odour somebody had let loose a rouser, the remains of which floated about, apparently unable to find any means of escape. John, forcing his way into the room behind Samuel, who was shouldering his way in, waved a hand in front of his face.

"Dear me, 'tis a bit noisome."

"It positively reeks. Are you sure you want to drink in here?"

"We're lying in wait for Zachary Flint, the constable, don't forget."

"Has he arrived?"

John nudged a farmhand. "Is Mr Flint here by any chance?"

"No, sir. He ain't. Mark you, he could be about official business. There's no saying whether 'e'll come or not."

The Apothecary produced a coin from his pocket. "My friend and I will be in the guests' parlour. If the constable should turn up, perhaps you would let us know."

He must be getting old, John decided. Where a few years ago he would have welcomed the bustle and thrust of the taproom — stinks and all — now he was positively glad to take a comfortable seat by the fire, a table in front of him on which he could lean his paper for making a list, and order two pints of ale from the serving wench.

"Age is catching up with me," he remarked to Samuel.

"Why so?"

"At one time nothing would have got me out of that place. Now I prefer sitting in the warmth and nodding off."

"You need a woman, John. You have been a widower long enough. I suppose there is no hope . . ."

"Of partnering me with Coralie? Sam, I truly don't believe so. We are very different people now from those we were long ago."

"And who would take on that horrible child?" said Samuel, downing a draught of ale moodily. "I think Coralie will be hard put to it to find another husband with that little beast lurking on the stairs."

"The child is disturbed. She's not evil."

"You may have your opinion, I have mine."

"Enough of that. I'm going to write a list."

John took a pad and pencil from his inner pocket. Heading a column "Suspects", he turned to Samuel.

"Well, who do we have?"

Continuing to look woeful, his friend answered promptly, "Lady Georgiana Bravo. I tell you, John, she may be young but she's the killer."

The Apothecary gave him a glance but said nothing and wrote the name down. "Now who else?"

"Dominique Jean."

"Surely not just because he's French. That would be most unfair."

"You know as well as I do why. He is owed a great deal of money and it rankles with him."

"Next?"

"Sir Francis and Lady Dashwood."

John scratched his chin with his pencil. "Him, I can imagine. But why her?"

"A woman with as dull a personality as she has is bound to have a secret life. Otherwise she would go quite mad," Sam announced in lugubrious tones.

John chortled. "What about Coralie and the sister?"

"Both are suspicious, whichever way you look at it. The pair of 'em seem to glide round corridors in the dead of night."

"Samuel, really! According to you they all could have done it."

"And don't leave out old Lord Orpington. He could have faked that heart attack and will no doubt make a magnificent recovery in time."

"The man's life hangs in the balance," John remonstrated.

"Then why have you left the house?"

246

"Because for the moment there is nothing further I can do for him. Besides, Lady Dashwood — dull or no — is quite capable of looking after the man."

Samuel finished his ale and called for another pint for himself and John. Settling back in his chair he said, "Well, it's up to us now to question everybody and draw our own conclusions."

John, ignoring the use of the plural, said, "Well, it will have to be done quickly. The party is breaking up. Besides, I have a mind to get back to London and put the whole thing before Sir John and Joe."

Samuel sighed gustily. "And I have been away far too long. A good thing Jocasta is such an understanding woman."

"Is she?" asked John, with just a tinge of envy. "Sam, are you happy?"

"I can say I truly am. She is a good wife, loyal and kind. And the birth of my son crowned my joy."

John, looking at him, thought what an extremely jolly ending his old friend had achieved. He felt a sudden rush of emotion.

"Samuel, don't let us quarrel ever again. I'm sorry I was neglectful but it was one of the truly terrible times of my life. I was forced to go on the run and you can believe me, that is the most wretched experience a man can suffer."

"John, I want to be your friend for evermore. I promise you that from now on I shall never take offence at anything you do."

"Well, that gives me plenty of leeway," John answered, and gave his friend an affectionate punch.

"Gentlemen, am I interrupting?" said Dominique, who had come into the room without them seeing him.

"Not at all. Take a seat. What can I get you to drink?"

"Tonight I feel like wine. Shall we have a bottle of claret?"

"Indeed we shall."

Dominique sat down between them and looked from one to the other. "You are discussing the recent deaths?"

"We were," John answered.

"Do you know I have been thinking about that night; the night that Lord Arundel died. I have been over and over it in my head and I remember now that there was yet another set of feet."

"Tell me the story from the start," said John, sipping his wine and looking comfortable, yet his mind sharp as a razor.

"I related to you that I heard someone go into Lord Arundel's room and then there came what sounded like a scream."

"Yes, I remember."

"Well, after that, between the feet clattering over the floor and someone shuffling down the stairs, I heard a person come along the corridor."

John sat forward. "Go on."

"This was the walk of somebody determined. I could tell by the way the shoes sounded. It was someone who knew where they were going in life."

"Was it a man or a woman?"

"I can't be sure. Whoever it was walked as if they were important, that is all I can say."

"I see. Thank you. It might be connected to the death. On the other hand it could be a midnight prowler. Tell me, who else slept on your floor? Besides Charles, I mean."

"Coralie and the child; Lord and Lady Orpington; Lady Juliana. I think that was all."

"Um." John looked thoughtful.

Samuel's face assumed the sort of expression which meant that he was about to ask a question and John braced himself for the moment.

"Tell me, Dominique, do you sleep well at home?"

"Usually like a log. But I told you, the storm kept me awake on this particular night and that is why I constantly woke up."

"And would you say the person who went into Lord Arundel's room first of all was a woman?"

"Yes, I should think it probably was."

"Well, that narrows the field." And Samuel looked so pleased with himself that John could have hugged him.

"Despite what you have to tell us I feel that I am no nearer solving the puzzle. In fact, I believe that the murderer will get away with his or her crime," he said reflectively.

"Why?" asked Dominique, looking surprised.

"Because all the potential killers are leaving and returning to their own homes. I have no jurisdiction to make them stay. I doubt that even Sir John Fielding could bid them to do so."

"But you can ask them where they live," the Frenchman answered. "Surely they would be obliged to tell you."

John gave a sudden smile. "You're right, of course. Tomorrow we shall present ourselves early, Samuel, and take everyone's details." He turned to Dominique. "And where do you dwell, my friend?"

"I live at 70, Charlotte Street. Close to the workrooms in Tottenham Court Road."

"I see. Do you walk there?"

"Indeed I do."

And with that it was almost as if Dominique Jean deliberately closed that line of conversation and began chatting about more congenial things.

CHAPTER
TWENTY-THREE

They journeyed home together and finally parted company in the Strand, both hiring hackney coaches to take them to their respective destinations. Early that morning they had come to present their compliments to Sir Francis and Lady Dashwood, this time accompanied by the village constable, who had appeared utterly over-awed by the fine company and had hardly said a word. Nevertheless, he had agreed to inform the Coroner of the deaths of Lord Arundel and Lady Orpington and solemnly watched the coffined remains be loaded on a cart and taken off to the nearest mortuary. John, surveying the couple's grim departure, thought of them in life, as anxious to get at one another as dogs on heat, and found it to be one of the saddest endings of an affair that he had ever witnessed.

Samuel, standing next to him, had said, "I wonder if their souls will be reunited."

John had answered thoughtfully, "I doubt that very much. They were neither of them pleasant people. Why should they be particularly smiled upon in the afterlife?"

Sam nodded, seeing the wisdom of this, then had said, "Do you believe we go on after we die?"

John had turned on him a face full of uncertainty. "Who knows?" he had replied.

But now they were climbing into their hackneys and bidding each other farewell.

"You'll keep me up to date, won't you?"

"You may depend upon it," the Apothecary answered as he headed off to Nassau Street.

The house was quiet when he entered it and John, enquiring from the footman who greeted him as to everybody's whereabouts, was informed that Sir Gabriel was in the library and Miss da Costa and Rose were out.

"But they will be back soon, sir. It will soon be time for Miss Rose to go to bed."

"Thank you."

He was just heading towards the library when the front door opened and there stood his child, hand-in-hand with the governess, both of them looking even lovelier than when John had last seen them.

"Papa," shrieked Rose, spying him, and she rushed towards him and was gathered up into his arms.

Sir Gabriel was having a pre-dinner nap but woke up the moment John entered the room.

"My dear, you have returned to us. Have you had a great adventure?"

"I have indeed. Let me pour you a sherry and then we can discuss it all."

He sat down opposite his adopted father and started to recount his exploits, carefully editing those of the Hellfire Club. Sir Gabriel raised a quizzical eyebrow.

"Obviously you enjoyed that part of the proceedings, far more, I believe, than you are telling me. However, you need say no more. I was a man of the world once, you know. Before I married your mother and my life changed for ever."

John smiled at him, wishing the wise old creature were immortal but realising that that was a dream which could never come true.

"Let me tell you the rest later. What I really want to know is how Miss da Costa has settled down."

"She has proved a treasure, my dear. Rose adores her madly, as do I. Indeed, as do several young men of our acquaintance."

"Oh? And who might they be?"

Sir Gabriel had looked austere. "I have not lowered myself to kitchen maid gossip yet. Those are facts you must discover for yourself."

"I am duly chastened," said John, looking morose, then twitched his mobile eyebrows at his father and burst out laughing.

Rose was allowed to stay up to dine with the older people and sat very straight and well behaved, keeping one eye on her father to make sure he approved. As the meal ended, John rose from his seat.

"Father, Octavia, please forgive me. I must go to the Public Office this evening. There is much I have to tell Sir John. I hope to see you both on my return."

"Octavia and I will probably be playing chess in the library. We will await your arrival."

"I shall look forward to it," replied John, meaning every word he said.

He had dined late, London fashion, and found that the summer sun was low in the sky by the time he alighted from his conveyance in Bow Street. Earlier on he had roused Irish Tom from his slumbers and told him that he must look to his laurels now that his master had returned.

"But, sorrh, I've been driving Sir Gabriel all over the place, so I have. I assure you that I have not been wasting my time."

"I see. Well, in any case I have returned and from now on will keep you occupied," John answered severely, and proceeded into the Public Office.

A Beak runner was attending the desk and his face lit up as he recognised the Apothecary.

"Goodness me, sir. I am sure the Magistrate will be delighted to see you. Would you like to make your own way up?"

"I'd be honoured." And John had proceeded up the twisting staircase to the Beak's private apartments which lay above.

Knocking politely, he stood outside the door of Sir John's salon and heard footsteps cross the floor, then it was flung open by none other than Joe Jago.

"My dear Mr Rawlings," he said, a great grin crossing his features, "a pleasure to see you back, sir."

John, who, when he had been on the run, owed his life to the foxy-headed clerk, pumped his hand warmly.

"My dear Joe, how goes it with you?"

"Very well, I thank you, sir."

From the depths of the room, just catching the dying rays of the day, a familiar voice was calling out, "Mr Rawlings, is it you? You were away so long I thought something had gone wrong."

John bowed, even though he could not be seen. "Things indeed took a turn for the worse, Sir John. I have come to tell you the entire story."

"Then enter, my dear fellow, and take a seat. Jago, fetch our friend a drink."

Half an hour later the Apothecary eventually finished his tale and saw a sight with which he had now grown familiar. The Blind Beak sat so still and so quietly that he appeared to have dropped off to sleep. Joe's eyes, meanwhile, had grown wide and a look of astonishment had appeared on his craggy face.

"So two people were murdered, sir?"

"It is my belief that they were. But the damnable thing is that I don't know how."

But further conversation was ruled out by a deep sigh coming from Sir John Fielding. "What a tangled web indeed. Tell me, Rawlings, do you suspect anyone in particular?"

"No, sir. It seems to me that the murders could have been committed by a number of people. In fact, Samuel Swann was convinced that it was the child — a girl of but a few years — who was guilty."

"Tell me again who they were."

"Well, there is the little girl, Lady Georgiana. Then there's her aunt, sister of Lord Charles Arundel — the murdered man. She is a spinster of about forty-five and her name is Juliana. Then there comes Charles's wife, the former actress Coralie Clive —"

Sir John interrupted with a deep chuckle. "Who, if memory serves correctly, stole your heart away when you were young and foolish and unmarried."

"She is still very beautiful," John replied earnestly, "but I believe that I have finally recovered."

"So I should think. But pray continue."

"Then there comes the dead woman's husband, the Earl of Orpington. He appeared to have a heart attack when I told him of her death but I treated him with foxgloves and this morning he was somewhat recovered."

"I see. And who else is there?"

"Three people. The notorious Sir Francis Dashwood, his wife Sarah, and finally Dominique Jean, son-in-law of the late Pierre Langlois, who was present at West Wycombe and apparently bears a grudge against the family because he is owed money."

"Quite a large field," said the Blind Beak slowly. "What do you think, Jago?"

"I wouldn't know until I've seen them, sir. But who stood to gain from the deaths? Anybody?"

"I suppose they all did in their different ways."

"Even the child," said Sir John heavily, "for she was much put upon by her father."

There was silence in the room and the noises from the street outside rose up and filled the upstairs salon. The Apothecary became acutely aware of his love of London and how much he had missed it while away in the country. The shouts of the hawkers, the babble

256

of prostitutes, the shrill voices of the beaux as they minced along, intermingled in some strange unearthly chorus which set his blood racing in his veins. He longed at that moment to be able to return to his shop and once more live a normal life, settling down with Rose and Sir Gabriel, and, who knows, even marrying again when the time was right.

His thoughts switched to Elizabeth, his dark lady, and he wondered how she was and if she ever had any regrets about turning him down. How much he had loved her, almost — though it shamed him deeply to admit it — from the time he had met her on his honeymoon. A mental picture of her lean, full-breasted body ran through his mind and he shifted uncomfortably in his chair.

Sir John was speaking. "They must have been poisoned, Mr Rawlings. But with what?"

"I don't know, sir. That's the devil of it. And how was it administered? I told you that Lady Orpington had a tiny mark on the back of her neck but it was scarcely bigger than a pinprick. Far too small for any instrument I know to have inserted it."

"And the man? Did you not say that there was not a mark on him?"

"Nothing. Except of course his chancre. He had syphilis, as I've already told you."

"Yes, I recall. Well, it seems to me that it must be a poison as yet unknown in this country which has its own peculiar way of administration."

"Tomorrow," said John with determination, "I shall go to Apothecaries Hall and make enquiries."

"I think, sir," said Joe Jago, who had been listening intently throughout, "that that would be a very good plan indeed."

As John stepped into the hall of number 2, Nassau Street, he was greeted with the wonderful and warm sound of a woman's laughter, joined a few seconds later by Sir Gabriel's chuckle.

"Ah, my dear, it is checkmate, is it not?"

"Indeed it is, Sir Gabriel. You are a master of the game."

Shedding his cloak, John headed straight for the library, where he found his father and Miss da Costa staring intently at the chessboard. Looking up, Octavia laughed once more.

"Sir Gabriel has won again. He plays such a daunting contest."

"Years of practice, my dear. You will learn some of my moves if you study carefully."

She stood up, smoothing down her creamy white petticoat over which her open robe of midnight blue hung attractively.

"And how did you fare, Mr Rawlings? Was it a successful meeting?"

"Yes and no. It has given me yet another task to perform tomorrow while I am anxious to return to my shop."

Sir Gabriel glanced up lazily. "The trouble with you, my dear, is that you hate to delegate responsibility. And yet because of your connection with Sir John you are being forced to do so all the time."

258

John laughed and said, "That, sir, is a slur on my character." He looked at Octavia. "Take no notice of what is being told you. I am extremely adept at leaving my affairs in the hands of others. Particularly someone as efficient as young Nick."

A light rose pink bloomed in her cheeks. "Yes," she said, "he seems a very reliable person."

"He is. He was apprenticed to me when he was somewhat older than is usual and had already had a full and interesting life by the time I met him."

"How old is he now?" she asked casually.

"About twenty-eight I think."

"A good age," she answered, and smiled attractively.

A warning bell was sounding in the Apothecary's brain as he considered why the girl was so interested in Nicholas Dawkins. Thinking he knew the answer he felt elated that Nick should have made so fine a conquest. Certain that the Muscovite returned Octavia's feelings, he decided to put the matter to the test.

"I see that you and he have got to know one another in my absence. Have I your permission to invite him to dine with us tomorrow?"

Miss da Costa became flustered. "Mr Rawlings, it is your house. I am only an employee. You may invite to dine whomsoever you wish."

He bowed politely and said gravely, "Thank you. I shall ask Gideon to deliver him a note."

Sir Gabriel, looking up, winked at John. "I like young Dawkins," he said solemnly. "He has called here several times while you have been away."

The Apothecary knew then that his suspicions were confirmed. He winked back at his father, making sure that Miss da Costa could not see him.

"Then we shall make tomorrow a special occasion, sir. I suggest that we dine at six o'clock and Rose may stay up and sit with us a while."

"That will give her great pleasure," Octavia answered solemnly, in control of herself once more.

Early next morning John set off for Apothecaries Hall, situated in Black Friars Lane. He had gone by way of the river, hiring a wherry as far as Black Friars Stairs. Normally he would have enjoyed the journey, loving water travel as he did, but today he was impatient to get the business over and done with, and to return to Shug Lane and all the old familiar matters of his everyday life. However, an enormous part of his curiosity had been aroused and he wondered if anybody might be able to help him in his search for the highly unusual poison that had been used.

As luck would have it the Master of the Society was in that day and John, feeling somewhat lowly and unimportant in the face of such high professionalism, requested an interview with him, little thinking that it would be granted. But to his amazement Master John Peck only kept him waiting fifteen minutes before the younger man was ushered into his presence.

The Master sat behind his desk, a dark, saturnine creature with a great hawk's nose which gave him a ferocious profile. He looked up as John entered.

"Well, Apothecary, what can I do for you?"

"Sir, I am here on behalf of Sir John Fielding of Bow Street."

Peck ceased examining the mound of papers in front of him.

"And what might your connection be with him, pray?"

"Master, I have worked with Sir John from time to time, and I am at present involved in a little scheme of his."

"And may I ask what that scheme might be?"

"I am afraid that I am not at liberty to reveal that. But I am allowed to tell you that during the investigation two people met their deaths in a quite inexplicable manner."

The saturnine face came alive with sudden interest and there was a definite gleam in the dark eyes.

"And what might that manner have been?" He motioned John, who up to now had been standing, to take a chair.

"I am not altogether sure but I am convinced there was foul play." And the Apothecary went on to describe the two bodies, particularly that of Lady Orpington and the small puncture on the back of her neck.

By now he had the Master's full attention. "It sounds to me, Mr Rawlings, as if a rare poison must have been used."

"I am aware of that, Master. The question is what?"

John Peck shook his head. "Of that I am not certain but I believe that I know someone who might be able to help you. My friend Dr Pitcairn, a physician at St Bartholomew's Hospital, was telling me the other night that he has a student from the Americas who is an expert on tropical plants, having been a medical attendant in both the West Indies and Surinam. I would imagine that a chat with him could be of great assistance."

"It most certainly would, sir. Might it be in order for you to reveal his name to me?"

"It would indeed. He is called Edward Bancroft but I have no idea where he lives. However, I can discover that for you quickly enough."

John felt like kissing the man's hand, so grateful was he. Instead he gave a deep and respectful bow and said, "Thank you most sincerely, Master."

"It is the least I can do to assist Sir John. Now to save me looking it up will you be kind enough to write your address on this piece of paper. I promise to be in touch with you shortly."

There was a silence while John scribbled his address, during which the Master picked up the sheaf of papers from his desk and started to study them once more. He looked up absently, clearly surprised to see John still standing there.

"You may go," he said.

"Thank you, Master," John answered humbly. But once outside the door he threw his hat in the air and caught it again. At long last he knew that he was on the trail of the murderer.

CHAPTER
TWENTY-FOUR

The next morning, true to his word, Master John Peck sent the relevant information by way of special messenger to John, working in his shop in Shug Lane alongside Nicholas Dawkins. It had been a happy day during which the Apothecary had hung out herbs to dry, and compounded and mixed several potions. He had also rolled quite a few suppositories, which had given him a certain satisfaction. Indeed, later he had been called out to visit a man suffering with painful haemorrhoids and was able to give him some freshly made samples from the ointment of Pilewort.

The dinner on the previous evening had been highly successful and John's earlier suspicions had proved correct, indeed he could not remember such a couple for exchanging looks and giving each other warm and affectionate glances. He could see at once that the Muscovite had made up his mind to marry Miss da Costa, and though delighted that at last his former apprentice was about to enter the state of married bliss, could not help but feel a tinge disappointed that this meant that Nicholas would be leaving him and setting up on his own.

Now he turned to the Muscovite as John Peck's messenger left the shop.

"Well, Nick, I reckon this is it."

"The address you sought, John?"

The Muscovite had only recently been finally persuaded to call his former master by his first name and it still sounded slightly awkward when he did so.

"Yes. This will bring me one step nearer to the solution, I feel certain of it."

The Master of the Worshipful Society of Apothecaries had written:

"I have Spoken to My Friend William Pitcairn and he Tells me that Edward Bancroft can be found at number Twenty-Four, Little Britain, in a lodging above a Book Shop. You can Catch Him there on most Evenings."

John looked up. "It's the address all right. The American lives in Little Britain, not far from St Bartholomew's. I shall go and see him this evening, as soon as we have closed the shop."

"Might I come with you, sir?"

The Apothecary glanced at him in some surprise. "Are you sure you really want to?"

"I would like it very much. After all, from what you have said, we can only learn from him."

"How true. I'll give a message to Gideon that they are not to wait dinner for me. And what of yourself?"

Nick's pale face took on a little colour. "I am on my own this evening, sir. There is no one to inform."

"But not for much longer, I believe."

The former apprentice glowed. "It may seem foolish to you, John, but I can truly say that Octavia and I fell in love almost immediately. I intend to propose in the next few days."

John smiled a crooked smile. "I do not find that foolish at all, my dear fellow. Was it not Marlowe who said, 'Whoever loved, that loved not at first sight'?"

"I believe it was, sir."

"Well, he knew everything, so that's settled."

"There is another issue, John."

"Oh? What's that?"

"After I am married I would like to open my own shop and have already started to look round for some premises."

"Well, that's understandable. Have you anywhere particular in mind?"

"Somewhere a little out of the heart of London. Perhaps Chiswick or Chelsea."

John smiled at him. "I can just see the pair of you living in the country and relishing it. I suppose I could not tempt you back to Kensington?"

"I would love to, but I want to work for myself."

"Quite right too," John answered, but in his heart of hearts he thought that everything was beginning to change and nothing would ever be quite the same again.

The address in Little Britain was relatively easy to find. John had picked up a hackney coach from the stand in Piccadilly, having lent Irish Tom to Sir Gabriel that evening, and had proceeded down the Hay Market to Charing Cross. Then they had gone up Fleet Street to St Paul's, then proceeded along St Martin's le Grand and finally turned left into the winding confines of Little Britain. A little further on, on the south side of West Smithfield market, to which livestock were herded through the open streets of the city, lay the great St Bartholomew's Hospital, occupying exactly the same site as when it was founded in the early twelfth century.

Little Britain abounded in bookshops but John and Nicholas identified the number fairly easily and climbed up the narrow staircase which lay beside the establishment. At the top they found a fairly decrepit front door on which the Apothecary was forced to bang with his cane, there being no knocker. As he could have predicted, there was total silence.

"What do we do now?" asked Nicholas.

"We seek him out at the hospital," John replied and proceeded back down the stairs. But he was forestalled, for a tall, slim young man wearing a tricorne hat which was just a fraction too large for him and was prevented from descending over his eyes by a pair of jolly jug ears, was starting to make his way upwards.

"Can I help you?" he asked politely, his accent revealing that he came from across the Atlantic.

"Dr Bancroft?" John enquired.

"Yes, sir, I am. How may I assist you?"

The Apothecary could not help but notice that the American's hand had gone to an inner pocket where he clearly carried a pistol.

266

John hastily added, "Your name has been given to me by Dr Pitcairn, so I do hope you don't mind me calling unannounced."

"And why did he give you my name, may I ask?" the other answered.

"Because, sir, it is known that you are something of an expert on exotic poisons."

Edward Bancroft visibly relaxed. "I see. May I ask who you are, sir?"

John fished inside his cloak. "My card, Dr Bancroft."

The man studied it carefully, then looked up and held out his hand. "I am delighted to meet you, Mr Rawlings." He peered at John in the gloomy light. "But your face seems vaguely familiar to me. Have we met somewhere before?"

John stared at him, then went bright red. "I believe it might have been at Medmenham Abbey," he said, and gave a wry grin.

"Well, bless me, so it was. I think we'd better step inside, Mr Rawlings." His look took in Nicholas. "And you, too, sir. Any friends of Sir Francis are friends of mine."

Nicholas merely smiled and the two of them were ushered into Edward's very neat and comfortable set of rooms.

Half an hour later they were seated by the fire, which Dr Bancroft had lit for the look of it, sipping dry sherry.

"So you were a monk, Doctor?"

"Yes, I have been for some time," the other answered carelessly, giving a broad grin.

John, considering how robust the monks were about their sexual excesses, totally unashamed and brashly honest about the whole situation, decided that rather than being embarrassed about his connection with the place, he might as well join in with the general hearty attitude.

"Terribly good fun, wasn't it?" he said, giving a rollicking laugh and at the same time shooting a glance at Nicholas, who, rather than looking shocked, appeared extremely interested.

"Yes. Suits me, anyhow," replied the American doctor, giving another broad smile.

"Tell me," asked John, "did you ever discuss any of these exotic poisons when you were at the Abbey?"

"Truth to tell, I did. Sir Francis seemed very interested and I discussed one poison in particular with him and the other apostles."

The Apothecary pricked up like a hound. "All of them or just a few?"

"About four. As well as Sir Francis there was Sir Henry Vansittart, Lord Sandwich and Lord Arundel."

"And what particular poison were you discussing?"

"One made by the Accawau Indians who live in Dutch Guiana. I was telling them how they make it, store it and then envenom the points of their tiny arrows, which they then blow through a pipe."

John stared at him as light slowly began to dawn. "You say that the poison is administered by use of a blowpipe?"

"Yes. The Indians hunt with them. The smallest quantity of the poison, conveyed by a wound into the

268

red blood-vessels of an animal, causes it to expire in less than a minute."

"So taken internally it would do no harm?"

"Precisely," Dr Bancroft answered. "It has to enter the blood to kill."

"Sir," said John solemnly, "there is something I have to tell you."

And there, in the quiet of the Doctor's apartment the Apothecary told him the entire story of the deaths of Lord Arundel and Lady Orpington, the two lovers finally united in hell.

Edward looked shocked. "I knew them both, as you know. And you say that the woman had a small mark on the back of her neck?"

"Yes. The only evidence I could find for her strange demise. Other than for that it could have been of natural causes."

"Then somebody has either acquired or made a blowpipe and blown a little arrow into her."

"And Lord Arundel? What of him?"

The Doctor shook his head. "You say the poor wretch had the Great Pox?"

"He did indeed."

"Was there a chancre anywhere on his body?"

"Yes, in his groin. But you don't think . . ."

"If a killer were to mix up a little poison and if that were put on the chancre . . ."

"What would be the results?"

"Why, in that case the chap would suffer muscle paralysis and might well go blind and stagger out into the gardens."

John stared at him aghast, while beside him Nicholas drew in a sharp breath.

"You are serious about that?"

"Completely," the Doctor answered. "That is what the effect would be."

There was a profound silence and then Edward Bancroft spoke again. "By the way, I dined privately with the Arundels, and his wife — the former actress Coralie Clive — expressed a great interest in the poison. So much so that I gave her husband a little of it. He said he wanted to experiment with it on a cat."

Outside in the street John leant hard against the wall, feeling slightly out of breath. "God's blood, Nick, that was something of a shock."

"I should say it was, sir. Let's go in here and have a brandy."

They were passing a tavern — a small disreputable-looking place — but still they made a concerted dive into the grimy confines.

"You look terrible, John," said Nick, who was none too calm himself. "Let me get you a drink."

He went to the bar, having found two seats in a dark, wretched corner first, and returned a moment later with glasses in his hand.

"What a revelation," he said.

"Yes," the Apothecary replied grimly. "But despite that I cannot believe she did it. I have known her for years and am certain that however immense the provocation she could not possibly have killed her husband."

270

"But, John, you were once in love with her. Surely that might prejudice your opinion."

The older man emptied his glass and sighed. "I suppose you're right. But who else? Who else? Who could have such a specialist knowledge of poisons?"

Nick shook his head thoughtfully. "Who is there? Well, the child is ruled out at least."

"Is she? Supposing she overheard a conversation and actually saw the substance they were talking about. After that she would be quite capable of forming some primitive wooden splint to act as an arrow, I feel certain of it."

"In that case the field is open, with Sir Francis Dashwood as favourite."

John nodded gloomily. "But you're not saying what you really think, Nick. Namely that Coralie, compelled by despair, actually got rid of her disease-ridden husband."

"And her rival for his affections? That doesn't quite make sense to me."

"No." John allowed a small smile to appear. "I would rather imagine that Coralie — being utterly sensible — would have thought poor wretched Lady Orpington was welcome to him."

Nick looked at him. "Who do you think did it, sir?"

John raised his shoulders. "I have absolutely no idea. But one thing is sure. We should search for that blowpipe. For I feel whoever has it will turn out to be the killer."

"But how do we go about that?"

"Let us call on each person in turn."

"But that could take some while."

"Nevertheless, it is what we must do."

So saying, John stood up and was making to leave when he suddenly sat down again.

"What is it?" whispered Nick.

"That couple who have just come in. I know them."

Nick stared and saw two people, both of whom looked extremely out of place in the dingy surroundings.

"Who are they, John?"

"None other than cronies of Sir Francis Dashwood and regular attendees at Medmenham Abbey. James and Betsy Avon-Nelthorpe."

John's voice must have carried more than he intended for two pairs of eyes swivelled round and stared at him. There was a momentary frisson, followed by a rapid glance of suspicion, then Betsy metamorphosed into her usual self.

"Why," she gushed, "if it isn't Mr O'Hare. How divine to see you. What are you doing in this part of the world?"

And without waiting for a reply she crossed over and joined him, elbowing Nick out of the way and leaning across the table in a most familiar manner. James followed more slowly, clearly embarrassed, though whether through being seen or by his wife's behaviour, John was not quite certain.

The Apothecary and his assistant rose to their feet and bowed, at which James returned the greeting.

"How do you do, sir and madam? How nice to see you again," John said politely.

"My dear, have you heard the news from West Wycombe?" asked Betsy without preamble. "Lord Arundel is drowned and Lady Orpington has died in the grounds. Isn't it terrible?"

"The fact of the matter is that they were both murdered," John answered, cutting straight to the point.

James looked shocked but John thought he detected a knowing look on Betsy's face. Despite this she said, "Oh, surely not. You must be mistaken."

John's vivid sense of recall brought back a picture of Sir Francis leering happily at his fellow monks as he had picked his "bride", Betsy Avon-Nelthorpe, and he wondered, as he had done at the time, exactly what her relationship with her husband could possibly be.

"I can tell you most assuredly, madam, that those are the facts. The pair of them were attacked with an exotic poison little known in this country."

"And how do you know all this, sir?" asked James.

"Because," John answered bluntly, "I work with the Public Office — Sir John Fielding himself, to be exact — and have done so for some years."

There was a silence during which James sat down, somewhat heavily.

"Well, we have nothing to say to you. We were not present at the time," he said.

"I am aware of that. But I am hoping that you might be able to tell me what the association between Charles Arundel and Sir Francis was."

"They were both apostles and took part in the monks of St Francis's secret ceremonies."

"Anything else?" John asked.

"No, nothing," Betsy replied. She looked suddenly militant. "But you were a guest there, Mr O'Hare. You should know."

Nick, who had remained silent up to this point, said, "Surely as an old friend of Sir Francis, you must be able to tell us something, madam."

Betsy regarded him coldly, taking in his pale, dark, arrestingly handsome looks. John watched her visage change and suddenly become both coy and arch.

"That's as may be, young sir. But I can tell you that Sir Francis was a better friend of my husband than he was of myself, wasn't he, James?"

"We played cards together occasionally," her husband replied shortly.

So was that the way of it? John thought. Did James Avon-Nelthorpe play deep with Sir Francis Dashwood and had the older man wiped out his debts in return for his wife? Not that he had received a very good bargain out of it, the Apothecary considered with a certain amusement.

James stood up. "Have you asked all your questions, Mr O'Hare? Are we free to go?"

"Of course. I had no intention of interrogating you. And by the way the name is actually Rawlings. I used the other to hide my true identity."

Betsy rose also, not sure whether to titter or be angry. "Well, good evening to you, sir. I trust that if we meet again it will be in happier circumstances."

The Apothecary and Nick both got to their feet and bowed magnificently.

"Good evening, madam. Good evening, sir." But as soon as the two of them were out of the door John turned to Nick and said urgently, "Follow them."

CHAPTER
TWENTY-FIVE

They hurried out just in time to see the Avon-Nelthorpes climbing into a hackney coach which had been pulling up outside St Bartholomew's Hospital. John looked round frantically for another but could see none. He turned to Nicholas.

"What shall we do?"

"We could beg a ride off that farmer."

John stared at him but indeed there was such an individual amongst the horde of drovers driving their cattle to market. With merely a look between them the two men raced towards the trundling cart shouting, "Stop, stop, we will make it worth your while."

The fellow looked over his shoulder, saw that his pursuers were well-dressed and duly pulled to a halt.

"How can I help you, sirs?"

"Can you follow that hackney coach?"

"The one just disappearing?"

"Yes. If you can keep up with it I'll give you a golden guinea," answered John.

They clambered on board the hay cart and proceeded back along the way they had come until, as they reached the Strand, the hackney coach veered off to the right.

"They're heading for Covent Garden," said John in amazement.

"Probably going to a brothel," Nick answered, not really meaning it.

For Covent Garden was infamous as the area of London with more prostitutes and houses of ill-repute per square inch than any other.

"I wouldn't be at all surprised," John answered.

The cart turned slowly to the right and the Apothecary asked the farmer to slow down.

"I think we'd better disembark," he said to Nick. "This is not the usual form of conveyance for this area."

"Do you think they have seen us?"

"Bound to have done."

And as the Apothecary gave the farmer his promised guinea he saw two figures scurrying into a house of dubious reputation, glancing over their shoulders as they did so.

"We daren't follow them in, dare we?" Nicholas asked.

"No. But we can saunter past and see what kind of things are on offer."

They walked onwards in a casual manner and went up to the door at which stood a huge negro slave. He bowed as they drew closer.

"Good evening, gentlemen. Can I interest you in a game of chance? Cards or dice? Or perhaps beautiful young ladies? Or why not have both? We cater for all tastes in this establishment."

"Thank you, but no," John answered. "Unfortunately we have another engagement. But we shall come back another night. You can be sure of it."

"Thank you, sirs. I hope to see you again."

The servant gave a deep bow and John and Nick walked quietly on.

"What shall we do now?" asked the Muscovite.

"We shall go and see Dominique Jean. I've a feeling he could be very useful to us."

They quickened their pace but as soon as they saw a hackney they hailed it as time was moving by and John could only recall where the Frenchman had his workshop. Or rather where his celebrated father-in-law had had his. Fearful that the place might be closed and Dominique returned home for the night, John felt a sense of relief when the driver put them down at the junction of Oxford Street and Tottenham Court Road, not far from the brewhouse, which stood in an alleyway leading off Bainbridge Street. There were lights on at the workshop and the Apothecary turned to Nick with a smile.

"Sombody's in there and at least they can tell us Dominique's home address." And with that he knocked loudly on the door of number 39.

From within the building they heard a French voice say, "*Merde*," and the two men turned to one another and grinned. Bolts were drawn back and eventually Dominique's face appeared in the crack. Lit from behind by a lanthorn which he held high, it had a strange, greenish pallor. Recognising John, the French-man broke into a broad smile and threw the door wide.

278

"Come in, *mon ami*. I was wondering if you might call. How are you?"

"Very well indeed." John motioned to Nick. "May I present Nicholas Dawkins, my former apprentice, now qualified and an apothecary in his own right."

"I am delighted to meet you. I have news for you, John, about one of your patients."

The Apothecary stared. "Who?"

"Lord Orpington, of course. I called in at West Wycombe on my way back to London and I can tell you the old boy was up and about."

John turned to Nick. "That just proves the efficacy of foxgloves given in small amounts."

"I shall remember that."

They walked into the workshop and John stood sniffing the air. From every corner the smell of beautiful wood filled his nostrils together with another odour, a strangely unique tang. He turned to Dominique.

"What a wonderful stink. What is it?"

The Frenchman smiled. "You are in the repair section at the moment. Wood comes to us from various places and brings with it an individual smell of its owner. The blending of their essences is what you can detect at present."

"I never thought wood to have a smell."

"Oh, but it has, my friend. Each piece that comes in is unique. Sniff them for yourself."

The Apothecary did as he was instructed and sure enough a faint aroma rose from each piece. Nicholas looked on fascinated and eventually joined in.

Dominique stood watching them, smiling at their astonished expressions. Then interrupted them by saying, "Gentlemen, would you like to see some of my father-in-law's work?"

Leading them through to the other end of the large workroom, John and Nicholas stood in silent admiration at the great things of beauty that had been fashioned by the hands of that master craftsman, Pierre Langlois.

"These are still waiting for me to put the finishing touches to them," Dominique said, feeling an exquisite piece of furniture with love.

"I wish I could have such a masterpiece in my home," John answered sincerely.

"Alas, these are all pre-ordered," the Frenchman stated a little sadly. His voice changed. "Now, *mon ami*, I am sure you had a reason for calling here. What can I do for you?"

John laughed. "Dominique, I want you to go to a certain house in Covent Garden for me."

The other looked stricken. "But John, I am a married man with a small child. My wife would kill me."

"Not if you explained to her first. All I want you to do is find out if it is both a gambling hell and a whorehouse. And anything else that might be of interest."

"Such as?"

"Two people whom you have already met patronise the place. I refer to Sir Francis Dashwood's friends Betsy and James Avon-Nelthorpe."

"But I saw them briefly once, that is all."

"Nevertheless, you would know them again." John's face took on an earnest expression. "It is quite important to me that you do this, Dominique."

"Why can't you?"

"Because they would recognise me," the Apothecary answered, and explained the events of the evening to the Frenchman, leaving out the reference to the unusual poison used to kill Lord Arundel and Lady Orpington. At the end Dominique pulled a face.

"Very well, I will go, provided I can explain to my wife. If she is agreeable I shall visit the place tomorrow and will call on you with the results. Do I have your card?"

John produced one with a flourish and the Frenchman studied it.

"Shug Lane, eh. A good address."

"Yes."

"Tell me, are you any nearer finding out who committed the murders?"

"I'm afraid not."

"Then perhaps you never will," Dominique answered and gave a Gallic shrug.

Outside Nick turned to John. "Do you think he was trying to hide something?"

"I don't know. But it occurs to me that he could very easily fashion a blowpipe. Don't you think so?"

"Very easily indeed," the Muscovite replied as they set their faces towards Oxford Street and the long walk home.

The next morning, Sir Gabriel having played cards the night before and remaining in bed for a while, John had an excellent opportunity to read the paper and an item of interest immediately caught his eye. "The Funeral of Charles William Montblanc Bravo, Marquess of Arundel, will Take Place at 2 o'clock at St James's, Piccadilly, Today."

So the Coroner had released the body and the murdered man was finally to be laid to rest. John glanced at his watch and saw that if he changed into his mourning clothes he could slip out of the shop and be at St James's in five minutes, leaving Nicholas in charge once more. He could also get a full morning's work in before having to do so. Consequently, he left the house arrayed in deepest black and hurried off to Shug Lane.

Both Gideon and Nicholas were there before he arrived and looked somewhat startled at his appearance.

"I'm off to a funeral later, my lads," John said briefly, and slipped off his coat and put a long apron over the rest of his sombre gear.

At half past one the solemn funeral bell started its melancholy single note and ten minutes later the Apothecary hurried from his shop and went down Shug Lane to Castle Street, turned left into Air Street and thus made his way to Piccadilly and the church of St James's. Pulling his hat well down, John stood behind a bush in the churchyard and watched the various arrivals.

Dignitaries came by the score and amongst them the Apothecary recognised several monks of St Francis. As well as the monks there were two apostles, namely Lord Sandwich and Sir Henry Vansittart, who made their

282

way inside to be followed a moment later by the arrival of Sir Francis and Lady Dashwood, he very florid, she looking disapproving and somewhat thin. Finally, the immediate family appeared escorting the coffin: Coralie — very pale and lovely — holding the hand of her pallid child, followed by Lady Juliana on the arm of an elderly aristocratic man who John presumed to be the dead man's father, the Duke of Sussex. Having checked that they were safely inside, the Apothecary slipped in and sat at the back where he could see everything that occurred.

Coralie was weeping, presumably remembering her husband as he must once have been, as was the old Duke, probably for the same reason. John wondered if the man had another son who would now inherit the title, and looking round those sitting in the front pew thought he identified a likely candidate. Lady Juliana sat ramrod straight, her lips moving soundlessly as if she were praying for the soul of her departed brother. Occasionally she would pat the hand of Georgiana, who sat next to her, her face utterly expressionless. John thought that if he had been asked to pick a murderer from among them his money would have gone on the child.

The service finally came to an end after several flowery funeral orations, one given by Sir Francis himself — by now puce in the face — which as far as John could see amounted to nothing more nor less than a series of totally false compliments. As soon as it was over he rose like lightning and made his way out to the churchyard. The freshly dug grave — like an open black mouth — yawned nearby, the gravediggers standing removed at a respectful distance. Down from the church wound the mournful dark procession and John secreted himself behind a large family grave with an overpowering angelic erection above. The line of mourners passed within a few feet of him and he found himself terribly aware of their individual smells. At the head of the file came Coralie, holding Georgiana by the hand, and John was instantly reminded of the many nights he had spent with her, locked in her embrace, inhaling that wonderful perfume of hyacinths which he always associated with her. The child smelt faintly of horses and John suspected that she had not washed since going for a ride that morning.

Behind them followed Lord Arundel's father, sister and brother; the old man smelling of shaving soap and ancient perspiration, she of lavender water, as if she had splashed a great deal on herself, the brother of costly scent. Sir Francis Dashwood stunk of stale alcohol, Lady Dashwood of vinegar, while Lord Sandwich had a musty aroma peculiar to him alone. Betsy and James Avon-Nelthorpe both wore outrageously expensive perfumes. There were a great many people walking to the graveside and from each one John detected a highly individualistic whiff as they passed him by in his hidden hiding place.

He was just about to creep away when a voice muttered in his ear, "Good morning, sir. I thought I might find you here." He looked up and straight into the fox face of Joe Jago.

"Joe!" John exclaimed at full voice and was instantly told to be quiet.

"Nobody knows you're about so let's keep it that way, sir."

The Apothecary looked contrite. "You're right," he whispered. "What brings you here?"

"Saw the announcement in the papers and Sir John suggested I come and have a look. He also suggested that if Sir Francis Dashwood were here then we head straight for West Wycombe and search the grounds before he gets back. Are you game, sir?"

"Of course I am. When do we leave?"

"Immediately. I have a coach waiting at the church gates. I also have a runner ready to deliver a message to your family."

John gave a smile that turned his mouth up on one side. "Poor wretches. It would never surprise me to walk in one day and for my daughter to say, 'Who are you?' "

Joe chuckled. "I am quite aware of how you feel, sir. So if you'd rather not . . ."

"I can't wait to conduct a search in your company, my friend. Let us go."

Half an hour later they had left London and were heading in the direction of Oxford. Four hours after that they stopped for refreshment at Henley-on-Thames. By now it was getting on for seven o'clock and though it would be light for another few hours — it being high summer — by the time they reached West Wycombe the shadows would be lengthening. They decided therefore to leave the coaching inn first thing in the morning and take a chance that Sir Francis would not travel home overnight.

"It is my belief he will enjoy the delights of London for a few days," said John.

"Let us hope you are right, sir. Otherwise I shall have to go all official and brandish my letter from Sir John."

In the event they arrived at West Wycombe House at seven o'clock the next morning and John, waving cheerily at the east gate lodgekeeper, managed to gain entrance. But once there the enormity of the task before them struck them both with force.

Joe gulped loudly. "The grounds are vast, sir. It would take an army of men a week to search them thoroughly."

"But you expected them to be large, did you not?"

"Yes, but not quite as big as this."

"Listen, Joe, let us start searching near the Temple of Venus — that is where the second murder took place — and work outwards from there. I have a feeling that if anything were dumped it would be close to that spot."

"Why do you say that?"

"Because the murderer must have carried Lady Orpington's body there. She was killed somewhere nearby and dragged or lifted up and put to lie in the temple. Clearly the killer's little joke about the girl's purity — or lack thereof. Anyway, the point I'm making is that if she was killed by a poisoned arrow it is more than likely that the murderer dropped the blowpipe in order to transport the body."

"And you're sure that's how she died?"

"Positive. I've spoken to the expert on such poisons and it was he who told me how it was more than likely done."

Joe looked slightly dubious but John ignored it and, leaving the coach — which stayed hidden in a thick group of trees and out of sight of the house — the two men began their search.

An hour later and nothing had come to light. Joe, clearly feeling ill at ease about the whereabouts of Sir Francis, constantly glanced across the lake towards the house, while John became convinced that they were on a fool's errand and that the murderer had kept the blowpipe about their person after the killing. Eventually they sat down to catch their breath and it was then that they saw the figure of the runner who had driven their coach making his way towards them. John noticed at once that the man was carrying something in his hand.

"Hello, Munn. What's that you've got?" Jago asked.

"Don't know, sir. But it looked like it could be important. I found it in the ashes of a fire which someone had started down by the lake."

He held it out and Joe took it, turning it over and over in his hands.

It was the charred remains of something like a recorder, except that there were no holes for producing the notes. John let out a cry.

"God's own life, Joe! That's it. That's what's left of the blowpipe. And home-made, too, by the look of it. The killer obviously tried to destroy it but never reckoned on this piece remaining."

Sir John Fielding's clerk peered down at the burned piece of wood. "It's so commonplace. I think I might have overlooked it. Well done, Munn. How did you find it?"

"I'd just gone to the lake to answer a call of nature and have a look at the boat and my foot kicked against something in the grass. I saw the remains of a fire and stooped down and picked it up."

John took the pipe from Joe and held it in his grasp. As he did so a faint smell rose from the thing and he raised it to his nostrils and sniffed. Marred as it was by the smell of burning, there nonetheless was a distinctive odour and one that he felt was familiar to him, though how he could not say.

"What are you doing, sir?" asked Jago.

"It has a slight smell."

The clerk took it back and sniffed it. Then he said a word and John sat stock still while a million lights went off in his head.

"Of course," he said. "Of course. I should have known before."

CHAPTER
TWENTY-SIX

They drove back to London as soon as it was light on the morning of the following day. John, being put down in Nassau Street, told Jago that he would call on Sir John Fielding that night but meanwhile must pay his compliments to his family. As soon as he was through the front door Rose came running down the stairs in a flurry of flying hair and outstretched arms.

"Oh, Papa, here you are. I've missed you so much. I do wish you would stop working for Sir John Fielding."

John picked her up and hugged her, answering, "Your mother often thought the same thing."

"How do you know that? What she thought, I mean."

He laughed. "I didn't. I am only guessing."

Rose wriggled to the floor. "I believe it is time, Papa, that you went to visit Mrs Elizabeth again."

"My dear child, I am not certain that she wishes me to visit her. Besides, it would be rude of me to call without an invitation."

"Yet I feel certain she is thinking of you."

He stared at Rose and she stared back, smiling, but with old magic in her eyes. After a few moments John tickled her under the chin.

"You wise child, you. Maybe I will write to her and ask how she fares."

"You promise?"

"Yes, I promise. But it will have to wait until I've solved this odd case."

"What is odd about it?" asked Rose, leading the way out into the garden.

John sat down and took the child on his knee, playing with her bright red whorls of hair.

"It was the method used to dispatch certain people."

"By dispatch I suppose you mean kill."

The Apothecary ruffled the curls and put her to stand on the ground, getting to his feet himself.

"Enough questions. Where is your grandfather?"

"He is packing in preparation for returning to Kensington. He says he is tired of London and requires a little country air."

As she uttered, the child unconsciously mirrored the way in which Sir Gabriel spoke and John had an extraordinary moment of comparing Rose with Georgiana, that sad and abused child. Speaking on impulse he said, "I wonder if you might like to play with a little girl I have met. She is the daughter of Lady Arundel, who was once the actress, Coralie Clive."

"Is she a nice child?" Rose asked.

"Not particularly," John answered, laughing at his daughter's directness. "But she is interesting."

"Then I would like to meet her," pronounced the youngest member of the Rawlings clan, and with that took John's hand and led him back into the house.

Climbing the stairs, John found his father taking his ease and directing his valet as to the arrangement of his clothes in his trunks.

"Father," said John, kissing him, "I hear from Rose that you are leaving London."

"Yes, my dear," answered Sir Gabriel, returning the embrace, "I think perhaps I am getting old. The noise of the city is too much for me. I desire nothing more than the quiet of Kensington, until that, too, bores me and I return once more."

"When will you depart, sir?"

"Tomorrow morning, if I may borrow Irish Tom again."

"Of course you can. But Father . . ."

"Yes?"

"I wonder whether you would mind if Rose accompanies you. I have to go away again for a few days and I am sure that Octavia da Costa will be much preoccupied with her forthcoming nuptials. You know how much the child enjoys staying with you."

"It would be a great pleasure to have her. I love her company. But where are you bound for this time, my dear?"

"To West Wycombe House, that is if Sir Francis Dashwood will allow."

"I see," replied Sir Gabriel with a wealth of meaning. "Do you?"

"I take it that you have discovered the identity of the guilty party?"

"I have, but on the flimsiest piece of evidence. Everything will depend on the way I handle the situation."

"My son, you will do it with ease. I have every confidence. And now, if you will leave me, I must dress and saunter forth. I promised to call on Lady Clydesdale this late morning."

"And she must not be disappointed," said John with a chuckle, and having kissed his father once more, left the room.

As soon as he had washed and changed his clothes, John made for Shug Lane, where Nicholas and Gideon greeted him with a great deal of fervour.

"We were so worried, sir, when you did not return from the funeral."

"I was called away on urgent business. But you know about that. A runner must have told you."

"He went to your home, sir. He did not come here."

"Oh well," said John, and grinned at them.

Later he drew Nicholas on one side and told him about the finding of the blowpipe. "It had a certain aroma, Nick, which proved to me who had used it."

"So you know who committed the murders?"

"Yes, though the evidence is thin."

"Have you told Sir John Fielding yet?"

"I shall call on him immediately after dinner."

And so saying John donned his long apron and went into the compounding room where, with much joy, he got to work. But this day was not destined to be peaceful, for a half hour or so later a stiff-backed lady's maid entered, peering about her and saying in an affected voice, "Is Mr Rawlings here?"

John came through from the back. "I am Rawlings."

"My mistress asked me to give you this." And she thrust a letter into his hand.

"Thank you. Could you tell me . . ."

But the woman was gone, having dropped a very slight curtsey and turning on her heel before John could question her any further. He broke the seal on the paper and scanned the contents.

"Sir, I beg of You to Call on me Tonight. There
is Much of Importance that I would say to
You. I shall Await You after Dinner.
I have the Honour to remain, Sir,
Yr Obedient Servant, Coralie Clive."

So she had used her old name and not bothered with titles or obeying custom. Something of the woman he had once loved came back to him, standing there and holding her letter, begging him to see her. He knew at that moment that he would go to her, however late at night it was, but first of all he must acquaint Sir John Fielding with the facts and ask for his help in setting the final scene.

CHAPTER
TWENTY-SEVEN

John Fielding was now forty-five years old, though through the years of hard work and strain he looked considerably older. He sat in the dying light, his trenchant profile turned to the window, his flowing white wig curling onto his shoulders, his handsome face beginning to fall slightly into a double chin, drumming his fingers on the arm of the chair. For once he wore the black ribbon that covered his lack of sight pushed up so that his eyes showed beneath the half-closed lids. John, regarding them, thought them a pleasant colour — a shade of calming blue — and regretted for the thousandth time that his great friend and mentor should have been blinded in an accident at the age of nineteen.

Also sitting in the room was Joe Jago, as cheerful as ever and hardly having changed at all in all the years that John had known him. His red unruly hair was distinctly visible beneath his wig, his light blue eyes danced in his craggy face, his figure was as spare as it had been when the Apothecary had first set eyes on him. He was a man of mystery, of little-known antecedents, yet he was omnipresent, Sir John's right-hand, his sight. But of his personal life John knew nothing and felt it beyond his business to enquire.

The three men sat in silence, waiting for Sir John to speak. From the street below the usual noises drifted upward but other than that there was no sound. The Apothecary felt that he was sitting on the edge of a precipice waiting for the Magistrate to tell him that what he believed was pure nonsense.

Eventually the Blind Beak spoke. "Pass me the remains of the blowpipe once more, will you, Joe."

"Here you are, Sir John," replied the clerk cheerfully, and handed the object to his master.

Very delicately the Magistrate raised it to his nostrils. "There is definitely an odour," he said at last, "though very faint and heavily masked by the fire."

"There is indeed, sir."

"And you think that this points the finger at the user of such a scent?"

"I have nothing else to go on, Sir John. It is our only hope."

"Um," said the Magistrate and relapsed into another prolonged silence.

Sounds of family life drifted into the room.

"Mary Ann, can you take the port to your uncle, if you please." This from Elizabeth, Lady Fielding.

"Very good, Mama."

And the door opened to reveal a beautiful young woman, now in her early twenties, who cast her naughty eyes round the room, saw John, and dropped a suggestive curtsey.

"Why, Mr Rawlings," she said, "I had no idea that you had joined the company."

John, perfectly aware that she had glimpsed his arrival some twenty minutes earlier, said, "Gracious, Mary Ann, I hope it is a pleasant surprise."

"Oh indeed it is, sir," she answered, and gave him a look full of mischief.

Adopted by Sir John, brought into the marriage by Elizabeth Whittingham, as Lady Fielding had once been, Mary Ann was regarded by everyone as Sir John's daughter and had even changed her name to Fielding. And with her had come a deal of trouble, for she flaunted her beauty for all she was worth and had indeed caused many a serious problem. At the age of sixteen she had driven Lord Elibank mad for love of her, he being nearly fifty years old and recently widowed and so vulnerable that he had fallen into a kind of hysterical fit at the very thought of her. But, strangely, she was still not married and rumour had it that she was holding out for a title.

John winked at her, he could not resist it. "How goes it with you, young lady?"

She winked back. "Very well, I thank you, sir."

"Did you know that my former apprentice, young Nicholas, is about to get married?"

Nick, too, had fallen victim to her charms in the dim and distant past.

"I wish him well then. I prefer the single life personally."

The Blind Beak interrupted. "Pour the port for Mr Rawlings and Jago, there's a good girl. And then if you don't mind making yourself scarce for we are in the middle of a most important meeting."

"Certainly, Uncle."

She passed John a glass with one of the sauciest glances he had ever seen, positively thrust one at Joe whom she disregarded totally, gave one to her uncle, then left the room with much swaying in her gait.

Just as well that the Beak can't see her, John thought.

"Now, where were we?" said the Magistrate.

"You were wondering whether Mr Rawlings had sufficient evidence to proceed," Joe reminded him.

"Well, as you say, my friend, it is very flimsy but it is the best chance we have. What do you want me to do?"

"Write to Sir Francis and suggest that he hold a reunion of all the people present at the time, plus others so as not to make them suspicious. Press on him how important it is that they all accept his invitation," said John.

"I can certainly do that but whether he will agree to it is an entirely different matter."

"And whether the guests decide that they want to go," the Apothecary answered gloomily.

"Perhaps," said Joe, "Sir Francis could disguise it a bit. Say he is holding some sort of celebration on the lake and it will all be excessively jolly and amusing."

"What about those ladies who are in mourning? To say nothing of old Lord Orpington."

"Well, suggest he uses his powers of persuasion," the clerk replied cheerfully.

"And could you also ask Sir Francis to invite Betsy and James Avon-Nelthorpe?" John added.

"I think in view of the number of requests I might go in person and see the honourable gentleman at his London address."

"A very good idea, sir. Leave the arrangements to me. I shall get on to them straight away, if you will excuse me."

"A good plan, Jago. See to it will you."

"Yes, sir." And having bowed to John, Joe left the room.

"A remarkable fellow that," said the Blind Beak.

"Does he still live in Seven Dials?" asked John.

"Oh yes."

John cleared his throat and dared to ask a personal question. "Tell me, sir, has Joe Jago ever been married?"

The Blind Beak's laugh rumbled round the room. "If he has, he has never told me of it. To be frank with you, Mr Rawlings, I know very little about his private life. It is something that we do not discuss."

"I quite understand, Sir John, it was forward of me to ask."

"Joe Jago is a man of mystery, my friend. And I feel certain that that is how he will remain."

Having left Bow Street, dusk just falling over London, John decided to walk to St James's Square, in which fashionable London residence Coralie Clive now lived. Cutting past the Theatre Royal, Covent Garden — a place infamous for unruly audiences to which prizefighters had occasionally to be brought to quell the rioters — he cut his way through various alleyways to St Martin's Lane and then down to Charing Cross.

From there it was but a stone's throw to St James's Square and, feeling a little shabby and poorly dressed, John rang the bell. A footman answered, clearly expecting him, for he was ushered immediately into a small salon in which Coralie, looking a little lonely and somehow bereft, sat by herself. She looked up as John entered the room.

"I wondered whether you would come," she said.

"You know I would answer any summons from you," John replied gallantly.

"You have dined?"

"Yes, at home. I came straight here from the Public Office. I'm sorry to be late."

"That is perfectly all right. Do sit down, please."

They were being terribly stiff and formal and John, thinking of all that had passed between them, longed to make the meeting more amicable. He sat down opposite Coralie and leaned forward in his chair.

"My dear Coralie, why have you invited me here? Remember that I have always supported you and I don't intend to stop now."

She turned away from him and said in a low voice, "Have you unmasked the murderer yet — if murderer there is?"

"It was an unlawful killing. Quite definitely so. And, yes, I think I know who did it."

She moved back towards him and fixed him with her dazzling emerald eyes. "But surely the death of my husband was accidental."

"I think not, madam. It is my belief that somebody dressed his chancre with a poison not known in this country until extremely recently. And the same poison was administered to Lady Orpington."

"How?"

"By means of a blowpipe and a small arrow."

The green eyes filled with sudden tears and before he knew it he was kneeling before her and had taken her in his arms.

"Oh, Coralie, don't cry. I implore you. You must know how it upsets me."

"Then I beg you to let the murderer go. Do nothing to apprehend them. Let this be the one crime that you do not solve."

He drew back, holding her at arm's length. "But why, sweetheart?"

"Because I wish it."

"And that is the only reason?"

She leant back in her chair, releasing herself from his grasp. "There is another reason, of course there is. But I would rather die than tell you what it is."

He stared at her aghast, a million thoughts racing through his mind. "But, Coralie, it is too late. I have just come from the Public Office, as I told you. Sir John Fielding and Joe Jago know the identity of the person. The inevitability of the law has begun."

With a great effort Coralie got herself together. "I see," she said in a strained voice.

"I'm sorry, my darling, but that is the situation."

"Would you care for a drink before you go?" she asked, her tone completely different.

John shook his head, not in refusal of her offer but in wonderment at her amazing control.

300

"Yes, I would like one very much," he said, and even to himself his speech sounded odd.

Coralie rang a bell. "I would prefer it if you address me as Lady Arundel in front of the servants."

Full of tension, John suddenly lost his temper. "God's life, Coralie, do you think I am a man from the sticks? I shan't stay for that drink after all. I am sorry that I could not meet with your request but it was too late. Good evening to you, madam."

And he swept from the room allowing himself only one backward glance at her, which revealed Coralie sitting ramrod straight, staring into the fire, her face turned away from him.

Outside in the street John swore violently and kicked at the kerbstone. Coralie's plea had put him into a state of terrible uncertainty. Had he been wrong in his identification of the killer? Was Coralie more heavily involved than he had thought? Deep in deliberation he started to walk back to Nassau Street, shoulders hunched and head thrust forward.

Had he really been in love with her? Yes, deeply, and a small part of him still was. That was why she had so much power over him to this day. That was why it was possible for her to upset him and hurt him. John's thoughts turned to Elizabeth and he determined that come what may he would write to her as soon as this sorry and tragic business had drawn to its terrible and final conclusion.

CHAPTER
TWENTY-EIGHT

There was one thing left to do before he departed for West Wycombe and that was to seek out Dominique Jean and discover the answer to his question about that extraordinary couple, the Avon-Nelthorpes. John left his shop in the care of Nicholas and hurried to 39, Tottenham Court Road, where he was lucky enough to find Dominique gilding an exquisite piece of furniture. On seeing his visitor, the Frenchman was abject in his apologies.

"My dear friend, I am so sorry that I have not yet given you the answer. As you can see I am inundated with work. This particular piece is a special order for the Duke of Bedford and he requires that it is delivered tomorrow. I am at my wits' end."

Despite his protestations he seemed calm enough, working at a slow and methodical pace while the commode grew beautiful beneath his hands.

John smiled at him. "Don't worry, please. But did you go to the brothel, that is what I really want to know?"

Very surprisingly Dominique Jean blushed a deep red and said, "Yes, I went."

"And?"

302

"You will never guess who the madam is. It's Madam Betsy herself."

"No! I can scarcely credit it."

"It happens to be true. As you thought was the case, the place is divided into two sections. Downstairs there are gaming rooms, and there the dissolute James sits and gambles away all his money, while upstairs his wife earns it all back again."

"Well, I'll be damned," said John, totally surprised.

He had thought something along those lines but that Betsy should be a madam simply had not occurred to him.

"But why on earth did James marry her?"

"That, *mon ami*, I do not know. I suggest you ask him."

"Maybe I will at that." John's face adopted his honest citizen look. "Have you had an invitation from Sir Francis by the way? Mine arrived in the post this morning."

"Yes. Apparently he is giving a *fête champêtre* and is most anxious that I should join the throng."

"I, too, am invited. Tell me, will you go?"

"Yes, I think I will," Dominique answered, "provided that I finish all my work on time."

"Oh, please do try," the Apothecary urged. "I am sure it will be a splendid occasion."

"The mystery is why he should invite me. After all, I am trade."

"So am I," John replied, feeling just a fraction guilty at lying to the Frenchman about why he was going to West Wycombe.

Fortunately Dominique Jean did not see through the deception and continued to work on his gilding. John, walking round the workroom, thought how cooperative Sir Francis Dashwood had been. Sir John Fielding had been to visit him in the House of Lords and appealed to him as a peer of the realm to assist in catching the murderer. For Sir Francis, as he was commonly called, had become Lord le Despencer in 1762, though few people referred to him as such. According to Joe Jago, who had been present throughout, his Lordship had become very grand and condescending and had agreed to do everything in his power to bring the criminal to justice.

"Sir John asked him if he would mind if I were present at the gathering," he had told John afterwards.

"No, provided he sleeps with the servants," had been the dignified reply.

John had shaken his head, wondering at the great social difference between those who worked for a living and those born to an extravagant and privileged lifestyle. Considering whether such an anomaly would ever change, he had felt fairly certain that it would not. And now, as he wandered amongst the fine example of tremendous craftsmanship and compared it with Sir Francis's decadent and full-blown lifestyle, it seemed to him that the whole structure of society was grossly unfair.

He looked up as Dominique laid down his tools and had a moment's rest.

"Tell me," he said, "did you enjoy your visit to the brothel?"

Again the Frenchman flushed a deep brick-red. "I only attended the gambling section," he said, looking embarrassed.

John smiled to himself. "Of course," he said, then he bowed and, bidding Dominique farewell, left the building and headed for Nassau Street.

Early the next morning he set off by coach for the final act that had to be played out in the drama. Beside him in the conveyance sat Samuel, determined to be in at the kill, as he put it. Opposite was Joe Jago bearing a warrant that gave him the power of arrest. The three men reached The Bear at Maidenhead by early afternoon, where they stopped to refresh themselves. Samuel, who had been apprised of the position, raised his tankard.

"Well, here's to the success of the venture," he said, more in hope than expectation.

"I am praying that, when faced with the crimes, the guilty party will confess," John answered.

"We're all praying that, sir," Joe Jago added. "Otherwise we're up the Nile in an oarless coracle."

"I wonder if they will all come," John said thoughtfully. "I mean, several of them could plead that they were in mourning and it would not be seemly for them to go to such a gathering."

"I believe, sir," Jago answered, "that Sir Francis, or Lord le Despencer to give him his correct title, went personally to visit several people in order to persuade them to be present. He has also asked a goodly crowd of other friends to make the whole thing seem natural."

"Well, let's hope that worked," said Samuel, and bellowed a laugh.

After an hour of these exchanged pleasantries the trio set off once more and arrived at the east lodge just as the sun was setting. The summer sky was a deep rich blue in which the sun was going down in glory, filling the sky with a golden glow that almost took the breath away. It was reflected in the lake and John, observing, saw that the ship had been tricked out with flags and that the Captain, in uniform, was standing on the deck looking through a telescope. This was in order to wave at the arriving guests then come smartly to the salute. Ahead of them, almost at the house, was another carriage which John remembered as the one belonging to the late Charles, Marquess of Arundel. So Coralie had come and presumably brought the child with her. The Apothecary let out an audible sigh of relief.

Samuel, hearing it, looked up. "I see that Coralie is here. I'll wager she took some persuading."

"I'll wager you're right," said John, thinking of the last time he had seen her and her plea that he should not reveal the identity of the killer.

"Excuse me, sir," said Joe Jago, clearing his throat, "but what exactly does a *fête champêtre* mean?" He pronounced the second word "shampeter".

"It means a country feast. What we would call a country fair."

"Oh, I see. Do we all have to dress as rustics then?"

"I shouldn't think so," John answered with a laugh, but a second later bit back his words as the coach drew level with the house and he saw that the servants and hostlers were all done up in breeches and smocks with beflowered hats adorning their heads.

"Gracious!" he exclaimed, and a second or two later positively gasped at the sight of Sir Francis Dashwood, who had come to the door to greet his guest wearing what appeared to be a bastardised version of a gamekeeper's gear.

"Ah ha ha," he roared. "Glad you could make it, O'Hare, or should I call you Rawlings? Come in, come in. I see you've brought some companions with you. Ah well, the more the merrier."

John stood astounded, wondering what could have persuaded the man to behave with such breathtaking bonhomie. He took a shrewd guess that the sight of Sir John Fielding had actually frightened Sir Francis, that he thought news of his scandalous behaviour at Medmenham Abbey had reached the ears of the law and that the whole thing might result in legal action against him. Whatever the reason he had thrown himself wholeheartedly into this amazing *fête champêtre* and for once was not being too fussy about who his visitors were — provided that they slept in the servants' quarters, of course.

The trio dismounted from the coach and went into the house, where Lady Dashwood, dressed in an excessively ornate country frock, was looking daggers at all and sundry. It was obvious that she had no wish to go through with this farce and was ill-prepared for an influx of visitors.

John went straight up to her and made his second best bow, followed by Samuel, slightly more effusive.

Last to make a salute was Joe Jago, whose wig had been dislodged by the removal of his hat, red hair more visible than ever.

"A pleasure to meet you, ma'am," he said.

She did not smile, considering this form of introduction to be beneath her.

John looked round the entrance hall to see who else had arrived. There were several people whom he did not know, though one or two of the men were recognisable as monks of St Francis. Coralie was present, dressed in black from head to foot, and looking pale and drawn as a result. Her sister-in-law, Lady Juliana Bravo, was also clad in deepest mourning, her features set and stern, her deep-set eyes looking round disapprovingly. Of the child Georgiana there was no sign and John realised with a feeling of sad gladness that she had been left behind. Even while he was thinking these thoughts somebody else came in, very noisily indeed, and he turned to see Betsy, hideously arrayed in a type of milkmaid's dress, with James lumbering along garbed as a shepherd.

"Good heavens," said Samuel at John's elbow, "were we meant to dress up?"

"It would appear so," the Apothecary answered quietly.

"No sign yet of the Earl of Orpington."

"Nor of Dominique Jean, though he informed me that he was coming."

"I doubt the Earl will be present in view of his recent ill health, to say nothing of his bereavement."

But at that moment Sir Francis, with an enormous display of jollity, announced loudly, "My dear good people, do not wait in the hall. Come into the saloon where some rural delights await you."

They all trooped into the huge room overlooking the lake, about twenty in all, to find some young girls dressed scantily as nymphs serving punch from a vast bowl draped with flowers. In the middle of them, somewhat purple in the face but other than for that showing no signs of his recent ill-health, was the Earl, his fingers laid lovingly on the behind of a nymphette. He snatched them away as soon as he heard the door opening. John went up to him.

"My Lord, I am so pleased to find you in better health."

Lord Orpington put on a dreary face. "I am recovered, thanks to you I believe, young man. But my poor wee wife is not here to join the fun with me. Woeful am I." He sighed deeply.

"Ah well, time heals all," John replied, thinking to himself that within six months there might well be an even younger Lady Orpington to grace the scene.

Lady Dashwood came in. "I hope you all have some punch," she said in the kind of voice that she must have used to the servants when asking them if the dogs had been fed.

"I haven't, madam," said James Avon-Nelthorpe brightly.

She cast an evil look at him and clapped her hands so that a young girl came scurrying. James cast an appreciative eye over the nymph but was interrupted by

Betsy saying, "You keep your gaze to yourself, d'ye hear, James?"

His reply was lost as the door opened again to admit Dominique Jean, dressed in what John could only think of as a French huntsman's outfit, looking totally splendid and, despite his earlier misgivings, appearing to be completely at ease.

"We're all here," bellowed Sir Francis, and made his way round the room introducing everybody to everybody else, even including people who already knew one another. Very conscious of Coralie watching him, John bowed and followed on this kind of introduction merry-go-round until eventually he came face-to-face with her.

"Good afternoon," she said coldly, and made him a small curtsey.

"Good afternoon, madam. I trust I find you well," he replied, equally curtly.

"As well as can be expected," she answered and was about to turn away when John seized her arm.

"Coralie, must there be this coolness between us? I am sorry if I upset you the other night but, as I told you, the law had already taken its course. Look, Joe Jago is here."

"I had noticed," she replied, loosening her arm.

"I see you did not bring Georgiana," he said.

Coralie shot him a venomous look. "I would not subject the child to such an ordeal," she answered, and this time walked away in the most deliberate manner.

"And what was all that about, sir?" asked Joe Jago, coming up silently with a brimming glass of punch.

310

"Her daughter," John answered shortly.

"Ah, that would be Miss Georgiana, would it not?"

"It would indeed."

"A rather nasty child from what you have told us."

"I know it is not her fault, that her father drove her to the depths of despair, but nonetheless she is rather horrible."

"I expect she will grow out of it now that he has gone," Joe answered and walked away to talk to an eager young blade who was most anxious to know who he was.

Eventually, some somewhat the worse for punch, they went in to dinner. Sir Francis sat at the head of the table with the two women in mourning on either side of him. Similarly, Lady Dashwood sat at the foot, Lord Orpington to her right, a minor nobleman from the crowd of others attending to her left. John found that he had been put next to Betsy, who leaned across him continually displaying a great deal of bosom. Opposite sat Joe Jago, who literally could not take his eyes off her. Thoughts of rabbits and snakes went through John's mind and he winked at Samuel. Unfortunately the Goldsmith was looking elsewhere at that moment and the flicker of the eyelid was caught by an anxious young virgin who was present with her mama and papa. She blushed deeply and whenever John looked up moved her head to show that she was not looking at him.

Eventually the ladies removed themselves and the men were left to drink port, smoke pipes, and use the chamber pots which were passed round, some remaining at table while they did so. Eventually the brimming bowls were handed to the servants to dispose of. Sir Francis, seeing all were comfortable, began to take snuff and roar with laughter for no apparent reason. His great gurgle was so infectious that others began to join in. Samuel took advantage of the noise to lean across his neighbour and whisper to John.

"I believe we are sharing a room on the third floor."

"So we're all up with the servants," said John, and laughed jovially. The port and punch were definitely weaving their spell and he felt as if tonight very little could bother him. He crossed to where Jago sat, talking to Dominique.

"Where are you two fellows sleeping tonight?"

"In the servants' quarters."

"How splendid. Shall we have a party?"

"No, sir. I don't think that would be wise. I'll tell you why later," Jago murmured, soft enough for the Frenchman not to catch his words.

But further conversation was impossible as a rustle of skirts told them that the women were returning.

Lady Dashwood looked grumpier than ever as she said, "My lords, ladies and gentlemen, would you be so kind as to make your way to the music room where a rustic amusement has been prepared for you."

They trooped off, Betsy leaning heavily on Sir Francis, who was leaning equally heavily on her. John, observing them, cast his mind back to Medmenham Abbey and decided that she had been in charge of most of the girls who had come. His thoughts went briefly to Teresa and he broke into a reminiscent smile.

"What are you grinning about?" asked Samuel as they progressed through the huge entrance hall.

"Fond memories," said John, and smiled all the more.

"I see. By the way, did you notice a missing button from a certain person's apparel?"

"No, I don't think so."

"Well I did," answered Samuel, and whispered a name.

The entertainment was most amusing, culminating in country dancing, the musicians sitting at one end of the room and the chairs being put round the edge. Everyone went to with a will and John caught sight of Joe Jago whirling neatly with a very comely lady.

"I'll swear that man has hidden depths," he muttered to himself.

But nobody took any notice of him and he found himself in a set for Blue Stockings. His partners were James, Dominique, and a group of unknown people. Neither Coralie nor Juliana were dancing but sat on the chairs provided looking somewhat grim in their black attire. Lord Orpington, on the other hand, had puffed his way through a couple of country dances and had been forced to sit down for want of breath.

"Look at those two black crows," James muttered.

"They're in mourning," John protested.

"Well, they needn't look so bloody miserable about it."

"*Monsieur*," remonstrated the Frenchman, "show a little respect."

"Ha ha," said James, and skipped away as the music began.

But suddenly everything seemed false and hollow, as if a picture were being painted, an illusion to trick the mind. John, looking round, could see nothing but painted faces and men leering. At that moment he felt that frisson of fear that always preceded a disastrous event. He finished the dance mechanically, like a puppet, then looked round the room once more to see that Coralie and Juliana had both vanished from sight.

CHAPTER
TWENTY-NINE

He hurried over to where they had been sitting, noticing as he did so that Lord Orpington was also missing. Quickly, he made his way to Sir Francis Dashwood, who by now was extremely merry, his dark eyes flashing over all the women, his hands wandering wherever they could.

"Excuse me, Sir Francis, have you seen the Ladies Arundel and Bravo?"

Sir Francis turned to him in slight annoyance, busy as he was chatting to the young virgin at whom John had accidentally winked.

"No, I haven't. I expect they've stepped outside for a breath of air."

John went out through the east portico and anxiously looked around him. Several people had wandered into the warm summer night to cool off after the hectic activity inside, and one or two were making for the shelter of the trees for purposes private. But of the missing women there was no sign at all. Turning back into the house, John sought out Joe Jago, who was leaning against the wall, looking around him with a shrewd but benevolent gaze.

"Joe, Coralie and Juliana have gone somewhere and I cannot see them. I intend to look for them."

"Very good, Mr Rawlings. I'll come with you."

"I was hoping you would say that."

They went outside once more and Joe scanned the distance with a light blue eye.

"Can't see 'em, sir. Shall we walk down to the lake and search there?"

"Good idea."

They hurried down the slope to hear a pair of heavy footsteps running up behind them.

"I say, wait for me," panted Sam, who was nothing like as fit as once he had been. "Where are you two off to?"

"We're looking for Coralie, who's not anywhere to be seen. Sam, I've got a strange feeling that something is wrong."

"Oh dear," said Samuel and attempted to look serious, which was a little difficult considering that he had sweat pouring down his face and had gone rather red.

Ahead of them lay the waterway, its glassy surface calm and still, the full moon shining down, lighting its way with a path of silver that looked almost as if one could walk on it. John, staring at the unearthly light, felt himself growing more and more uneasy. In the distance he noticed Dominique Jean, who must have slipped out of the ballroom as soon as the dance ended. It seemed that everyone was out here except the one person whom he was urgently seeking. And then, very faintly, he heard a definite splash.

John broke into a run, Jago at his heels, Samuel following at some distance behind them. But they had a long way to go as they rushed round the perimeter of the lake, trying to identify the place from whence the noise had come. And then suddenly, hastening towards them through the trees, they saw a woman's figure running in their direction. For a moment the Apothecary thought it was Coralie and he increased his pace but then he realised that it was Juliana, her clothes disarrayed, her hair wild and flowing.

"Oh help me," she was shouting. "My sister-in-law has fallen in the lake and is drowned."

"Where?" John asked urgently.

"Down there." She waved a vague arm in the direction of the cascade.

Without waiting for any further explanation John shot past her and ran as if his very life depended on it towards the place where he had found Coralie's husband dead as beef. And then, just as he thought his lungs were going to burst, he saw her, floating so quietly and still, her skirts holding her up in the water as if they had filled with air. Without hesitation John kicked off his shoes and dived in, taking Coralie's body in his arms and swimming with it towards the shore.

Jago, a minute or so behind, knelt down and helped pull him and Coralie out of the water. The Apothecary was filled with a terrible sense of déjà-vu as he sat with the dead woman in his arms, transported back in time to that dreadful night when he had found his wife dying in the snow, her blood so red on the purity of the whiteness. Then he pulled himself together and, turning Coralie over, thumped her on the back violently, then lifted her with Joe's help so that she was facing downwards. The water poured from her mouth and she gave a great gasp, and John wept with relief that she was still alive. He leant over her.

"Coralie, you're going to be all right."

Her eyes rolled in her pale face. "Juliana . . ." she whispered.

"Yes, she saved you. She came running for help."

Coralie gave him a despairing glance and shook her head. "She pushed me in," she said, so quietly that he had to strain his ears to hear her.

Dominique ran up, hotly pursued by dear old Samuel. Joe Jago straightened up.

"Good timing, gents. Now, if you will carry Lady Arundel back to the house, Mr Rawlings and I will go in pursuit of that other woman."

And he set off at speed once more. John, following and running uphill, decided that he really must get fitter and that he would take up some sporting activity when things finally settled down. His admiration for Joe Jago grew by the minute as that lithe man, older than John but in far better shape, sped ahead of him towards the house.

As they neared the great east portico he slowed his pace so that he was doing little more than walking rapidly. John, relieved that they were easing up at last, finally caught up with him.

"Where is she, Joe?"

"That, sir, is what I'm about to find out." Jago looked round and seeing a young chap hurrying inside, called out, "Forgive me, sir, but do you know Lady Juliana Bravo?"

"Yes, I do."

"Can you tell me where she is at present?"

"I believe I saw her going round to the stable block."

But that was enough for Jago who sped off once more, leaving John to follow on as best he could. And when he arrived, following rapidly on Joe's heels, it was to a scene of great drama. Looking wildly disarrayed Juliana was ordering her coachman to get the horses in the traces as quickly as possible.

"But, madam, they aren't rested."

"Do I care? Take any two that you can lay your hands on."

"That would be theft, my Lady," said Joe, stepping silently up to her.

She turned on him like a fury. "I'll ask you to mind your own business, sir."

"That is precisely what I am doing. And, madam, I must warn you that I am placing you under arrest for the attempted murder of Lady Arundel."

There was a long silence during which Juliana, white-faced as if she too had recently been drowned, gazed at him, then she said in a hoarse voice, "She is still alive?"

"Yes," answered John, appearing out of the shadows to stand at Joe Jago's side, "you should have used your tried and trusted method, madam."

"What do you mean, sir?"

"This," he said, and he produced the remnants of the blowpipe from a back pocket of his evening suit and thrust it into her hands.

She stared down at it. "What is this thing?"

"I think you know that only too well, madam," said Joe Jago succinctly. "You see, it has the faint smell of lavender about it, a scent that you use, I believe."

There was a moment's silence and then Juliana's face contorted horribly and she threw the blowpipe on the ground. Her nails raked within an inch of Jago's face but he caught her wrists and held them in an iron grip.

"Mr Rawlings, be so good as to secure this woman, would you."

"Gladly," said John, and seizing a leather strap bound Juliana's hands in front of her.

"Now, madam, let's hear the truth, if you please," Jago said, and even John flinched at the tone of his voice.

Lady Juliana began to sob, deep heart-rending cries that would have made him pity her but for recent events.

"Yes, it's true. I killed my brother and the bastard deserved it. For years he had abused me when we were children and then he turned his attentions to his own daughter. He made her life hell, my poor little Georgiana. I lived for that child, she was my only reason for being alive."

"And what about Lady Orpington?" Joe asked in a much kinder voice.

"She was out and about that night, the night I did for Charles. I'd been in to see him earlier and changed the dressing on his chancre, put poison in it so that it would enter his bloodstream. How he must have suffered and how well he deserved everything he got."

"The girl; his mistress?" Jago reminded her.

"I thought she had seen me when I went outside to check what had happened to him. She was wandering about in the grounds, knowing that Charles wasn't in his room and had gone searching for him. But I couldn't take the risk of her having seen me and betraying me. So I poisoned her with a little arrow which I blew into the back of her neck. Then I put her in the Temple of Venus, where the pox-ridden little creature belonged." Juliana gave a terrible laugh. "They say that Sir Francis Dashwood has founded a club called Hellfire. Well, that's where those two people have ended. May they rot in hellfire for all eternity."

"And what about Coralie?" John asked quietly.

She turned on him a look of pure contempt. "That empty-headed woman. That 'actress'. She's not fit to be a mother. Georgiana doesn't love her, she loves me. And now as her sole living relative the child will be handed into my care for me to bring up as if she were my own."

"But as I've already told you, Coralie is still alive, Lady Juliana."

She literally writhed in front of them and spat upon the ground. And it was at that moment that John realised she was quite insane and felt a moment's intense pity for such an unhappy woman. He turned to Joe Jago.

"What shall we do with her?"

"We'll get Sir Francis to lock her up overnight and at first light I'll take her back to London and deliver her into the hands of Sir John Fielding."

"What will happen to her?"

Joe lowered his voice. "She'll probably end up in Bedlam," he whispered, and John shivered at the very prospect.

An hour later he was allowed to go and see Coralie, who was lying in bed, very pale but very much alive.

"I'm afraid it was Juliana who killed your husband and Lady Orpington," he said quietly.

"They both deserved to die," she answered. "I know it is wrong of me to say that but it would be hypocritical of me to do otherwise. Dr Bancroft gave him some of the poison to do experiments with on a cat. Charles showed the results to Juliana when she came visiting and she must have stolen some at the time."

John nodded, afraid to say anything.

"And now," Coralie continued, "I must devote my life to my daughter. She has had a terrible start and I must do all I can to make sure she grows up into a fine young woman. Do you know, John, I grew to suspect her all over again. That is why I begged you to let the case drop. I thought she had killed Charles and his mistress out of revenge."

"Poor, poor Coralie. What a burden for you to have to bear." There was a long silence, then he said, "Perhaps she would like to come and visit Rose some time."

She covered one of his hands with one of her own. "Oh, my dear friend. What a life we both have led. Tragedy has struck us and yet we are here to tell the tale."

"I think, Coralie, that we were both born to survive."

She smiled at him. "I expect you are right. I will not marry again. As I have said, I shall now devote myself to my child to the exclusion of everyone else."

He looked at her, just a little sadly. "If you are sure that that will be enough for you." He stood up. "Goodbye, Coralie. I wish you well."

"I shall never forget you, John. You have saved my life on more than one occasion and you know what they say."

"I do indeed. Farewell, my dear."

And with that he left the room.

The next morning he woke to find that Joe Jago had already left in the Bow Street coach and that he and Samuel were dependent on Dominique for a lift back to town. Sir Francis, though, despite the contretemps of the night before, was still intent on enjoying his party and was challenging everyone present to a walk through the grounds ending in an outdoor feast, after which he intended to have a mock battle on the lake. John, strangely depressed by last night's events, refused politely, as did Samuel. The Frenchman, too, made his excuses.

"Forgive me, my dear good sir, but I have a mass of work to do. I am afraid that I must bid you adieu. I shall head back for London if you and madam will allow."

"Talking of madams," John whispered to Samuel, "any sign of Betsy?"

"She was last seen going into a thicket with old Lord Orpington."

"He'll probably die of a heart attack."

"Oh, but my dear John, what an exit!"

His humour somewhat restored, John travelled back to town in good company and was dropped off at the corner of Gerard Street. Walking to Nassau Street and letting himself in with a key he went through to the garden and sat down on a seat.

He knew now that his lifelong preoccupation with Coralie Clive had finally come to an end. It was finished and he must move on. He asked himself, then, why Elizabeth had been so quiet and what she could possibly be up to. He decided that a letter to her was long overdue. But just as he was going to the library to write it the front door opened and Rose shot through and seized him and hugged him and gave him many kisses.

"Oh, sweetheart," he said, "how pleased I am to see you."

"Have you finished your work for Sir John, Papa?"

"Yes, darling, it's all done."

"And will you be at home for a while?"

"I shall indeed."

"Then when you are not working you can take me out for walks like Miss da Costa does?"

"I certainly will."

Octavia, who had followed Rose in, twinkled her blackberry eyes. "I'm not getting married for a couple of months so that we can still go out together, Rose."

"Yes, of course we can. But I enjoy walking with Papa too."

"It's really good to be home again," John said, and picking Rose up in the air he swung her onto his shoulders.

CHAPTER
THIRTY

That September, on a golden morning, John, dressed in his very best clothes, accompanied Nicholas, also dressed very finely, to St Ann's, Soho, where the Apothecary took his place as bridegroom's man. He felt that with this wedding an era was ending and that from now on he would have to spend more time at his shop in Shug Lane and could no longer go wandering about the countryside at the behest of Sir John Fielding. His trusted friend and former apprentice was on the edge of starting a new life and as a result everything would alter drastically.

The arrival of the bride caused a stir and John turned his head to have a swift glance at her. She came up the aisle slowly, walking on the arm of Sir Gabriel Kent, she not having a father of her own. Sir Gabriel was dressed in a stunning silver suit trimmed with black jet, but for once he was outshone by the bride. She wore white and blue and had on her head quite the most glorious hat with long turquoise ribbons hanging down behind. The colours enhanced her dark eyes and colouring and John thought she was one of the most beautiful brides he had ever seen. And the sight of his father, well in his eighties, walking beside her caused his eyes to fill with tears. He looked at Nicholas and saw that he too was emotional and moved by the charming vision.

In the front pew on the left sat Rose, quite alone, wearing a dress of emerald green which enhanced the redness of her hair. She waited for her grandfather to give Octavia to Nick and then, when Sir Gabriel sat down next to her, held his hand. And as the couple left the church together she threw rice in their path together with rose petals.

Amongst the guests were Sir John and Lady Fielding, for Nick had been rescued from terrible circumstances by the Magistrate and owed everything to him. Joe Jago, also an old friend, had been included, and Samuel and Jocasta were present, he grinning heartily and she looking thin and somehow a little unbending.

"We'll soon put a stop to that," said Sir Gabriel, and poured her a large glass of champagne as soon as she came through the front door of number 2, Nassau Street.

Sam came bustling over. "A fine show, John. Truly excellent. I suppose there's no hope of you . . .?"

John looked at him with a sad smile. "I know what you're going to say and the answer is no. Coralie is devoting the rest of her life to her daughter and has no intention of marrying again. And how could I continue my adventures with a wife?"

Sam looked a little chastened but said, "No, I suppose not. But all the same it is a pity."

"And a pity it will have to remain, my friend."

Sir John Fielding came to the Apothecary's side, led by his wife, who settled him in a chair.

"Well, Mr Rawlings, you're going to miss young Nick. Indeed, what are you going to do without him?"

"I don't quite know, sir. But no doubt I'll think of something."

In the corner of the salon the musicians started to tune up and John knew that from now on everything would be devoted to dancing and conversation would become almost impossible. But as he wove his way in and out of the sets, partnering all Octavia's young friends, he wondered if this was to be his fate, a widower in his mid-thirties, always popular, always jovial, and always alone.

Joe Jago came over as John eventually paused for breath.

"A very joyous wedding if I may say so, sir. I am delighted to see young Nick settled at last."

"Indeed. I'll never forget the first time I saw him. Dragging logs upstairs for Mr Fielding — as he then was — so pale and limping so wretchedly."

"He's a different person now," said Joe with a great deal of satisfaction.

"Yes, and with such a beautiful girl."

Joe looked at him seriously, reading John's mind. "Oh, you'll find somebody for yourself some day, sir."

"Do you really think so?"

"I'm certain of it. An older lady. A person who has been married before."

"But where is she, I wonder?"

"You'll have to go looking for her, I think."

John smiled wryly. "I also have to earn a living, Joe. Let us hope that one day she will cross my path."

"Indeed, sir."

But both men were being called upon to join the next set and their private conversation ended there.

Later, after the bride and groom had left and people had started to head for home, John drank one last glass of champagne with his father and Rose, who sipped on a cordial.

"Well, I thought it all went off splendidly, my son. And I was so honoured to give the bride away."

"You looked magnificent, Father. A truly resplendent figure. And so did you, Rose. You were a good girl and behaved perfectly."

"It was a wonderful day, Papa. Thank you for my new dress."

She gave him a look which was so like Emilia that he drew in his breath sharply.

"What's the matter?"

"Nothing. It's just that you reminded me of your mother, that is all."

"I am sure that Emilia was with us in spirit," Sir Gabriel announced, and looked very wise.

At that moment, like a portent, there was a knock on the door and a footman stood there.

"Yes?" said John, looking up.

"A letter has arrived for you by the late post, sir. I have taken the liberty of putting it on the desk in the library."

"It's from Mrs Elizabeth," Rose stated into the silence.

"How do you know that?" John asked, surprised.

"I just know," Rose answered, and would say no more.

And strangely enough when John went into the library and opened the letter he saw to his astonishment that it was from the Marchesa di Lorenzi.

"My dear John," *he read.* "It is several
Months since we last had Communication but
now I Feel It would be Right to Speak to You.
There is something of Interest I have to Tell You
and I would be Obliged if You could arrange to
Call on Me in the next Month or so.
I remain Yr Obedient Servant, E di Lorenzi."

John sat looking out of the window with a strange joy in his heart. Elizabeth had not finished with him but wanted to see him and about something important.

Standing up, his limbs aching from so much dancing, he decided that next month, if he could find an apothecary to run the shop while he went away, he would go and visit her before the cold weather set in and the ways grew foul.

"Elizabeth," he said under his breath, and just for a moment he had a clear mental picture of her, with her dark, dark hair streaming out behind her and her lips drawing back in a smile.

Historical Note

John Rawlings and Sir John Fielding both lived in eighteenth-century London. John Rawlings, as my regular readers will know, was made a Yeoman of the Worshipful Society of Apothecaries on 13th March 1755, giving his address as 2, Nassau Street, Soho. John Fielding was knighted in 1761, when he was forty years old. His work in assisting his brother Henry, the author of *Tom Jones*, in founding the Runners, later known as the Bow Street Runners, is well known.

There are several other characters from real life featured in this book. Sir Francis Dashwood, Lord le Despencer, and his famous Hellfire Club have been frequently described. Let me just say that I could find no evidence of Satanic worship, a myth which gained currency during the nineteenth century, though there were certainly mock religious ceremonies at the annual election of the Abbot and during the induction of new members. It is believed, however, that the goddesses Demeter and her daughter Persephone were represented by naked young women made to lie across the altar with their legs spread open and that aristocratic women sometimes volunteered to represent these goddesses.

What is known for certain is that good-class whores were hired in London by Paul Whitehead and conveyed to Medmenham Abbey by coach for the pleasure of the assembled company. But the main purpose of the club was, in John Wilkes's own words, "a set of worthy, jolly fellows, happy disciples of Venus and Bacchus, got occasionally together to celebrate woman in wine and to give more zest to the festive meeting, they plucked every luxurious idea from the ancients and enriched their own modern pleasures with the tradition of classic luxury".

Pierre Langlois was a cabinet maker of great renown, crafting furniture of enormous beauty for the aristocracy, whilst his son-in-law, Pierre Dominique Jean, was equally highly regarded in his day. Their bills — and the amounts owing to them — are still extant.

A fascinating character was the American, Dr Edward Bancroft. He was born in Westfield, Massachusetts in 1744. He was a physician, scientist, philosopher, politician, novelist, technical expert in dyes and a philanthropist. He also introduced Woorara or Indian Arrow Poison into this country, in which he arrived in 1765 or 1766. This poison later came to be called Curare. In his book published in 1769 he added the footnote, "As the Author has brought a considerable quantity of this Poison to England for the use of any Gentleman, whose genius may incline him to prosecute these experiments and whose character will warrant us to confide in his hands a preparation capable of perpetrating the most secret and fatal villany, he may be supplied with a sufficient quantity of the

Woorara, by applying to Mr Becket in the Strand." It can be seen from this that the stuff could fall into the wrong hands with the greatest of ease. Incidentally, in the American War of Independence, Bancroft became a double agent, apparently spying for Britain but in reality working for Benjamin Franklin, the colonial agent for several colonies. A man of many parts indeed.

Also available in ISIS Large Print:

Special Assignments

Boris Akunin

A Jack of Spades and his fragrant accomplice; an eager young deputy and a fugitive countess; a game of cat and mouse and a series of savage murders: the dashing, inimitable Erast Fandorin finds himself juggling them all . . .

His first adversary is a wickedly mischievous swindler and master of disguise, whose outrageous con tricks and machinations are sending ripples through the carefully maintained calm of late 19th-century Moscow. His calling card is the Jack of Spades.

The other is a brutal serial killer — nicknamed "The Decorator" — driven by an insane, maniacal obsession, who strikes terror into the heart of the city's slums, and who may have more in common with London's Jack the Ripper than just a taste for women of easy virtue . . .

With twists and turns around every corner, Fandorin's powers of detection are tested to the limit.

ISBN 978-0-7531-7996-3 (hb)
ISBN 978-0-7531-7997-0 (pb)

My Lady Judge

Cora Harrison

1509. The Burren, on the western seaboard of Ireland, was a land of stony fields and swirling mountain terraces. The people of the kingdom lived peacefully by the ancient Brehon laws of their forebears.

On the first eve of May, hundreds of people from the Burren climbed Mullaghmore Mountain to celebrate the great May Day festival, lighting a bonfire and singing and dancing through the night, then returning through the grey dawn to the safety of their homes.

But one man did not come back down the steeply spiralled path. His body lay exposed to the ravens and wolves on the bare, lonely mountain for two nights . . . and no one spoke of him, or told what they had seen.

And when Mara, a woman appointed by King Turlough Don O'Brien to be judge and lawgiver to the stony kingdom, comes to investigate, she is met with a wall of silence . . .

ISBN 978-0-7531-7984-0 (hb)
ISBN 978-0-7531-7985-7 (pb)